D

JAN 1 9 2018

Crossing the Animas

Center Point
Large Print

Also by James D. Best and available from
Center Point Large Print:

The Steve Dancy Tales
 The Return
 Jenny's Revenge

**This Large Print Book carries the
Seal of Approval of N.A.V.H.**

Crossing the Animas

A Steve Dancy Tale

James D. Best

CENTER POINT LARGE PRINT
THORNDIKE, MAINE

This Center Point Large Print edition
is published in the year 2018 by arrangement with
the author.

This is a work of fiction. The names, characters, places,
and events are the work of the author's imagination.

The text of this Large Print edition is unabridged.
In other aspects, this book may vary
from the original edition.
Printed in the United States of America
on permanent paper.
Set in 16-point Times New Roman type.

ISBN: 978-1-68324-656-5

Library of Congress Cataloging-in-Publication Data

Names: Best, James D., 1945- author.
Title: Crossing the animas : a Steve Dancy tale / James D. Best.
Description: Center Point large print edition. | Thorndike, Maine :
    Center Point Large Print, 2018.
Identifiers: LCCN 2017045625 | ISBN 9781683246565
    (hardcover : alk. paper)
Subjects: LCSH: Large type books. | GSAFD: Western stories.
Classification: LCC PS3602.E785 C76 2018 | DDC 813/.6—dc23
LC record available at https://lccn.loc.gov/2017045625

For Diane
It's been a great life together

Contents

Chapter 1

cock-and-bull story

"Seven!"

The croupier yelled the number to smiles and cheers. He scooped up the dice with practiced élan and ceremoniously handed them to the grinning winner

I didn't understand craps, but I knew the shooter had won. The jubilant crowd around the table made working our way around to the back of the saloon difficult for Jeff Sharp and me. We weren't here for a drink or to gamble. Our mission was to sell Edison electrification to a big mine operator in Silverton, Colorado. Success would mean the first sale of Edison's inventions for mining. We needed a contract. After we had been delayed by the shooting kind of trouble in Carson City, Edison had sent a flurry of telegrams insisting that he needed to see progress, not excuses. We had signed a contract to light the welcome arch at the Denver train station, but we needed a bigger deal. Otherwise, Edison might withdraw our license for the western states.

Sharp and I had ridden horses up from Durango, along the path of construction for a new fifty-mile rail line the Denver & Rio Grande was carving through the mountains. Lumbermen had cut down trees, and dynamite had blown away rock so track could be laid along a precarious ledge that looked straight down to the Animas River. It had been a beautiful ride, but we'd made slow progress threading our way between construction workers, wagons, tents, and building material that clogged the way.

I owned stock in the Denver & Rio Grande, and the trip was a rare opportunity for a shareholder to get a close view of company operations. D&RG officials had wired instructions to treat us like owners, which we were in part. We ate with the workers, drank the night away with the superintendent, and slept in a company tent with construction supervisors. Sharp only dabbled in railroads, but I invested heavily in lines I thought had big potential. Some in the East believed that out West, money came from cattle, but real fortunes were built from mining and servicing the gold, silver, and copper mines. The new Denver & Rio Grande line promised hefty profits hauling bullion out of the San Juan Mountains.

It took us three days to traverse the clogged fifty miles, although we did spend more time than necessary being entertained by the construction crews along the way. To avoid wasting any more time, we made our way to the Claim Jumper after checking in to our hotel. As we approached the back of the rowdy saloon, I spotted a group of men sitting in a line with their backs against the wall. A narrow table stretching the length of the row of oddly seated men offered a place for them to rest their beer and whiskey glasses. The group carefully watched the activity at the gambling tables and seemed amused by the titter-totter emotions of the crap players as they won or lost. The dice game certainly generated more noise, back-slapping, and boot stomping than poker.

The two men sitting on the outside looked hard, as if they might be hired guards, but the other three could have been bookkeepers. My suspicions were confirmed as the two ruffians shifted menacingly in their seats at our approach.

"I'm looking for Mr. Phelps," I said. "Would that be one of you gentlemen?"

I didn't make eye contact with either of the sentinels.

"Who would be asking?" one of the clerkish men asked.

"Steve Dancy and Jeff Sharp," I answered. "We sent a telegram."

The man next to him nodded. "I'm George Phelps. Sit."

We swung over two chairs from another table and sat facing Mr. Phelps. Besides this saloon, Phelps owned the biggest mines in Silverton. He also had an express company, a hotel, and a gang

11

of brutes to make sure he kept it all. He was our number-one target for Edison electrification.

"Can I buy you a beer?" Phelps asked.

"Two, if yer inclined," Sharp answered.

Everyone laughed except the guards, who maintained stoic demeanors. We shook hands with the three bookish-looking gentlemen. The guards were not introduced.

Phelps was a dandy. His suit cost a great deal and looked to have been tailored in the East. His starched, pristine white shirt was a rarity in a mining town. He sported a thin mustache that must have taken a half hour to groom each morning and slicked hair with not a single strand astray. The two clerks, although dressed as respectable businessmen, looked slovenly next to him. I guessed that he was younger than my thirty-two years, and he looked even more citified than me.

Appearances can lie. I had asked around about Phelps before we made our journey. While I was raised in New York and educated at Columbia, Phelps grew up dirt poor in Arkansas, with a patchy education. While I inherited wealth, he scratched the earth to build his own fortune. It appeared that Phelps only pretended to be cultivated. I found this amusing, because I pretended to fit into my new home on the rough and tumble frontier. We all have affectations, I supposed.

"So, you claim to have a license for Edison's inventions?" Phelps asked without ordering the previously offered beers. "Do you have proof?"

I drew a contract from my coat pocket and handed it to him. He read it thoroughly before handing it back.

"Do you believe I should recognize Edison's signature?"

"No, and I'm aware that cheats plague mine owners. Jeff here was a mine owner for years. At one point, he was the largest mine operator in Nevada."

"A short time," Sharp chuckled. "An' only due to the untimely death of a larger competitor."

Phelps jerked back, startled. His guards stiffened at his sudden movement.

"Did you kill him?" Phelps asked. "I don't find that an endorsement of good character."

"No, sir," Sharp replied quickly. "I had nothin' to do with his demise."

I was grateful Sharp didn't mention that his mining competitor had been killed by none other than me. No sense muddying the water with events I would just as soon forget. I needed to get the conversation turned in a positive direction.

"Did you telegram Mr. Edison after you received my message?"

Phelps's expression turned smug. "No, didn't bother. Not interested." He flicked an imaginary piece of lint from his coat sleeve. "Too expensive

13

to electrify a mine. Lanterns work fine. I asked you to sit because I thought your cock-and-bull story might be entertaining."

Sharp explained, "Stringin' copper wire ain't as expensive as you might think, an' Edison's inventions go beyond lightin' excavations. His motors can bring fresh air down to the deepest shaft."

"My men breathe just fine. I don't need motors and hoses and generators and expensive engineers to make them breathe easier. If they want fresh air, they can get a job on the surface . . . for half the pay."

Sharp leaned forward. "A man with lungs full of oxygen works a damn sight harder than a man strugglin' to breathe. An' good light gets 'em workin' on the right vein. Ya might not want to dismiss this so quick."

"That's your pitch? Hell, I make good money with things the way they are. Why should I hand over my hard-earned gains to the likes of you?"

"Ya ain't been down to the mines, have ya?" Sharp asked with an edge.

Phelps expression instantly turned sour.

Uh oh. Sharp knew mining and how to lead men in other dangerous professions, but he was no salesman. He spoke his mind, especially when it came to the handling of hired hands. Men eagerly worked for Sharp because, though he would not abide slackers or miscreants, he treated everyone

14

fairly. He ran a quality crew, paid them well, and kept them safe. I suspected he was about to lose his temper with this pretentious grandee.

Phelps wasn't our only opportunity, but we needed a solid sale in Silverton. He had major competitors and a number of lesser lights, but Phelps was the largest operator, and his youth had led me to believe he would be receptive to doing things in a new way. I was apparently wrong, but insulting him was not the way to change his mind.

I said, "Mr. Phelps, I understand your position, and you're right, the investment goes beyond the purchase of equipment. You'll need to hire an electricity engineer, but Mr. Edison sells only rigorously tested equipment that lasts and is easy to maintain."

"Where do you live?" Phelps asked in a tone that was none too friendly.

"We rode up from Durango," I offered.

"You didn't answer my question. Where do you live?"

"For the time being, we live in Durango, but don't worry, if you make a reasonable order, we'll hire a man and locate him in Silverton."

"A man? Not an engineer?"

"Anyone representing our company will—"

"I don't know you." He waved at Sharp. "Nor your ill-bred friend. I don't hand money over to strangers who reside hell knows where and

15

promise to leave some out-of-work lollygagger as their company representative. I built my operation from nothing, and I didn't get where I am by being played for a fool. Good day."

The guards took a slightly more belligerent pose, but they didn't worry me. I was more concerned with Phelps's business associates. They didn't look intrigued, concerned, or irritated. They looked bored. They had witnessed this little drama before. Phelps had been serious when he said he'd agreed to see us to be entertained. He enjoyed belittling people.

I stood to leave. Sharp remained seated.

He leaned forward on his elbows. "Ya say ya built yer operation from nothin'. I don't buy that. Ya ain't got the character to build it on yer own. I bet ya stole it."

Phelps flew to his feet, the two guards only a moment behind. Sharp maintained a relaxed posture and looked amused.

"Get the hell outta my saloon!" Phelps yelled.

Sharp slowly stood, never breaking eye contact with him. I ignored Phelps and kept my eyes on the guards. I didn't get the sense they were eager for a fight.

When Sharp was upright, he said, "Thank ya for meetin' with us, Mr. Phelps. We won't bother ya any further."

We walked out of the saloon with every eye on us, but I noticed most of the patrons appeared quizzical instead of hostile. I assumed they had never seen Phelps treated in this manner. I was worried. If Phelps was tightly connected to the other mine owners, he could squelch any deal we might make. I left the saloon hoping he had bigger things on his mind than holding a grudge.

Chapter 2

till hell freezes over

"Now what?" I asked, a bit testy.

"Ya sound like ya think I messed up the sale. I didn't. That prissy bastard was never gonna buy from us."

We walked away from the saloon in silence. I was angry. Sharp could size up a man faster than it took to complete a handshake. It irked me that he was seldom wrong. I didn't like Phelps, but I could have done business with him. Sharp didn't do business with men he couldn't trust to hold his purse. If I approached business like him, I wouldn't have made any deals in New York City. Yet both of us got wealthy doing things in our own fashion. Then a thought occurred to me. I'd trust Sharp with my purse . . . and I had trusted him with my life. I also trusted Virginia Baker, my fiancée and previous business partner. Sharp and I had owned a general store in Leadville, Colorado, and we had hired Mrs. Baker to run it for us. At that time, she was a near stranger, yet we gave her authority to draw on our bank balance to restock the store. I also trusted our mutual friend, Joseph McAllen. I realized I had done better when I dealt with honest, forthright people. Sharp was right. In New York, every business transaction had to be shrouded in legal contracts written by high-priced sharpies. Then I chuckled to myself.

"I say somethin' amusin'?" Sharp asked.

"No. In *Henry VI*, Shakespeare wrote, 'the first thing we do, let's kill all the lawyers.' It occurred to me that if only honest men did business, we could put most of those lawyers out of work."

"Let's keep a few around like Mac Castle in case I get arrested again."

Castle had successfully defended Sharp at a trial for a hanging offense. Despite the fact that McAllen and I had tracked down the real culprit, Sharp continued to hold Mac Castle in high regard. His solid defense of Jeff made him one of the good practitioners of law, but the prosecutor had ended up going to jail. I guess it was like any other profession: Good men practice law and so do scoundrels. Just like good men own mines . . . and Phelps did as well.

"I got an idea, but ya ain't gonna like it," Sharp said.

"Try me." I walked a couple steps before adding, "By the way, you were right back there. Phelps would have made a lousy customer."

"Hell, if ya agree with me, then this ain't such a good idea. It had to do with lurin' Phelps back to the bargainin' table."

"Let's see the other mine owners before we go

19

courting Mr. Phelps again. I want to do it fast so we can head back. Virginia won't wait forever for a wedding ceremony."

"Ya got that wrong. She'll wait till hell freezes over. For the life of me, I can't understand her, but that woman's deep in love with ya."

My relationship with Mrs. Baker had developed slowly, and its fruition had flabbergasted me. I hadn't been looking for a wife, and our early dealings had been contentious. That all ended one day when she suddenly kissed me. From that moment, I knew I really had been looking for a lifetime companion and had found the perfect woman.

"By the way, what was your idea?"

"Illuminate a competin' saloon. I thought that would get Mr. Phelps's attention."

I stopped walking. "Jeff, that's a great idea. Let's find a competing saloon *and* a competing mine owner. In fact, Edison will be happier if we illuminate the city of Silverton rather than some dank, dark hole. Phelps will come along or not, but it will be on our terms, not his."

"The biggest saloon is the Silver Nugget. Start there?"

"Lead the way," I said cheerfully.

Chapter 3

rude question

The Silver Nugget was nearly twice the size of Phelps's place. A loud three-piece band sat below and to the side of the stage at the rear. Worn-looking women kicked their legs high in the air, exposing ruffled undergarments. I walked right up to the stage and peered over the rim to examine the lighting, standard brass gas lamps overlaid with colored cloth. I was about to show Sharp when a burly ruffian put his hand in the center of my chest and pushed me away from the stage.

"Stand back . . . three feet," he said.

"I want to see the owner."

"Them's his rules. Stay away from the girls."

"I don't care about the girls. I want to see him about better stage lighting. Is he available?"

"Don't want men closer than three feet to the stage. Peddlers no closer than fifteen." He pushed me slightly harder. "So ya gotta move even further back."

The barrel-chested man stood over six feet and moved with a smoothness that defied his heft. Braces kept his general-store pants up over a generous gut. He wore no beard, his boots were clean, and his threadbare flannel shirt freshly washed. In general, he looked like a lumberman, not a saloon bouncer.

Sharp grabbed my elbow. "Come on, Steve. Let's go. We'll finish our deal with Phelps."

"Whoa! Wait up a minute. What've you got going with Phelps?"

The man's diction suddenly sounded like a man with some education.

"He wants Edison illumination," Sharp said matter-of-factly. "Says he's gonna build onto his saloon if we get him the genuine stuff."

"Can you?"

I answered. "We have a license to sell all of Edison's inventions west of the Mississippi."

"If you can prove it, I can get you in front of the boss."

I pulled out our contract and handed it over.

The big man read it, then handed it back. His next words startled me.

"Edison doesn't sign with his whole name."

"He signs his full name on contracts," I answered, surprised that this ruffian would have that kind of knowledge.

"Let's go to my office."

He whirled around and marched past the stage to a narrow staircase leading to a second floor. We followed, perplexed. He knew how Edison signed papers, his English suddenly displayed erudition, and he had said "my office." As I climbed the stairs, I glanced back at Sharp, but he shrugged confusion as well.

The man walked through a tiny spartan office and led us into a comfortable sitting room. As he waved us to seats, I noticed another door that probably opened onto a bedroom. These were the owner's private quarters.

"Do you own this establishment?" I asked.

"Establishment has a ring of permanence. Nothing lasts in a mining town, but yes, I own the Silver Nugget." He reached behind and grabbed a bottle of Scotch whiskey. "Drink?"

"Yes, sir," Sharp said, looking pleased with himself.

His ruse about returning to Phelps had procured us an audience with the owner of the largest saloon in Silverton. He had a right to look pleased.

"How do you know Edison doesn't normally sign with his whole name?" I asked, accepting a glass loaded with a double shot of Scotch.

"I have several letters from him over in that drawer." He pointed to a rolltop desk in the corner.

"You know Edison?"

"No. Do you?"

"We've met . . . we did some work for him in New York."

He gave me an appraising stare, so I sipped the whiskey. It was first-rate. Sharp swallowed about half his glass in a single gulp and sighed pleasurably. He preferred Irish whiskey, but appreciated expensive Scotch, bourbon, or rye. All Sharp needed to make him content was a smooth whiskey and a comely woman. He possessed half of those essentials sitting here in—

"Excuse me," I said. "I think we forgot introductions. I'm Steve Dancy, and this is Jeff Sharp."

He reached over and shook our hands. "Michael Fletcher, but everyone calls me Big Mike. Before this goes any further, what have you got going with Phelps?"

"Well, we—"

"Nothin'," Sharp said before I could say anything further. "Don't like the man. Just said that to get yer attention." Sharp raised his whiskey glass. "Worked good too."

Fletcher didn't see the humor. "What else have you lied about?"

"Nothing," I added quickly. "We have a bona fide license to all the territory in the western United States, except for San Francisco. You can telegraph Edison for confirmation."

"I'll do that before any money changes hands. Why not San Francisco?"

"Edison had already granted a license for that city before we met."

He smiled. "Just the kind of detail a shyster uses to build credibility."

"Seen a few of them?" Sharp asked pleasantly.

"More than my share. Now tell me something that will make me want to pour you boys another round of drinks."

"Why do you have letters from Thomas Edison?" I asked.

"That's none of your business," Fletcher answered, "and a rude question won't get me to lift this bottle again."

I thought it might be our business. I owned the license for his products in this region, and I was a shareholder in his company. Fletcher had to be in correspondence with Edison on one of those two issues. Instead of pursuing the subject, I said, "If you have real letters from Edison in that drawer, they're signed with an E. One initial only."

Fletcher visibly relaxed and poured us another drink. "You earned another drink, but I still intend to get confirmation from Mr. Edison."

"Wouldn't 'xpect nothin' less," Sharp said.

"Did you come here from Phelps's place?"

"We did," Sharp answered. "Threw us out. Not a pleasant meetin', that's for sure. Didn't even order us the beers he promised."

Fletcher appeared puzzled. "Ben Law there?"

"Ben Law? Don't know the man," Sharp said.

"Law runs protection for Phelps's mines and saloon. Phelps wouldn't last a minute out here without him. Law's got lots of hard men on his payroll. Runs a damn tight operation."

"Two men flanked Phelps and a couple of underlings," I said. "He didn't introduce the hard-looking men, but they were obviously personal guards."

"Did one of them wear a bright red bandanna?" Fletcher asked. "Law wears it all the time. Supposed to be a warning or something. Man's got a big head."

We both shook our heads.

"You're lucky. Law's tough . . . and mean. He enjoys taking care of Phelps's problems. Be careful with Phelps if he's around. Law won't verbally throw you out. He and his men will hurt you. Bad."

"We don't intend to do business with Phelps," I said. "Neither of us liked him."

"Good to hear. Tell me what you want to do for me."

"Make yer saloon bright as day," Sharp answered. "No hissin' from gas lamps an' no dirty smoke. Yer girls'll be dancin' on a glowin' stage. They'll look like angels cavortin' on the clouds."

Fletcher laughed, which made me uncomfortable. We needed this sale, and Sharp had just made our best pitch. Damn, selling illumination was harder than I'd anticipated.

"You boys sold any Edison illumination yet?"

"Denver bought Edison's system for their new welcome arch at the train station," I said.

"Barney Ford bought from you?"

26

"He did," I answered. Big Mike seemed to know everyone. "He's also the landlord for our warehouse."

"I'll send Barney a telegram as well. If this checks out, we'll talk money, but I want a heavy discount for leading the way in southwest Colorado. If you illuminate the Silver Nugget, then all of Silverton and Durango will follow."

"We'll make ya a good deal," Sharp said. "Ya own any mines?"

"Mines?"

"We want to illuminate mines an' bring fresh air down the shafts."

Fletcher rubbed his chin. "I prefer house odds, but I know a few mine owners who'd love to steal a march on Phelps. Fresh air in the mines? If you can pull that off, the other mine owners could peel off some of Phelps's best men." He looked us both in the eye. "If you do right by me, I'll organize a meeting with his competitors."

I downed my whiskey and stood, extending my hand. "We'll do right by you."

After shaking all around, Sharp said, "It's been a pleasure, Big Mike. We'll get out of yer hair so you can send Barney that telegram. If ya run this saloon near as well as he runs his hotel, ya must be doin' pretty good."

"Let me give you some advice. Stay away from Phelps. That man and his gang are more than dangerous, they're crazy wild."

"No problem," Sharp said. "We'd rather do our drinkin' lookin' up ladies' undergarments anyway."

Fletcher turned to me and said, "Mr. Edison is a shareholder in Denver & Rio Grande. It's no secret that I send him progress reports on the new line. If that contract is not legitimate, he'll tell me straight out. Then you'll need to stay away from me as well."

I was surprised. "How did he come to contact you?"

"I'm related to his wife. Did you meet her?"

"Mary? We did. She appears fit and happy. A little bored with the isolation of Menlo Park, but otherwise content."

I wasn't going to elaborate about her frustrations with her husband's obsession with work. If she wanted Fletcher to know, she could tell him herself.

"How are ya related?" Sharp asked.

"She's my niece. I'll telegraph her as well."

"Good," I said. "By the way, the next time we meet, I'd like to talk about another subject."

"And what would that be?"

"I'm also a shareholder in the Denver & Rio Grande. We rode up along the line. Perhaps we can exchange observations."

He looked intrigued but merely nodded. As Sharp turned to go, Fletcher slapped him on the back and kept his arm on his shoulder as he escorted us out of his private quarters. It was obvious that Sharp had established a rapport with Fletcher. I was jealous of his knack for comradery with men and women. Then I remembered that, despite his lascivious wiles, I had been the one to win Virginia's heart.

Which reminded me of something. We needed to conclude our business in Silverton so I could get back to Durango.

Chapter 4

bygones be bygones

Our hotel in Silverton might have lacked fancy decoration, but maids kept it spotless. Frequent scrubbing of the soft pine floor planks had revealed the relief in the grain, and the serviceable couches and chairs were whisked morning and afternoon. Each customer received fresh linens, and the aprons worn by food servers seemed to be washed daily. In all, Sharp and I were pleased with the accommodations, that is, until we spotted a man with a red bandanna in the sitting room, watching the front door.

We tried to ignore him as we asked for our keys. No such luck. He came right up and tapped me on the shoulder. I took my time accepting the key and then slowly turned to look him in the eye.

He was a thin man, with no facial hair. He was dressed casually as a drover, not a miner. All his clothes, including his boots, were tan except for that bright red bandanna, which also appeared to be the only item of clothing washed on a regular basis. He wore a Colt high on his hip, canted forward. Overall, he looked dangerous.

After glaring at us for a long moment, he said, "Don't bother Mr. Phelps again, ya hear?"

"Rest comfortable," I said. "Mr. Phelps is not worth the bother."

"What the hell does that mean?" He appeared genuinely perplexed by my answer.

"It means we won't have any trouble complying with your request," I answered.

"Ain't no request, pretty boy." He poked me in the chest with a finger. "It's an order."

Sharp smiled friendly, "Don't get yer dander up. We'll leave yer boss alone."

"Shut up. I'm talking to yer starchy friend."

"Ya talk to him, ya talk to both of us," Sharp said.

Law flicked his wrist, and two arrogant men sauntered over, eager to join a fracas.

I moved in close to Law, leaving only inches between us.

I whispered, "Don't move or interfere."

Sharp's fist clobbered the first man to arrive, and when he grabbed the second by his shirtfront, Law reached for his gun, only to find my hand covering his pistol. Sharp jerked the second man forward and down until his head hit the edge of the reception desk. He fell to the floor like a limp rag doll.

I slowly drew my own Colt and slightly lifted Law's chin with the barrel.

"We don't want trouble. We're just a couple of businessmen that made an offer to your boss. He declined, so we won't bother him again. There's no reason for you to get involved."

31

"Ya just gave me reason," Law sneered.

"We don't take threats lightly, gent," Sharp said as he also crowded forward to go eyeball to eyeball with Law. "Pick up yer friends an' let bygones be bygones. That . . . or I'll break yer arm in more places than ya can count."

Law looked as angry as any man I had ever seen. He opened his mouth to say something, but I lifted his chin further with my pistol barrel. "Don't say anything more," I said. "You don't want my friend to make you a cripple, do you?"

His mouth shut tight.

"Now take your hand away from mine," I ordered.

He withdrew his hand from my hand, which I had been using to keep his pistol in place. I took his gun with my left hand as I holstered my own. Then I flipped open the loading gate with my thumb and used my other hand on the ejection rod to cycle all of the cartridges onto the floor. The first cartridge was still bouncing against the wood planks when the last hit the floor. I performed this little ceremony to show my skill with firearms. I wanted him to have second thoughts about challenging us again.

I slipped his empty Colt back into his holster.

I said, "Now go . . . quietly."

The man Sharp had punched to the floor struggled to his feet and looked quizzically at Law. He nodded, and they each grabbed an arm of their unconscious partner and pulled him toward the door.

Law turned to say, "Ya don't know who yer dealing with. Ya got the best of me this time, but this won't be the last ya see of me."

Sharp said, "Mr. Law, stay away from us an' hope we never spot ya again. There won't be no walkin' away next time."

At first, Law appeared startled that Sharp had used his name, but then he turned contemplative and calmly reassessed us. I knew what he was thinking. We knew who he was, yet met his challenge anyway. I bet that experience was rare for him. I hoped he had learned a lesson and would give us a wide berth in the future. Then another thought struck me: It could go the other way, and he could become even more of a threat. Small-time tyrants can't allow public humiliation. If the townspeople lost their fear of him, he might not be able to control them. His empire was at risk.

Damn, I didn't want this kind of trouble just before my wedding.

I marched over to Law, drew my pistol, and jabbed it hard in the middle of his chest, knocking the wind out of him. He doubled over, gasping.

I leaned in close and whispered, "If I see you again, I won't kill you, but I'll maim you for life. Think about the people here in Silverton. Any you hurt. Any who might want to get even when you no longer can use a gun or knife."

The look in his eye told me he had bullied or assaulted enough people to make an enfeebled life miserable.

Sharp added, "Ya got three choices. Ya can let it be . . . git . . . or come after us. We've handled yer kind many times, so it makes no difference to us. There's a peckin' order, an' as long as we're around, ya ain't at the top no more."

Law gasped as he struggled to exit the hotel with his two impaired partners.

After they were gone, I asked, "What do you think?"

"We gave it a good try, but I doubt he'll be warned off." Sharp kept his eye on the door. Then he shook his head. "Not him."

"How much should we worry?" I asked.

Sharp shrugged. "Not much if we stay away from Phelps an' his saloon. I don't think Law will come lookin' for us . . . but I could be wrong."

I also looked at the now-empty doorway. "We plan to do business in this town. We may not be able to avoid him forever."

Sharp remained silent so long, I thought he had no further comment. Then he said, "Yer right. Sooner or later, we'll need to deal with him. Next time, don't maim him. Kill him."

"I just said that to give him pause. Men like him fear being weak more than death."

"True, but I've never feared a man with six feet of dirt holdin' him down."

Chapter 5

unbecoming for an old man

Unbeknownst to us, our little ruckus had attracted gawkers to the hotel lobby. As soon as Law left, men and women came out from behind walls and furniture. Several men stepped forward to congratulate us but backed away after seeing the look in Sharp's eyes. He didn't challenge armed men to entertain people, nor had he put Law and his cronies in their place for the benefit of the townspeople. He would fight his own fights but seldom got mixed up in the troubles of people he didn't know. I was surprised that his countenance softened with a question from an attractive woman who looked to be in her early forties.

"You haven't changed, have you, Jeff?"

Sharp tipped his hat, making a half bow from the waist. "Well, ya don't look to have changed a bit yerself, Nora."

"Kind . . . but untrue. I'm six years older. So are you, I might add. You need to quit beating on people. It's unbecoming for an old man."

"Ain't all that old." Sharp winked. "Everythin' still workin' like it used to." He made a show of looking around the lobby. "What about your husband? Did ya stay married?"

She shrugged. "After a separation, we reconciled."

"He around?"

"My husband was murdered by one of those outlaws you threw out of here. My compliments, by the way."

Sharp instantly appeared sympathetic. "I'm sorry to hear that."

"Almost two years. It still smarts."

Sharp introduced me to Nora West. From their banter, I assumed that Sharp was intimately familiar with Mrs. West. I also expressed my condolences. I wanted to ask about how and why her husband had been killed, but this woman was Sharp's lady friend, so I kept quiet and let him lead the conversation.

"How are ya gettin' on?" he asked Nora.

"I do fine. I run my husband's mine. It's not a big claim, but I'll be damned if I'll let Phelps get his dirty hands on it. That's why they killed him. As long as I'm alive, I'll make sure Phelps never gets the Galena Queen."

I was confused. "They leave you alone?"

"They haven't sunk to killing women . . . yet, but they put offers in front of me all the time. None good." She straightened her shoulders. "Since I've been running it, the mine produces steady."

"Ya run it yerself?" Sharp asked.

"I have a foreman. Good man, but I keep an eye on the ore."

"Ya always was a smart woman. We'll be in town a couple days if ya need help."

"I've handled Phelps for nearly two years. I think I can survive the next two days without your manly protection." Her stern expression conveyed more than her words. "What're you doing here, anyway?"

"Sellin'. I'm a peddler now."

"I hope you're selling manure. You've got an endless supply."

Sharp laughed. "Nope. Me an' my partner are sellin' electrification. We can light yer mine an' bring fresh air to the deepest shaft."

She looked between us. "You're serious?"

"Very," I answered. "Jeff and I have a regional license for Thomas Edison's inventions. We can make you a good deal if we can use your mine to demonstrate our wares."

"How good?"

This was interesting. Phelps had nearly thrown us out of his saloon because he had no interest in improving the working conditions of his miners, while Mrs. West seemed receptive right away. Perhaps we should light up a mine he once killed to own, as well as a competing saloon.

"Our cost," I responded.

"Less. My mine is close to town, above ground, and famous because of Phelps's treachery. If your lighting works at my claim, everyone will see it, and you'll sell dozens of installations."

"I'm confused," I said. "Why would you want Edison's electric lights if your mine is above ground?"

"She wants to work the claim 'round the clock," Sharp answered.

She nodded appreciatively at Sharp. "You have your faults, Jeff, but you always were clever." She addressed me. "If I can illuminate the dig, I can work double shifts and get out of here twice as fast."

"Do ya want to sell it outright?" Sharp asked, with kindled enthusiasm.

"Jeff, the Galena Queen is too small for you. Hell, I'm lucky to clear a thousand a month from her."

"Can ya show it to me? Then we'll talk. Maybe over dinner?"

"You want me to go to dinner with you?" she asked. "I can't believe it. I take that back about you being clever."

"Show me the mine . . . then we'll see what happens." Sharp sounded ill at ease.

"Hell no. Have you forgot you left me high and dry? Not happening again, Jeff."

"I'm talkin' 'bout yer mine. Only yer mine. If ya want to leave, maybe I can make it quicker for ya."

She stared at Sharp for a long moment. "Go find someone else to rescue. I'm busy."

She turned on her heels and stomped up the stairs.

When I looked at Sharp, his expression surprised me. I had never seen him look sad. My first impulse was to rib him for being snubbed by a woman, but evidently this was no ordinary woman. I had many questions, but Sharp would tell me about her in his own time.

"Jeff, I like the idea of buying a mine," I said, trying to be helpful. "Let's keep an eye out for other opportunities."

"I need a whiskey," he said abruptly.

As he left the hotel, he added over his shoulder, "Alone."

Chapter 6

ill-mannered bunch

When I returned to the hotel, I lay down to rest but dozed only for a bit and, an hour later, felt wide-awake. I'd never be able to get back to sleep. I began to worry. The last time I'd gone to bed when Sharp tried to drink away a foul mood, he'd been arrested for murder, and I'd spent weeks trying to prove his innocence. My friend might be in trouble.

I had to get up. Damn. Before swinging my legs off the bed, I blindly brushed my arm along the floor to locate my boots by touch. I didn't look forward to trying to corral him. If he was in a sour mood, Sharp could be harder to handle than a raging bull. I sighed. Better do it now. The less inebriated he was, the better.

I decided to visit the Silver Nugget first—ladies' underthings and all. Besides, Sharp wasn't dumb. He'd figure Big Mike might help if he got into too much trouble.

The packed saloon held twice as many men as when we had visited in the afternoon. The mood was rollicking, with loud music, dancing girls, and shouts from the gambling tables. The day shift had ended, and miners had charged in to see how fast they could dispose of their pay. I didn't see Sharp at first but then spotted him alone at a table at the extreme edge of the stage. His morose demeanor discouraged anyone from sitting near him.

I sat at his table.

"Buy you another?"

"Yep."

After I ordered beer for both of us, Sharp asked, "Here to keep me from punchin' someone?"

"Can I?"

He laughed and relaxed a bit. "Everybody's too damn polite here. Thinkin' of wanderin' down to Phelps's place to find an ill-mannered bunch."

"You talk like you already know that's a bad idea."

"At the moment, but I may forget after a couple more drinks. Maybe those dancin' gals can distract me. If not, bludgeon me if I head in that direction."

"With pleasure." I smiled to show I wasn't entirely serious.

I said nothing more. By nature, I talked too much and asked too many tactless questions. This situation might become hard to control, so I needed to watch and listen. If he wanted to tell me about Mrs. West, he would. If he didn't want to tell me, asking about her would only ignite his temper. So I sipped my drink and watched the dancers. There were six women now, all young and pretty. Some even showed talent. It appeared that the better performers worked nights, and once they started looking worn or weary, Fletcher relegated them to the afternoons.

After two dance numbers, Sharp said, "Thanks."

I nodded. I knew he was thanking me for keeping him company without prodding. We had spent a couple of years together, in towns, on trains, and on trails. We had fought side by side more than a few times. We knew and understood each other—our good points . . . and our bad.

In the time I had known him, Sharp had been cavalier about women. Polite, successful, and transitory. He allowed no woman to get a hold on his heart, at least none that I had witnessed. It took all the discipline I could muster not to ask a fusillade of questions. Instead of opening my mouth, I signaled for a hostess. Perhaps another round of drinks could elicit more information than pestering.

After our new drinks arrived, a pretty solo singer started her act. She must have been a relative or bedmate of Big Mike, because she sang like an overly pampered child screeching disharmony to the applause of parents and hapless relatives. I winced on the occasions she tried to hit a note beyond her vocal range.

I grew to love her singing when Sharp became bored and started to talk.

"Nora was the only woman I ever loved." He studied his beer. "Damn. I wish I had never seen her again."

"How long?" I asked.

"She said six years, but it's been over seven. December 24th." He shook his head. "Hell of a Christmas."

"She said you left her," I said.

"Half the story. The half that makes her look the innocent party."

I sipped my drink and tried to ignore the irritating trill from the stage. Despite the sparseness of the explanation, Sharp was at least talking instead of throwing punches at some poor miner unaware of his transgression.

The men were now jeering the singer, and some were yelling at her to strip. I didn't think that likely. She looked very proper, both in dress and deportment. I felt sorry for her. Someone of her beauty could satisfy this mob of inebriated men without being overtly sexual, but she would need a good voice and a song that would put toes to tapping. She continued haltingly. When the men sustained their insults, she bashfully raised her skirt to display an ankle, then a little calf. These maneuvers only served to encourage the boisterous crowd. Men yelled obscenities or demanded that the dancers come back on stage. As the frenzy neared its peak, the tiny band hit a hard beat, and the singer grabbed her skirt, and in one practiced motion, ripped it off. Suddenly, the tune turned saucy, her horrible voice melodic. She ripped off her clothing one piece after another while sensually dancing. The laughter and banging of beer mugs indicated that this was a nightly ritual. As I laughed with the rest of the men, I admired her lithe figure and teasing gyrations that were smooth and effortless. The underwear-clad woman continued singing, her voice one of the finest I had heard on the frontier. I looked around. Despite having seen this act many times, the audience whooped and stomped their feet like it was the first time. I glanced at Big Mike standing to the side of the stage, and he winked. I saluted his showmanship with my beer mug, and he smiled in satisfaction.

Sharp no longer appeared morose. He clapped and stomped with abandon, never taking his eyes off the erotic exhibition. I hoped this diversion would take his mind off Mrs. West, but as soon as the actress exited the stage, Sharp's expression turned serious.

"Right smart show," he said.

"Had me fooled," I responded.

Sharp gulped the last of his beer and signaled for another.

"Nora had me fooled too," he said.

When I remained silent, he added, "Caught her with another man. Left right after. Didn't even stay to celebrate Christmas."

He fell silent, so I asked, "Had you planned to marry?"

"We did . . . as soon as she got divorced."

I was stunned. I had assumed this relationship had happened before her marriage. Sharp flirted with every woman, but I had never known him to cavort with a married one. In fact, he seemed to have a proclivity for widows. Then an awful thought struck me.

"Who did you catch her with?"

"Her husband."

Chapter 7

love is blind

After the next act, I led Sharp back to our hotel to finish our drinking in the lobby bar. The hotel had the advantage of being relatively private with a bed in near proximity. During the short walk, Sharp offered no clarification as to why he found a wife in bed with her husband offensive. He seemed to have it backward. To my way of thinking, the husband should have been the offended party.

We switched to whiskey, and once settled in front of a fire with drink in hand, Sharp said, "Nora promised she was goin' to get a divorce. I loved her. Thought she loved me. That night, I discovered she was playin' me for a fool. I was just a dalliance."

"Jeff, what did you catch them doing? Kissing or more?" I asked.

"Kissing? Come on, Steve. Ya think I'd react like I did because of a kiss?" His voice had grown loud enough to attract the attention of other guests. "Damn it, they were . . ." He lowered his voice, trying to appear relaxed, because everyone in the lobby was listening. "They were goin' as far as a man or woman can go . . . an' both enjoyin' it . . . immensely. She was not sayin' goodbye."

"Perhaps she couldn't find a gentle way to break it to him."

"So she made the beast with two backs instead. Come on, Steve, I was cuckolded."

"Cuckolded? Perhaps her husband would have had a different opinion."

"Ya think I'm an idiot?" Sharp snapped. "She claimed they hadn't had sex in years. No intimate relationship with her husband. None. It was supposedly one of their problems. Well, I can tell ya, it didn't look like much of a problem. Not from what I saw."

"So you just up and bolted. You didn't even wait for an explanation."

Sharp grew angry, or I should say, angrier. I thought I might be on the receiving end of one of his dangerous punches. When he spoke, it was in a low growl. "An explanation? What conceivable explanation could there be? She said they didn't have sex. She said she loved me. I committed myself to her. She said she would get divorced so we could marry. What I saw put a lie to everything. Her husband may have had grievances, but they came from the same source as mine. Her goddamn lyin' an' cheatin'."

I waited for Sharp's temper to cool before asking, "Why did she say you were the one to leave her high and dry?"

47

"I thought I just told ya . . . she's a liar."

"Something's not right," I mused.

"What do ya mean?"

"I mean you're a good judge of character . . . especially women. How could you be fooled so badly?"

"Damn it, Steve, have ya never heard that love is blind?"

"I've also heard about love at first sight. Is that what happened to you?"

He became thoughtful. "No. We knew each other for months before things got serious. Her husband an' I were partners in a mine. In fact, he's the one that got me started in minin'. He had me over for supper on occasion. That's how I got to know her."

Now I was more suspicious. "So you had plenty of opportunity to judge her character before you fell in love?"

Over the span of a few seconds, Sharp's face registered every emotion known to man. He ended with a look of consternation as he finished his drink.

After a heavy swallow, he said, "I haven't had supper. Have you?"

"No, but it's late. I don't think the kitchen's open."

"Let's go to the Silver Plate. They stay open for the miners who prefer to visit a saloon before eatin'. I hear they serve good steaks an' chops."

Without another word, we left the hotel and followed the boardwalk a long block to the restaurant. In the daytime, I preferred walking in the street, because each business maintained its portion of the boardwalk, sometimes inadequately. Boards could be uneven enough to trip you if you weren't careful. The risk of falling was greater in the dark, but less dangerous than being ridden over by a horse whose rider was too drunk to see straight.

The Silver Plate had two large windows that shone brightly in the night, illuminating the boardwalk and the street. Inside, a dozen hissing gas lamps made the place bright as day, great advertising for a diner that specialized in late-night fare. We would need to approach the owner about installing silent electric lamps. After we sat down to a white tablecloth table, I noticed the plates were polished pewter, not silver. I hoped their steaks were genuine beef.

In an improved mood, Sharp bantered until our steaks arrived. They were perfect. The potatoes and corn were good as well. At least when we had future business in Silverton, we would have a dependable place to eat, a rarity in the West, where a slab of meat might remind you of shoe leather or worse. Cooks generally overcooked beef and vegetables, and their idea of sauce would be salt and pepper. I always avoided stew. These dark concoctions made from spoiled food bred bugs that churned the stomach and made diners disgorge the lot. Better to go hungry and avoid week-old swill that unpleasantly got you to the same place anyway.

A woman's voice behind me said, "We need to talk."

I glanced over my shoulder to see Mrs. West. She looked determined. Damn, and the meal had been congenial until now.

"About what?" Sharp asked. "Yer silver claim?"

"There's no need to discuss anything else until we resolve the problem between us."

"We have a problem?" Sharp acted befuddled, which he wasn't.

"We do, and you damn well know it."

"Where'd ya come from?" Sharp asked. "I didn't see ya at one of the tables."

"I work here. Mostly cook. I'm trying to save enough money to move to New Orleans. I waited for you to finish your meal so I could ask your gentleman friend to leave."

"His name is Steve Dancy. Ya met before, if ya recollect."

She looked at me with a steady gaze. "Will you please excuse us, Mr. Dancy? This is a private matter."

I stood without waiting for Sharp's concurrence. I wanted this problem resolved as well. Sharp was my best friend, and I didn't like to see him troubled. Either they would talk things out satisfactorily, or Sharp would vent his anger. In either case, I would get my friend back in a better mood. At least, that was my hope.

"Steve, hang back. Ya know how I tend to punch people that provoke me."

"Nonsense," she said as she took my seat. "You may leave, Mr. Dancy. I'm not afraid of Jeff's bluster. He's never hit a woman . . . no matter what the provocation."

"Just remember your surroundings, Jeff," I said lightly. "These fine folks don't want their meals disturbed."

I meant it as a joke, but Sharp looked around as if noticing the room for the first time. When he returned his attention to Mrs. West, he appeared uncertain. Finally, he made up his mind and dismissed me with a wave of his hand.

As I turned to leave, I heard Mrs. West say, "Jeff, why did you run off like that? Did I do something wrong?"

Chapter 8

played for a fool

The next morning, after breakfast, I met up with Sharp at the livery. He had been there for over an hour. When I arrived, he seemed preoccupied, so I said a perfunctory good morning before checking on Liberty, my horse. We proceeded to waste time grooming our already well-cared-for animals. While I absentmindedly brushed Liberty, I thought about our purpose in Silverton. This was supposed to be a quick trip. I wanted to conclude a sale and ride back down to Durango. I began to wonder if Edison's license was worth the trouble. When I'd decided to pursue the right to sell his inventions, I'd needed a purpose for my wanderings. Perhaps I didn't need the hassle now that I would soon be married. Besides, I could always write another book if I got bored. Sales of my first novel had started slowly but picked up enough pace that my editor had sent a telegram encouraging me to write another.

Sharp interrupted my musing. "She says it wasn't her."

"Who wasn't her?" I asked confused.

He tossed his brush into a wooden bucket. "She wanted to know why I left without a goodbye, so I told her. She claimed that the woman in bed with her husband wasn't her. Says it was his mistress."

"You don't look happy. Shouldn't that make you feel better?"

"I'm not sure I believe her. Hell, even if I did, why should it make me happy? If she's tellin' the truth, it means I made a big mistake an' wasted seven years." He shook his head. "If she's lyin', I don't want her 'cuz she'll lie again." He kicked some hay. "No, I ain't happy. Not by a long shot."

"Didn't you see the woman clearly?" I asked.

"The man was on top, but I know her sounds . . . an' body."

"Could you have been wrong? Men get attracted to the same type of woman over and over."

Another futile kick at wispy hay. "Hell, I don't know. It was a long time ago." He went over and pulled the brush out of the bucket and brushed his horse again. "At the time I was certain. Dead certain."

I didn't know how to respond. Should I tell him to trust his instincts from seven years ago, or believe her today, or tell him it no longer mattered, and he should do whatever felt right? Instead of offering advice or trying to make him feel better, I uncharacteristically kept my mouth shut.

"She offered to sell me her mine," Sharp said

as he continued to brush his perfectly groomed horse. "She badly wants to get out of Colorado . . . an' the West for that matter."

"And?"

"An' I told her I'd take a look at it this mornin'."

"Ride out now?"

He kept brushing. "In a minute."

Sharp busied himself for the next few minutes with the hooves of his horse, followed by an elaborate inspection of his saddle and harness. Next, it looked as if he were going to clean his rifle, but he slipped it back into its scabbard.

Finally, he said, "Let's saddle up."

"What's bothering you?" I asked.

"If we buy her mine, she's gone for good. Maybe that's for the best, but damn, I'm not sure."

"What happened last night?"

"What? Last night? What do ya mean?"

"I mean did you and Mrs. West retire to the same room?"

"That ain't got nothin' to do with this."

"You know it does."

I prepared to duck a punch, but Sharp looked forlorn, not angry.

"Yep, we made up for lost time. Seemed fine at the moment, but this mornin' it gives me pause. Am I bein' played for a fool . . . again?"

"Let's find out. If the mine is producing close to what she said, and her price's fair, then you probably aren't being played."

That got a small grin. With a smooth practiced motion, Sharp slung his saddle over his horse's back and cinched the flank strap. I followed suit, happy that we were at last taking positive action that might expedite our departure from Silverton. If we could buy a mine to demonstrate Edison illumination and sign a contract to set the Silver Nugget ablaze, our work in this town would be done for the present. I didn't have an inkling whether Sharp and Mrs. West would sort out their problems, but Virginia and I were eager to get married and visit San Diego for our honeymoon.

Mrs. West's mine lay only a half mile out of town, so the short ride wouldn't qualify as good exercise for the horses. After examining her claim, we could visit other mines surrounding Silverton to get a feel for pricing and production.

I remained on horseback when we got to the Galena Queen. Sharp swung down and spent about twenty minutes talking to the foreman. Then he chatted with each of the four miners under the foreman's direction. Finally, he remounted, and we walked our horses away from the surface mine.

"The foreman an' his crew verify Nora's assertion. Production runs about a thousand a month. They keep hopin' for a new vein, but nothin' yet. Most mines the Galena Queen's size produce more than five times as much. A few, even more. After wages an' supplies, Nora probably clears only a few hundred a month. Enough to live comfortably, but not enough to get rich."

"Odd," I said.

"Why odd? It's exactly what she told us."

"Let me ask you a question. If you were of Phelps's temperament, would you kill to get a mine that grossed $12,000 a year?"

Sharp pulled up. "Damn, yer right. Why would Phelps want this claim?"

Looking back, we saw that the miners were ignoring us as they bent to their work. To find potential buyers for electrification, we had investigated mine operators in Silverton, so we knew a bit about Phelps's operations. This mine produced a pittance compared to his other holdings—and it wasn't as if it were the only one left to grab. There were plenty of other, more valuable claims around Silverton. What made this mine so important?

Sharp snapped his reins against his pants, and his horse ambled forward again. We rode silent for a few moments, and then Sharp said, "We need to look at this more carefully. If Phelps knows somethin' Nora don't, that foreman's got to be in on it."

Suddenly, he wheeled his horse around. "Let's go back. I got some new questions."

Chapter 9

waiting to be harvested

The foreman was displeased to see us return. This time I dismounted with Sharp. If his questions provoked these men, he might need help. I studied the foreman and his crew. None appeared to be carrying a gun, but each had a long-bladed knife hanging from a belt. The knives were probably viewed by the miners as tools, not weapons. Sharp seldom wore a handgun, so he would be vulnerable unless he unsheathed his rifle. He didn't. I hung back and stood slightly to the side so I could keep an eye on all five men.

"Forget somethin', stranger?" the foreman asked.

"Yep. A small question. How do ya sneak silver past Mrs. West?"

That answered my question about whether Sharp intended to provoke.

The foreman angrily threw down his shovel. "What the hell you talkin' about?"

He took a step toward Sharp and put his hand on his knife, so I moved abruptly till I was square with him and put my hand on my gun. He noticed my motion out of the corner of his eye and turned his head to look me over. We held eye contact for a couple of seconds, and then he removed his hand from the knife. I waited a beat and allowed my hand to fall to the side of my holster. I smiled friendly. No one relaxed, however.

"How much did this mine produce two years ago?" Sharp asked. "Ya might as well tell me the truth, 'cuz Mrs. West will anyway."

"Ain't got nothin' to do with today."

"Tell me."

"About five thou a month, but those veins played out."

"I want a look-see," Sharp said as he started to walk around the foreman.

When Sharp got within arm's reach, the foremen put his hand on his knife again. He looked serious.

Sharp said, "Steve, kill these other miners if they make a move toward their weapons. Never mind this asshole."

"Ha, you think you can win a barehanded fight against a knife? I've torn open many a man before you, and I'll slit more after you're long gone."

Sharp made a feint like he was going to roundhouse the foreman, but instead grabbed his right hand with his left. He jerked the hand away from the knife, twisting it savagely. A scream accompanied a sickening crack of bones. Sharp didn't relent. He twisted in a new direction and shattered fingers as well as the wrist. I had drawn my pistol, but the rest of the miners remained still as threatened possums. I wasn't sure if they felt little loyalty toward their foreman, or the swiftness of the action delayed their response. In either case, they wanted nothing to do with this fight. I reholstered my pistol.

Sharp grabbed the foreman by the ear and marched him up the slight incline to the diggings.

"How do ya hide the ore?" Sharp demanded.

Sharp got a yelp from another twist of the foreman's hand.

He breathed deeply before saying, "We haul it in buckets up to the top of the hill. Phelps has a claim just over the ridge. Mrs. West keeps an eye on what comes down, not what goes up."

"In broad daylight?" Sharp sounded incredulous.

"She ain't out here much. We dump it up there and cover the ore with slurry. Phelps's people come after dusk and carry it down the other side to their crusher."

"How much?" Sharp demanded.

"How much? You mean how many buckets?"

"No, ya dumb ass. How many dollars?"

"Dollars? Hell, I don't know. More than we take down the hill, I can tell you that."

"Double?"

"More. The claim probably yields the same as before her husband died."

"Yer fired," Sharp said as he twisted him around and shoved him down the hill. Then he turned toward the other miners and yelled, "The lot of ya!"

"You can't fire us!" one of the miners yelled back. "You ain't our boss."

"Yer right. My mistake. Stay right where ya are. I'll get the marshal an' have ya arrested."

All five men looked at each other and scrambled down the incline, scooting in the direction of town, while the foreman held his hand tight against his chest to keep it from jostling.

"Now what?" I asked.

"I'm thinkin' we take us a look over that ridge," Sharp answered.

He walked back down the incline and retrieved his rifle from his horse, then pulled the lever down far enough to make sure a cartridge had been chambered. Satisfied, he marched up the hill as I scrambled to catch up. When I noticed that large rocks had been positioned to make rough steps, I fell behind, rather than beside him.

From the top, the slope descended further than the one we'd ascended. About two dozen men worked in a wide shallow valley that stretched about a quarter mile in either direction. At the base of the hill stood a crusher and other mining apparatus manned by a few more men. One of them noticed us and pointed in our direction. I couldn't hear what he said, but our presence soon had the attention of every man working around the equipment.

Each man used his hand to shade his eyes from the sun behind us. We must have presented quite a sight. Two armed men silhouetted against the sky. They probably weren't sure who we were, but I doubted that the foreman or his men ever came up this hill armed with anything other than their knives. They had to be wondering how we had bypassed Mrs. West's, or perhaps I should say Phelps's, crew that was partially paid by Mrs. West.

Sharp handed me his rifle as he nodded toward the men below. He wanted me to keep an eye on them. Presumably, both eyes. I felt, more than saw, Sharp drop to one knee. I heard him digging with something. I stole a quick glance and saw that he was using a stick to scrape away the surface dirt and debris. I returned my attention to the men down the hill. We may have presented a bit of an apparition against a bright sky, but that also meant we presented easy targets. Sharp's rummaging in the dirt wouldn't encourage them to view us as friendly either.

"They weren't lyin'," Sharp said. "Decent ore. My guess is three or four bucket loads. Probably somewhere near two hundred dollars in silver there just waitin' to be harvested by our friends down below."

He stood and reached for his rifle.

I handed it to him. "Now what?"

"Thinkin'."

After a moment, he said, "Go down the hill an' bring back two buckets an' a shovel."

"Jeff, there's more than a dozen men down there. I don't think you should stay up here by yourself."

"Hell, I can lay below the ridge line an' kill every one of 'em that don't hide behind a piece of hard equipment. Don't worry about me. Yer the one who needs to be careful. Those men might come back with reinforcements. Yer the one gonna be exposed."

I smiled. "I believe you're right. Trade places?"

He pretended to think about it. "Naw. Just hurry yer sorry ass."

I did. In short order, I had returned with an empty bucket in each hand and a shovel tucked under my arm. I had seen no one around Mrs. West's claim.

At the crest, Sharp stood straight, his rifle lazily nestled in his folded arms. He looked like he didn't have a care in the world. When I examined the encampment below, I got another impression entirely. Almost all the men in the valley had congregated around the machinery, most brandishing rifles. I wished I had foregone the shovel for my Winchester. A pistol from this distance would only make a lot of noise.

"Dig," Sharp said as he kept an eye on the activity below.

He really meant shovel, because the loose ore

needed only to be scooped up. I quickly had two buckets full of rock. When I finished, I noticed Sharp examining the ground around my feet.

"Steve, I'll keep these men at the bottom of the hill while ya carry the buckets down. Dump them near the trail an' throw a bush over 'em. Bring the buckets back. Ya got one more good load."

I hefted the buckets and groaned. "Hey, you're the miner. Next time I stand guard and you haul pails of rocks."

"Next time, be smart an' bring yer rifle." I saw only the back of his head, but I knew he was grinning.

When I returned, I carried the two empty buckets and my rifle. As I crested the hill, I got a view into the valley below. I grew uneasy.

"Where did all those men come from?" I asked.

"Probably Phelps's other digs."

"Seen Phelps or Law?"

Sharp pointed toward the valley entrance. "Law's comin' along now with a few of his henchmen. Don't bother fillin' the buckets. Time to git."

With that, Sharp turned on his heel and started slipping and sliding down the slope in the direction of Mrs. West's claim and our horses. Halfway down the hill, we spotted Phelps with about a half dozen men. We kept moving in their direction.

As we approached, one of the men was untying

a miner's short shovel from his horse. When Phelps flicked his fingers, the other men spread out in a semicircle. The man with the shovel used it to roll away a bush I had pulled from the ground and laid on top of our liberated ore. Sharp pulled the hammer back on his rifle, and I followed suit.

"Touch that ore, an' it will be the end of yer boss!" Sharp yelled over the remaining distance.

After a few more steps, he slid to a stop, pulled his rifle up hard against his shoulder, and pointed it at Phelps. Phelps looked as out of place as a dusty cowboy walking down Broadway in New York City. He sat astride a horse, but he remained neatly attired in his eastern-style suit, including a derby hat with a black satin ribbon.

"You stole that ore from my claim," Phelps said.

Sharp said, "Hell, that ore's kinda restless. Keeps movin' around. At the moment, it sits on Mrs. West's claim." He smiled. "We plan on keepin' it. If ya got other ideas, tell yer men to shoot away."

Sharp kept a steady bead on Phelps. I pointed my rifle toward the man at the right hand of Phelps but used my peripheral vision to sense movement from the others further out. I tried to appear unconcerned, but in truth I worried that Law might climb over the hill and come at us from behind. I needed eyes in the back of my head.

I stole a glance at Phelps and felt relief. I could tell from his face that he was going to relent.

"There's not even a hundred dollars' worth of silver there," Phelps said. "I won't kill you for that pittance, but I will kill you if you ever step on to one of my claims again. Do you understand?"

"I do," Sharp answered. He paused dramatically. "An' if men under yer employ steal from this claim again, I won't hire a lackey. I'll kill ya myself."

Then I heard words from behind that chilled me.

"Ain't no lackey."

It was Ben Law.

Chapter 10

the victor

One of us needed to assess the threat from behind, but if we both turned, Law would assume an attack, and we would die in a hail of bullets fired by Phelps and his men. Sharp had the bead on Phelps, so it had to be me.

I told Sharp, "I'm turning around to say howdy to our friend. If Law shoots me, kill Phelps."

I made an unhurried turn, my rifle pointing toward an unoccupied portion of the hill. I didn't want to get shot because Law thought I might try firing first.

What I saw made my stomach tighten like a towel wrung dry after washing. Ben Law aimed a scattergun at my stomach. He was alone, which was probably why we hadn't heard him descend the rock staircase. One man walking carefully can be silent. I felt real fear because Law appeared smart as well as brutal . . . and he held a grudge for the little shindig in the hotel parlor. I never doubted that he would enjoy blowing me down the rest of the slope.

"Law has a shotgun on me," I said, as matter-of-factly as I could manage.

"Too bad for ya," Sharp responded over his

shoulder. "If he kills ya, I'll make a mess of Phelps's face."

Nobody uttered a sound. No one breathed heavy. Not one person flinched or twitched. It was deadly still.

Sharp chuckled. "What now, Mr. Phelps? Yer call."

"Now? Now, nothing. But keep a watchful eye. We'll meet again. And don't tread on any of my claims. From now on, my orders are shoot to kill."

Throughout, Sharp had kept his rifle aimed at Phelps's head. I held mine easy and pointed slightly away from Law. I was not eager for a muzzle flash to be my last memory. Slowly, and with a wicked grin, Law gradually lowered the scattergun so it pointed at my knees. I grew even more apprehensive. Did he intend to blow off my lower legs? My instinct was to bring my gun around and try to get off a first shot. Thankfully, I resisted the urge. That's what Law wanted. When I didn't comply, he dropped his aim until the shotgun pointed at the ground between the two of us. The huge barrels were no longer aimed in my direction, but Law's wicked grin remained fixed on me. I watched him closely and noticed that his smirk did not extend to his lifeless eyes—they remained emotionless and calculating. He had manipulated our encounter so that the contest was generally even now. Was he still goading me into a fight? I became certain. He wanted me to make a move.

I did.

I lowered my Winchester a smidgeon.

Law's grin turned into a big smile, one that now encompassed his eyes. He had won. To him, it didn't matter if we shot it out, or I chickened out. Either way, he went away the victor. That's what was important to him. The silver didn't matter. Phelps didn't matter. For that matter, I didn't matter. After me, there would be others—until there weren't. To Law, these encounters were a game, like kids playing king of the mountain. He had played it many times and had always won. And he would keep winning until he lost.

Phelps said, "Ben, climb back over to the other side. If anyone lifts his head above the ridge from this side of the hill, blow them away. No excuses. You and your men are paid to protect my property. Make sure your guards do their job. No more damn slipups. You hear?"

Law instantly became furious.

"George, don't bluster at me, you goddamn daisy. Weren't no slipups by my men. I'm tired of you prancin' about and actin' like some kinda fancy lord."

"You work for me, damn it. My money pays you . . . and your men. I can bluster at you any time I want. Treat me with respect or claim your last pay envelope."

"Treat *you* with respect? Hell, you better treat me with respect. If I kill you, I can just take yer damn money." He shifted the aim of his shotgun slightly. "If you got a lick of sense, you'll ride off now . . . quiet-like."

Phelps's mouth moved, but no sound came out. He clearly wanted to say something more, but in the end he rode off . . . quiet-like. Phelps had bought a wild animal, a beast that could revert to his feral nature at any moment. I wondered if Phelps could continue to control Law? After this display, I doubted it.

Law looked at us, and I could see his fury abate.

"I've worked for that man three months, and he ain't got a clue what I'm about. Dumb ass." He took a step up the hill and then turned back. "Don't think you can start a row between Phelps and me. I got honor. I do my job. Mr. Phelps and me get along just fine most-wise . . . except when he acts like he owns me. Can't abide that. If he does it too much, I'll kill him. I don't care who he is or his pa."

He took another step, then turned again to issue us a warning. "Please stick your head up over that ridge. My boys and me need target practice." He laughed. "Maybe you can bob up and down a little for us. Make it a challenge."

He took two more steps and turned around yet again.

"Hey, Dancy, smart move. I woulda killed you." He guffawed. "Hell, that would've been a sight. Your guts splattered all over Mr. Sharp there. Take him a week to wash you off."

With that he climbed the rest of the hill, laughing raucously.

I ceased to believe the man was sane.

Chapter 11

imagined slights

We gathered up the silver I had dumped by the trail and stuffed the rocks into our saddlebags. We both looked longingly at the top of the ridge but decided to leave the remaining silver for nocturnal bandits. No use getting killed for a hundred dollars or so. I put a greater value on my life.

When we got back to town, Sharp insisted on seeing Mrs. West immediately. Finding her took time, but we eventually discovered her at a seamstress shop. We had to wait in a vestibule until her fitting was complete. When she emerged, Sharp informed her that he had news about her claim and invited her back to the hotel for coffee. She directed us to a small café instead. I thought it was a good choice. The feminine décor and clientele would never attract Law or any of his men.

After we explained what had happened and showed her the silver, she grew agitated.

"You mean if I hadn't been robbed, I could have escaped months ago? Now I'm delayed even further. I need a new crew . . . and guards this time to keep them honest."

"Or ya could sell the claim to me," Sharp offered.

"How much?"

"Thirty thousand," Sharp answered.

"No, Jeff. That's too little. It would have been fine when I first offered it to you, but not now, not if it produces five thousand a month. Besides, you'll make millions off those Edison inventions. My mine opens up all of Silverton to you."

"Yer mine comes with risks," Sharp said, shaking his head. "Could be near played out. There's Law to contend with. Thirty thousand, plus what ya already got, will give ya a fine life. A comfortable life . . . away from here."

"You sound eager to see me gone," Mrs. West said.

Sharp shrugged.

"I'm confused. I thought last night set things right between us."

"Been thinkin' on it. Best we take this slower," Sharp said.

"If that's how you feel, I'll sell to Mr. Phelps. If what you say is true, he knows the real worth of my claim . . . always has . . . and Ben Law presents no risk to him."

"Not sure about that," I said.

She whirled around on me. "What do you mean?"

"Steve's just jabberin'," Sharp said. "Sellin' to Phelps might be the smart move." He shrugged again. "Course, he always knew what yer claim produced. Didn't up his price none when ya sent him packin' time after time . . . just continued to steal yer ore. Can't see how that will change."

"Blast you, Jeff." She sat back in her chair with a pout. "That's a bad offer, and you know it. You're trying to get even for imagined slights."

"Ain't got no imagination. Remember ya sayin' so yerself."

If I said anything one way or the other, I'd get in trouble, so I sat there and sipped coffee and nibbled biscuits. I had no inkling who was right, but having sex with her husband didn't seem like an offense worthy of a six-year grudge. I knew Sharp would say the issue was trustworthiness, not infidelity, but how would he learn the truth without giving her a chance?

"What's your best offer?" she said in a huff.

"Thirty thousand," Sharp repeated. "I expect that's considerably more than Mr. Phelps's last offer."

She threw her napkin at him. "Draw up the papers, you damn fool. I don't know why I ever loved you in the first place." She reached down and hefted our saddlebags. "These are mine, including the bags. Get new ones with your first diggings."

She stormed out.

Sharp did not appear happy.

"You decided against starting up with her again?" I asked.

"Not yet. Still thinkin' on it."

He gazed after her with a forlorn expression.

Finally, he stood. "Let's find a lawyer. Any ideas?"

"I always go for the best in town," I answered. "Let's ask the hotel clerk."

After returning to the hotel, the clerk directed us to the most successful lawyer in town. We got two contracts written up, one for the purchase of Mrs. West's claim and the other to electrify the Silver Nugget. The second contract had no price, so we traipsed over to the saloon to negotiate a final deal.

When we walked in the door, Big Mike directed us over to a quiet table. After we got beers, Sharp slid the contract over.

Without picking it up, Big Mike contemplated the contract. "Thought you boys might not come back. Lots of men with big ideas hereabouts."

"Not as big as ours," I said. "You'll notice the amount needs to be filled in. Are you still willing to introduce us to Phelps's competitors?"

"I am."

I gave him a figure that represented our cost and told him he would get ten percent of all sales resulting from the meeting he organized.

He read the contract carefully. When he satisfied himself, he said, "This looks okay, but no cash in advance. If I give you half, you'll disappear faster than a pigeon flapping away with a scrap of food. I'll pay on completion."

I had anticipated this response. Mining towns were rife with shysters.

"Twenty-five percent on delivery of product to a location of your choice. Another twenty-five percent on your accepting our engineer. Twenty-five additional after we light your place. The final twenty-five percent thirty days after our illumination works properly."

He thought only a few seconds and extended his hand. "Deal. Fill in the specifics."

As I recorded our agreed terms, Sharp said to Fletcher, "Ya know anythin' 'bout Phelps's pa?"

"Guess he must have had one," Fletcher said, "but I never heard any mention of him. Why?"

"Law said he didn't care who Phelps's pa was—like he was important."

"Phelps puts on airs, like he's a gentleman. Probably bragged up his pa to Law, but I bet he really was a dirt-poor sodbuster."

"Makes sense," Sharp said. "I presume ya checked our bona fides with yer niece."

"Mary and Mr. Edison confirmed your story, but don't ask for cash in advance. They say you got a license, but that doesn't mean you can do the work."

"Fair enough," Sharp said. "I like doin' business with a careful man."

Fletcher said, "I like doing business with honest men." He looked us over. "I'll be watching . . . careful-like."

We finished signing the papers and then went

to see Mrs. West. That contract signing went just as smoothly. I was a happy man. We had accomplished what we had come to Silverton to do. All that remained was for Sharp to hire a mining crew to work his new claim and for me to send a few telegrams. One telegram to arrange for equipment to be shipped from our warehouse in Denver, and another to request an engineer from Menlo Park. Edison wanted us to use only engineers he had selected and trained. We certainly had no reason to disagree.

With everything done, we would be able to leave for Durango the next day at first light. As we left the telegraph office, we were met by Phelps and Law on the boardwalk. I didn't like their self-satisfied expressions.

"How much you pay for that West claim?" Phelps asked.

"None of your business," Sharp answered.

"I'll give you ten thousand."

"Far short," Sharp said.

"Good. Wouldn't want you to come out whole. I'll have our common lawyer draw up papers."

We had asked for the best lawyer in town, never dreaming that Phelps would have an attorney put legal flourishes on his shenanigans. I should have anticipated that he would engage the finest legal counsel in town. That was a boneheaded error. Not only had we hired the same lawyer, but he was disreputable into the bargain. Lawyers aren't supposed to blab about the business of their other clients, but ours hadn't hesitated to let his more lucrative boss know what we were about. Damn.

"The claim ain't for sale," Sharp said.

Since we hadn't returned to our hotel rooms, Sharp still carried his Winchester. He lazily swung it into his arms so it lay across his chest. For some reason, this maneuver amused Law. He twitched a finger, and two men sauntered up from a bench in front of the telegraph office. I glanced behind me and recognized them as part of Phelps's escort at the claim site. I was fed up with these two and wanted to shoot Law dead right there on the street. I told myself to relax and let Sharp take the lead. He had handled many similar situations over the years and knew how to get us out of this predicament without bloodshed.

"If yer boys step any closer, I'll kill ya where ya stand."

Damn. Everyone bristled, including me. I shifted sideways to Sharp to get out of his way if he swung his rifle into action. It also put me sideways to the two on the boardwalk. I wanted Law, but taking care of the two to our back made more sense. Besides, I didn't think Phelps presented a threat to Sharp, so he would concentrate on Law.

"Now, now, boys," Phelps said. "No need for hostilities. We only made a business offer. Take it or leave it."

"Leave it," Sharp said.

"Too bad. Nobody in town will work that claim," Law said. "In fact, no one works on this mountain without my say-so."

Phelps grinned. "It saddens me to see a decent silver vein go fallow, but Ben's right. He's president of the Miners' Guild."

"We'll find men," Sharp said.

"No . . . you won't," Law said, overly pleased with himself.

"Ten thousand," Phelps repeated.

"Go to hell," Sharp answered.

The situation grew tense, but only for the slightest moment.

"Have it your way," Phelps said, turning to leave. He half-twisted to face partially toward us. "By the way, the offer goes down a thousand a week."

"Nice to know," Sharp answered amicably. "Can't wait for ten weeks to pass so I won't hear any more of yer foolish palaver." He let his rifle fall to his side. "If this business meetin's over, we got things to do."

Phelps waved his arm graciously, like a noble granting us leave to go. "Then by all means, don't let us stop you."

We walked away.

Once out of earshot, we stopped. Looking back, I said quietly to Sharp, "Law said nobody works without his say-so. If that's true, he can bring Phelps to heel any time he wants."

"Yep. Phelps is a fool. Law has designs on his whole empire. When he takes it, it won't be pretty."

"What are we going to do?"

"Nothin'. Go back to Durango an' wait for our equipment." Sharp leaned forward as if to walk away but pulled back. "On second thought, let's telegraph to cancel the engineer an' shipment. We'll reorder when we find men. I don't want to come back here with only the Silver Nugget." He shook his head, displeased. "I'll explain to Big Mike. Wasn't comfortable havin' the mine worked in our absence anyway."

"Will Phelps work it while we're away?"

"Naw. Too risky, us with clear title an' all. He believes we'll sell when we can't work the claim. He's got lots of other mines to keep him busy in the meantime. That silver ain't goin' nowhere. He believes it'll still be waitin' for him when we settle cheap."

"But you won't." I said this as a statement, not a question.

"Not on yer life."

I laughed. "I hope *that* was a slip of the tongue."

Sharp gave me one of his wicked grins. "Naw. Picked it on purpose."

Chapter 12

a confident man

As a child, I often went bird hunting with my father. We'd stay away multiple nights, camping in the woods, usually alongside a creek or stream. On several occasions, I watched beavers work tirelessly to construct dams. I was fascinated by those industrious amphibious creatures, but they had nothing over the land-based variety known as railroad workers. Since we had traversed this trail a few days earlier, the D&RG had worked feverishly on the narrow-gauge line. Rail workers may have made rapid progress up the mountain, but we couldn't get any speed going down. When we weren't ordered to halt because of blasting, we had to tread our way between men, wagons, mules, stacked supplies, tents, and huge tools scattered along every foot of the mountain ledge that represented the sole trail between Durango and Silverton. Often, we got stuck behind slow-moving wagons hogging the entire space allocated for travel alongside the construction.

It may have looked like bedlam, but only organization could achieve this relentless progress. The frenetic motion only appeared uncontrolled; foremen, supervisors and a superintendent orchestrated every action. Everyone worked with purpose, and everyone worked to a plan.

On our way up to Silverton, we had become friendly with Karl Werner, one of the supervisors. He oversaw the teamsters and express crews that moved and staged material, men, foodstuff, and living quarters. He took his job seriously. Hundreds of men could be idled if he failed to put the proper material in front of the moving line. This task was difficult enough on flatlands, but it was an unremitting challenge on the mountain precipice that ran above the Animas River.

We met up with him a half-day's ride out of Silverton. Werner greeted us like close friends. Actually, he greeted Sharp as if he had sincerely missed him. I received a polite hello and a perfunctory slap on the back. I wasn't sure if I came across as patrician or unfriendly, but I never prompted the kind of comradery that Sharp engendered with men or women. Werner asked us to ride ahead about a mile until we saw his tent and to wait for him there. He promised steak and the best whiskey between Durango and Silverton. Since only rock-ledged wilderness separated the two towns, I felt confident his boast would prove true.

Werner rode up late in the late afternoon, as Sharp and I lounged in camp chairs outside his tent, sipping a decent rye whiskey. We had occupied ourselves by watching men organize tools and materials for the following day.

"I see my assistant served refreshments," Werner said.

"Fine lad," Sharp said as he saluted with his glass. "Saved some for ya."

Werner laughed. "One of the good parts of my job is that I always have someone riding to town for something or other. I usually have an item or two I want him to pick up for me. We may be out in the wilds, but I never want for food, drink, or a clean change of clothes."

His assistant opened another camp chair and handed his boss a generous glass of whiskey. Werner sat with a sigh. After settling, he told his assistant, "Tom, we move tomorrow. Break it all down at daybreak, and I'll send a wagon back about noon. I got a spot in mind with a small waterfall. You'll like it."

"How close to the blasting?" the assistant asked.

Werner laughed again, obviously relishing his assistant's discomfort. "Close, by god. The crews will awaken us at first light, and you'll be cleaning dust off everything all the day long."

His assistant winced, which only further amused Werner. He sat quietly for a bit, savoring his drink as he watched the men work. After a heavy sigh, he said, "I love end-of-day chores. By dusk, the whole place will be organized and structured. Everything tidied up and readied for an early start. Makes you proud to be a railroader."

"When do ya 'xpect to finish?" Sharp asked.

"Hopefully, before October. Need to be finished in case of an early winter storm. Unless something unforeseen happens, we should make it easy."

"What happens to yer workers when ya finish?" Sharp asked.

The way Sharp asked the question, I suspected he wasn't concerned about their livelihood.

"Move to wherever we decide to lay the next rail . . . unless we tell them not to bother. Only a couple won't get a new job. Petty crooks, troublemakers, and cheating gamblers for the most part. A bad element is not good for morale. We've got to weed them out constantly."

"Will the Denver & Rio Grande start service immediately?" I asked.

"My hope is that we can hold them off till we finish." Werner waved his arm to encompass the men in front of us. "Men and materials cost plenty. The bosses want to start shipping ore as soon as they can. Sooner if they can figure out a way to run an engine up this hill without tracks." He laughed at his own attempt at humor.

I spoke to Sharp. "With the new line in place, we can recruit miners from Nevada or Leadville and get them here lickety-split."

"We'll need guards as well," Sharp mused. "Do all of yer security move on to the next line?"

Now I was sure I understood the reasoning behind Sharp's questions. We needed mine workers and guards to keep them safe. Both had to be independent of Phelps and Law. That meant they needed to come from somewhere else, needed to feel safe, and we had to pay them enough to keep them from jumping over to Phelps.

Werner asked what this was about, so we told him everything.

After we had finished, he shook his head and said, "You're in trouble, for sure. The Miners' Guild will try to get to your new men. No doubt about it. You'll need some ruffians to fend them off . . . and a boss that's tougher than Phelps."

"Are you applying?" I asked.

He sipped his drink and gnawed on a piece of jerky he had fished out of a canvas bag.

After chewing a few moments, he said, "I love this job. I love putting things in order. I love working for the Denver & Rio Grande. Good bosses. Pay's terrific. But I'll never get rich working for another man. My family lives in Denver and I miss them. So . . . if you match my pay and give me twenty percent ownership, I'll be your supervisor of operations."

"Pay's not a problem," Sharp said. "But twenty percent won't make ya rich. The mine produces only five grand a month. After expenses, you won't net more than two-three hundred. Good, but not great."

"Shame. Kinda liked you men. But I can't—"

I interrupted. "We can make you a better offer."

For the first time in this conversation, he gave me serious consideration. "And what would that be?"

I explained our arrangement with Edison and our plans to illuminate Fletcher's Silver Nugget and use the silver claim to demonstrate the use of Edison's inventions in mining. I told him we had a warehouse in Denver as a hub and intended to expand across the West. We needed someone who knew how to control inventory, handle men, and move goods. I had his attention.

"I'm not an electrical engineer," he said.

"Fix things that break around here?" Sharp asked.

He shrugged. "Got to."

"So yer handy. Educated?"

"Some college in Germany. Got antsy, so I came to America to make my fortune."

Sharp and I excused ourselves and stepped away for a few moments. We agreed on an arrangement like the deal we had made with Virginia to manage our general store in Leadville. As a sweetener, Sharp suggested a five percent commission for any sales he made.

When we returned, Karl Werner had refilled our glasses. A confident man.

We offered Werner ten percent now and an additional ten percent once he doubled first year profits. His percentage would include an ownership interest in both the mining operations and our electrification business. His monthly compensation would be the same as his salary with the D&RG. We would promote him to superintendent of operations, and his responsibilities would include hiring, firing, the warehouse, materials, transport, demonstrations, and installations for both enterprises. He would run our company for us.

When I had finished, Werner gazed off for only a few seconds, and then said he had one condition: We had to wait until completion of the Durango-Silverton line. That bothered me because I always wanted to move fast in business. But I had seen Werner's work, and he was worth the wait. Then a thought occurred to me. Edison would insist that he come to Menlo Park for training. Damn. We needed to put our mine and the Silver Nugget in abeyance for a couple of months. Oh well, better to hire a good man than to make a hasty start. We told Werner we agreed to his condition but had one of our own. He needed to go to New Jersey to secure approval by Edison; otherwise, we would need to restrict him to mine operations. Sharp promised that if necessary, he would expand the Silverton holding so Werner's twenty percent would become substantial. We also agreed that his family could accompany him to New Jersey with all expenses paid by us. This appeared to be the clincher, because Werner had always wanted to take his family on a long train ride.

Werner shook hands with his future bosses and poured drinks around for us to toast our arrangement.

He started to raise his glass, but I stopped him. "Before we toast, I need to warn you that this position has risks. Serious risks. We've made enemies of Ben Law and George Phelps. Law claims to run the Miners' Guild, and he has a small army of hard men as enforcers. You can hire anyone you think you need, but people in Silverton have warned us that he's dangerous."

"I know Law. Or at least, I know of him. I also know Big Mike. We sat many times in these same chairs." He took a healthy swallow of whiskey. "If you allow me to pick my crew, I can handle Law and his enforcers."

Chapter 13

a prison wall

I had been away only six days, but I felt excited as Durango came into view. Mrs. Virginia Baker, my fiancée, had remained in town to plan our wedding. At least that was her excuse for not accompanying me. After Leadville, I don't think she had much enthusiasm for mining towns. Durango acted as a supply depot for Silverton and served as a transport hub, but the actual mining occurred fifty miles north. Her engineer husband had been killed in a mining accident in Leadville. Mrs. West and Mrs. Baker had something in common: They both found it difficult to escape from a male-dominated culture that charged an arm and a leg for food, lodging, clothing, and everything else a person needed or wanted. Many women of ill repute were drawn to mining camps because they went where the men with money lived, but other women fell into prostitution because it was the only way to eat. Widowed women were especially at risk. Mrs. Baker and Mrs. West had the will to find another way. My fiancée became a shopkeeper, and Mrs. West continued to run her husband's mine, not as well as it could have been run, but well enough that she could remain independent.

Our wedding shouldn't have been hard to plan. The only guests would be Jeff Sharp, Joseph McAllen, McAllen's daughter, Maggie, and McAllen's ex-wife, because her new husband, the local preacher, would officiate. Didn't seem like Virginia would need to do much planning.

I believed the real reason Virginia stayed behind had more to do with our cottage. We had bought a two-bedroom clapboard house built for an attorney who had then moved his practice to Silverton. We still intended to roam the West, but Virginia had suggested that we acquire an abode that could serve as a refuge when we took breaks from traveling. Since McAllen owned a ranch nearby, and Virginia had grown close to Maggie, Durango made sense as our hometown. I hesitated owning something that stayed put like a house, but a base with nearby friends seemed like a fine idea. Virginia also pointed out that by not staying in a hotel suite, the house would pay for itself in short order. I wasn't too sure about her arithmetic but didn't want a heated argument with my future bride, so we bought the house.

After we closed the deal, I realized she was right. The cost to me was minor, and we could travel anywhere by train with speed and comfort. Telegrams provided nearly instant communication with anyone, anywhere in the nation. These inventions had shrunk the size of the country by making the movement of people or correspondence easy, quick, and reasonably priced. I loved the West . . . but I loved it more when equipped with modern conveniences.

We left our horses at a livery and walked to my street. I felt relaxed until I saw the house. How long had I been gone? Not even a full week. The house had been whitewashed, a waist-high fence had been built around a newly planted garden as neatly arranged as my mother's drawing room, lace curtains adorned the windows, but most startling of all, a raw-lumbered porch extended the entire width of the house. Had I made a mistake? This place didn't look like a provisional abode that we could leave whenever we wanted.

I stood stunned until Sharp broke my stupor by laughing uproariously. I gave him a dirty look.

Getting control of himself, he said, "Welcome to matrimony."

I looked around to see if any neighbors were peeking through their curtains. Sharp certainly laughed hard enough to draw their attention. Six houses and a few empty lots occupied the quiet street that gently climbed a foothill leading toward the San Juan Mountains. I saw no one, not even at the window or door of my own house. Where was Virginia?

I opened the picket gate and stepped up to the porch that had miraculously appeared in front of my otherwise simple house. Sharp had calmed to a chuckle that I found even more irritating. When I turned to face the street, I saw a spectacular view. Our lot was situated toward the end of the street, which gave it enough elevation to overlook the town and countryside. It would be a great place to while the day away in a rocker when I grew old, but at this point in my life, the waist-high picket fence looked like a prison wall. I was about to open the front door, when Sharp warned me to hold up because a buggy was approaching. Virginia snapped the reins to hurry the horse up the hill. She looked put out. More worrisome, three heavily loaded wagons followed behind, struggling to get their loads up the hill. What had I gotten into?

"Steve, stay away from that door," she ordered, her voice loud enough for neighbors to hear.

She swung the buggy onto a dirt lane that ran alongside the house and pulled to a stop opposite a side gate in the fence. She jumped out, ran up the few steps, and leaped into my arms.

After a chaste kiss, she said, "I wanted to be here when you came home. You haven't been inside, have you?"

"Uh no . . . there's more changes inside?"

"Not as many as there will be in an hour." She checked the progress of the wagons coming up the slight grade of the hill. "You just arrive?"

"We did," I answered.

"Then you and Jeff go have a drink and come

back in an hour . . . no, two hours. Everything will be ready for you then."

"Everything? I thought this was a simple place to stay between our travels." I waved at the garden. "This'll need tending."

"Of course, silly, but not by us. I've already made arrangements with two kids. They'll take care of it." She gazed at the garden with obvious pride. "To get vegetables, all we need to do is step out of the door."

"Two kids?"

"Maggie when she's in town, and another boy when she's at her aunt's or father's." She smiled. "Unfurrow that brow, nothing's changed. This isn't an anchor. But it is our home, and we have the money to make it nice. Now move so our furniture can be unloaded from these wagons."

I shook my head in wonder, or perhaps relief. "How did you do all this so quickly?"

"The same way I managed our general store. Now, git. Those men are paid by the hour."

As Sharp and I walked to a local saloon, I wondered where *our furniture* had come from. When we bought the house, it had included some furniture, so why did we need three wagons of new stuff? I glanced at Sharp, but he looked far too amused for me to give him an opening. I kept my reservations to myself.

Soon we were sipping beer, and I felt better. When Virginia had taken over our general store, she had immediately whitewashed all the interior walls, hung colorful paintings, and used numerous lanterns to chase murkiness from the corners. She had also created a cozy seating area around the stove to draw miners in from the cold. She did all of this without asking permission, and the profits showed that it was smart salesmanship. Why should it surprise me that she had taken the initiative in decorating and furnishing our new house? Or that she had pulled it off with the speed of a cavalry charge.

"Steve, yer smilin'. Ya figured it out yet?"

"I was remembering the Leadville store. She gave that more than a whitewash."

"That she did. Worked out fine, if I recollect."

"I should trust her."

"Ya should trust her," Sharp repeated.

We returned after two hours and three beers. Sharp wanted to retire to his hotel, but I insisted he come along. I not only needed his moral support, but I also knew that Virginia would want to show off her handiwork. As we approached the house, I was pleased to see the wagons were gone.

I stood on the new front porch and started to knock. Feeling ridiculous, I suddenly pulled my hand back to turn the door handle. Sharp stifled a laugh. His merriment at my predicament annoyed me. Upon opening the door, the first thing to strike me was the smell of freshly baked apple pie. My mouth watered immediately. Then my eyes scanned the most comfortable room I had ever seen. Not a room for show, a room to relax. Heavy furniture that looked sturdy and ready for use. Pale yellow walls, well-executed landscape paintings, big comfortable-looking chairs upholstered in chocolate-colored cloth with bright highlights woven into the fabric, and two oval braided rugs, one in the sitting area and another under a table in the dining room that could seat eight for supper. I wanted to sit down and read a book. Then I corrected myself. I needed to start writing a book.

The next sight was even more beautiful. Virginia entered from the kitchen wearing a white apron over a yellow form-fitting dress. Her fresh attire made her look as bright as a spring field in bloom. She was carrying not an apple pie, but a heaping plate of apple fritters.

"Those sure smell good, ma'am," Sharp said.

"They're Mrs. Paul's recipe. You remember her fritters, don't you?"

"I sure do, best little café in Leadville," Sharp said. "If these are half as good as Mrs. Paul's, ya need to bring a second plate."

"Take a seat around the table, boys. I'll be back with coffee."

Before she wheeled away, we traded smiles. Mine a bit wan, hers a glorious burst of sunlit good cheer. As she turned, she kept her head cocked, looking me in the eye, and then just before she swiveled completely, she winked. Damn. What did that mean? I suspected that she found my unease as entertaining as Sharp. Why was I so flummoxed?

Before I could figure it out, she returned carrying a steaming pot of coffee, using the bottom of her apron to keep from burning her hand.

As she poured, she said, "Steve, now would be a good time to say you like what I've done with the place."

"I'm stunned," I said. "It looks like the kind of room a man wants to spend time in. Where did you find this furniture?"

"Around. Not in one spot. I shopped while I hired men to paint, hoe the garden, and build the porch. Do you like the porch?"

"I do." Then I smiled genuinely. "Did you use witchcraft?"

"No. That's later."

"Later?"

"Yes, later . . . when I show you the room you'll really want to spend time in."

Chapter 14

rather be ornery

The next morning, Sharp and I rode out to McAllen's spread, which was twelve miles to the west. I didn't think of it as a ranch, because McAllen had little more than grass. Lots and lots of grass.

Joseph McAllen had recently retired from the Pinkerton National Detective Agency, where he had run a multistate operation out of Denver. Sharp and McAllen had been friends for many years, while I had come to know them both after venturing West a couple of years before. I had first encountered McAllen when I hired him and a crew of Pinkertons to protect me in a feud with a Nevada mining baron. Since then, the three of us had become fast friends. We made an odd team. I was in my early thirties, McAllen in his mid-forties, and, while Sharp had never disclosed his age, I believed he was approaching sixty. I had been born and bred in New York City, educated at Columbia University, and inherited wealth. Sharp was born who-knows-where, and with little formal education, had built a substantial fortune in mining. McAllen, a creature of the West, had seen it at its worst, and in fact, had probably arrested or shot many of its worst. He had been married at one time, and his daughter lived with her schoolmarm mother and her new stepfather, the sole preacher in Durango.

We found McAllen's ranch by spotting the tent he was living in while he built his barn and house. He was pounding stakes into the ground on top of a treeless hillock. The flat plateau must have been nearly two acres. I swung around in my saddle and examined every direction. The distant mountains to the east presented a majestic view, and the prairie gradually fell away to the west, the dozens of miles of grasslands interrupted only occasionally by a scrub oak. This was a fine spot for McAllen to build a ranch, but the stakes he had pounded into the earth outlined an odd structure.

"House?" I asked from horseback.

He didn't stop working. "Glad to see you boys. Lumber arriving this morning. Could use help unloadin'."

We both groaned dramatically.

McAllen was not amused. "Not a house. This is my stable and corrals. That tent's my house for the time being." He stood straight and stretched his back. "Climb down. There's coffee on the stove."

"Did ya make it?" Sharp asked with distaste.

"See anyone else around?"

Sharp dismounted and made a show of looking

around. "Damn, no one I can see. I guess that means I'll need water to thin yer sludge."

"Plenty of water in the creek," McAllen said, pointing to a trough at the base of the knoll about forty yards away.

"Year-round running water?" I asked, as I dismounted as well.

"Yep. Paid an ol' sod to check it once a week for the last year." He pointed toward the mountains. "Water comes straight from the snow up there. Nobody can remember seein' them peaks without snow all over 'em, and sometimes the snow lasts till summer. Good spot. Nice flat area for buildin', grass for feedin', and water for me and the horses." He pointed west instead of toward the mountains. "My land stretches that way, but at this end, I'm only twelve miles from town . . . and Maggie."

We peeked into the tent McAllen called home, and *Spartan* would be a generous description. A cot, camp chairs, lanterns, tools, and boxes upon boxes of supplies. Outside, a stove and fire pit finished off the modern conveniences.

Sharp said, "A woman ought to find this a comfortable spot . . . if ya plant a few trees."

"Woman? What are you talkin' about?"

"Joseph, yer settlin' down. Don't tell me ya can't see a woman in this place."

"I can, but not for a few years." He rewarded us with one of his closed-lipped smiles. "No need to hurry Maggie into womanhood."

Sharp shook his head in disappointment. "Take on a woman if ya want, Joseph . . . but don't take on humor. It don't become ya."

I hated to interrupt the friendly joshing, but I felt compelled to ask, "Joseph, have you ever built anything?"

He sniffed. "I'll learn. Can't be that hard. Dunderheads do it."

"Those stakes aren't square," I said.

"Horses won't know the difference," McAllen said weakly.

"Do you understand breeding?" I asked.

"Damn it, Steve, course I do. Grew up on a ranch. Since I was little, I always wanted to be a rancher. I know horses as well as guns."

"Did it take learning to understand breeding?"

He gave me a wary look. "What are you gettin' at, Steve?"

"It takes know-how to properly build stables and a house."

"I said I'll learn. If I make mistakes, I'll tear it down and do it again. It's not magic."

"May I offer help?"

"What? Now you're a builder? You got know-how?"

"No, but I can get one." I waited for the explosion. McAllen didn't accept help gracefully.

He stomped around for only the briefest of moments. "Where?"

"Virginia. She had a porch built on our house.

99

Whoever did the work knew what he was doing and got it done fast. It's straight and plumb and sturdy." I paused again for an explosion, but again it didn't happen. "Joseph, you've helped me time and again. I'd feel privileged to hire and pay this man for you."

"Accepted." He pointed at a wagon bouncing through the long grass. "Here comes the lumber. Let's get it unloaded."

I looked at Sharp, but he was as bewildered as I. McAllen accepting help? Readily? I studied the ground around his stakes. There were numerous lines drawn with the edge of a shovel. None were straight, nor were the stakes aligned with any of them. He had no idea how to proceed. Then I examined the wagon. The behemoth teamster gnawed on a cigar stub and looked as indifferent as a soldier on mess duty. As it pulled up, I saw nothing but siding planks. No wood for framing. McAllen didn't even know how to order supplies.

"Where's the framing lumber?" McAllen yelled at the teamster.

"Next trip. This was easier to load. Rob'll be at the mill this afternoon to help with the heavy stuff."

"Take it back," McAllen ordered.

"No, sir. Mr. Blackman told me to haul this load out here and return for the rest of your order. You gotta pay for this whether you accept it or send it back."

"Blackman told me he'd send two wagons."

"Rob got hungover, but he'll be at work by the time I get back. Ain't my fault."

"This plankin' is useless without framin'. You want me to sit and admire it until you get back? These men rode out here to help. By the time you drive twenty-four miles round trip, they might as well have stayed home."

"If you make me haul this back, you'll pay for it and pay to have me haul it out here again. That's the way it is."

"You need this wood, Joseph," Sharp said. "The sooner we unload, the quicker he'll get back."

"No!" McAllen barked. "He won't come back today because he'll have to drive back after dark. He won't return and this cow pie knows it too. Turn the wagon around and tell Mr. Blackman I'll see him at the mill in the mornin'. First thing."

The teamster turned red and started to climb down from the wagon.

McAllen stepped forward, and the look on his face stopped the teamster in mid-motion. After a second's hesitation, he climbed back into the seat.

"I heard 'bout you," the teamster said. "They say you was hard. Well, Mr. Blackman got some hard men working for him too."

"Hard like you?" McAllen said. "Big strong guy and you can't load framin' lumber. You gotta wait for Rob. And I don't see you climbin' down off that wagon."

"There's three of you . . . and Rob's the junior man. He's supposed to do the shit work."

McAllen spoke in the quiet tone he used to intimidate bad men. "Leave now . . . before I bust you up . . . or worse."

The teamster snapped the reins and pulled them to the side to turn the wagon around. He didn't look back. I didn't blame him.

McAllen looked at his camp, then at me, and then at Sharp. He said, "Let's break the tent down so it doesn't stick up in the air for people to see as they ride by. These supplies and equipment cost a lot. Then I'll ride into town with you boys. Maybe we can talk to that carpenter you mentioned."

"Stay with us tonight," I said "Breakfast with Virginia will keep you from being too ornery when you go to see Mr. Blackman."

McAllen marched toward the tent. Over his shoulder, he said, "What makes you think I wouldn't rather be ornery?"

Chapter 15

payday's a coming

Virginia worked hard to entertain our first house-guest. She prepared a roast with all the fixings for dinner and chops and eggs for breakfast. The extra bedroom suited McAllen. Like the remainder of the house, she had furnished it with big, comfortable pieces that were neither overly masculine nor dainty. She had struck the exact right balance to satisfy man, woman, or even a couple.

The carpenter, a rough-hewn middle-aged man named Tom, also met with McAllen's approval. He stood only about five foot six, and his sturdy build and wide stance made him look hard to knock down or tip over. He wore heavy, threadbare clothes that appeared regularly washed, and his hair and body were scrubbed. McAllen's favorable opinion was fortuitous, because Tom would need to live with McAllen at the ranch. Riding back and forth from town would waste too much time. I wondered how he would survive for weeks or possibly even months with McAllen as a sole companion until I noticed that Tom never said anything needless. He and McAllen would get along fine, since silence was the only form of communication that sooner or later McAllen didn't find objectionable.

After breakfast, McAllen asked me to accompany him to Blackman's Lumberyard. He claimed he might need my business experience. I hoped that was true, because I didn't want him needing my gun. I suggested we pick up Sharp at his hotel, but McAllen told me he needed lumber, not fisticuffs. I reminded him that Sharp got along with workingmen and had been on friendly terms with teamsters when we were in New York. Besides, a show of force might avert conflict. McAllen changed his mind, a rare occurrence. We went off to gather up Sharp and found him in the dining room of his hotel. He eagerly agreed to accompany us.

The mill was about two miles outside of town, close to the forest where the lumbermen harvested trees. It was far enough to ride horses, and when we arrived, five tough-looking men lollygagged around the yard. They appeared unarmed, but nasty lengths of lumber leaned against the mill wall within easy reach. The pieces of wood had been turned on a lathe until rounded nearly like a baseball bat. They quit chatting when they spotted us. Each turned in our direction and assumed a belligerent pose, although none picked up a length of lumber.

As we rode up, Sharp said, "This ain't good."

McAllen whispered, "Stay mounted."

We halted in front of three of the men, all of whom wore sour expressions.

"I'm here to see Mr. Blackman," McAllen said matter-of-factly.

"He's busy." The spokesman was the same cigar-chewing teamster from the day before. "Told us to collect twenty dollars from you for yesterday's wasted trip. When you pay, we deliver your order."

"I'm not payin' extra. Tell him to have both loads on their way within the hour."

"You'll pay 'cuz there ain't no other lumber mill 'round here," the teamster said. "Mr. Blackman also wants the second half of the payment up front. Says he can't trust you, so now it's cash on the barrelhead."

McAllen nudged his horse so it stepped sideways and suddenly pushed the men against the mill wall. Instead of trying to escape, the men seemed more concerned that the horse didn't step on their feet. Sharp and I spread out facing the other two men in the yard. Both threw their hands in the air and retreated into the building. They were evidently not part of our welcoming committee. The three men McAllen had shoved against the wall yelled for help, so we kept an eye on the door.

McAllen spoke to the men squeezed tight against the building. "I'm goin' to get off this horse and walk into that mill. If I don't find

Blackman, I'm comin' back to leave a message with you three."

McAllen checked to make sure we were ready and then smartly spurred his horse away from the men. Sharp had already dismounted and positioned himself between them and McAllen, who calmly climbed down and tied up his horse before walking into the mill.

One of them asked Sharp, "Yer 'sposed to keep us here?" He glanced at me swiveling my head back and forth between them and the open door to the mill. "All three of us?"

He started to laugh, but Sharp hit him with a straight jab to the nose. The man yelped and grabbed his face. Blood oozed from between his fingers. He began an angry retort, but Sharp silenced him with a single upraised finger.

Even though the three appeared unarmed, I kept my hand on my gun in a gesture of intimidation. They were smart not to carry guns. If they could keep the confrontation restricted to non-lethal means, most opponents would feel intimidated. As the advertisement went, God made men, but Sam Colt made them equal. Remove the option of guns, and these tough, hard men held the advantage.

No one spoke. We waited.

In less than two minutes, McAllen came charging out of the mill, dragging a man along by the scruff of the neck. I assumed the reluctant gentleman scurrying to keep up was Blackman. Several men chased after them, so I shifted my attention and position to face the gathering mob. They looked like mill hands, with a few teamsters mixed into the lot. Every last one of them appeared ready for a brawl. They probably had been talking themselves into a bloodlust all morning. Damn. I was good with guns, not fists.

McAllen pulled the man up short in front of the three teamsters.

"Tell them to get my order ready." Blackman said nothing. "Now!" McAllen barked.

"Go to hell. Men, do your—"

McAllen wrenched Blackman's arm high up behind his back. He shrieked in pain.

"If any of your men step in this direction, I'll break your arm. Tell them to return to work . . . which includes loadin' wagons with my order."

McAllen and Sharp could hold off a man with a flat, stern expression, so I tried an even gaze on the men congregating outside the main doorway. Instead of looking rough and ready, they now appeared confused. The mill hands had been eager for a break in their workday but didn't want to lose their jobs because their boss got hurt due to their actions. Everyone was held in check.

McAllen again bent the arm up enough to cause a brief spasm of pain.

After a grimace, Blackman yelled, "Back to work!"

"Assign a team to my order," McAllen said evenly.

"Mark, load his order."

"I said a team."

"Mark's a foreman. He knows I meant his team."

Everybody but the three teamsters slowly shuffled back into the building. When Blackman nodded his head toward the door, they left as well. McAllen spun Blackman around so that he faced him, then released his arm.

"Were you at the mill yesterday mornin'?" McAllen asked.

"I had a lodge meeting."

"Masons?" Sharp asked.

Blackman's head spun in Sharp's direction, surprised at the query. He nodded uncertainly.

Sharp shook his hand, using his body to partially block our view. Blackman smiled, then glanced warily at us. Sharp shook his head slightly.

"Ya need to settle yer differences with Mr. McAllen," Sharp said. "I won't intercede."

Blackman faced McAllen, evidently somewhat mollified that at least a lodge brother stood witness.

"What did your man tell you?" McAllen asked.

"Mark told me he hauled lumber out to your ranch, and you were rude, threatening, and refused delivery. Said you insisted I come out with the next loads to ensure that everything was done proper. I don't abide someone threatening my men. You can take your business elsewhere."

"Did he tell you he brought only one wagon-load? Sidin', no framin'."

Blackman suddenly went from looking frightened to perplexed, but he said nothing.

McAllen continued, "I refused delivery because sidin' did me no good until I had my barn framed. Claimed he would return in the afternoon with the framin', but he was lyin'. He'd never make it back and forth before dark. My threats came after that big man of yours started after me. Did you know Rob showed up late for work?"

Blackman ran a hand up and down his arm. "How would you know that?"

"Your man told me. Said it was Rob's job to load heavy stuff, not his. Rob hadn't showed up in the mornin' because he was hungover."

Blackman quit massaging his arm. He looked at Sharp, and Sharp nodded to confirm that McAllen had told him the truth.

"Damn," Blackman said. "Give me a minute?"

"Yep," McAllen answered.

Blackman marched back into the mill. In a few minutes, we heard angry voices. In a few more minutes, two men slunk out of the mill. They were heading toward the street until they saw us. The one called Mark suddenly veered in our direction.

"You son of a bitch. How do I feed my family?

109

My kid needs a doctor. If he dies, it's on your shoulders."

McAllen looked as angry as I had ever seen him. "You have a family . . . and you cheat and lie? You load of shit. Your heedless actions are what hurt your family, not me. I ought to beat you to a pulp."

"This ain't my doing!" he yelled. "You caused Mr. Blackman to fire me. I owe you, and payday's a coming."

Sharp grabbed McAllen's arm. He meant to restrain him from tearing the other man's arms off, but McAllen twisted away with little effort. He did not intend to attack.

"Go," McAllen said. "You're not worth another moment of my time."

"Don't turn your back on me. Ever! You ruined my life, and now I'm gonna fix yours."

Blackman had come back into the yard. He said, "Mark, go home. If you make any more threats, I'll dock your final pay envelope."

"You can't," Mark said. "You owe me."

"I can. I'll take that twenty dollars for that wasted trip out of your pay. Now go."

Mark's expression turned even more belligerent, but he physically retreated. Just before he turned onto the road, he hollered at McAllen.

"Payday's a coming!"

Chapter 16

a different way of living

Sharp and I left McAllen because he had promised to meet Tom the carpenter in town and show him the way to his ranch. We boarded our horses and walked to my house. So far, I thought of the cottage as my house, not my home. Truth to tell, Virginia's machinations in sprucing up the place still unsettled me. Was she trying to send me a message? If so, she needed to be more direct. I couldn't hear subtle.

All kinds of thoughts went through my head. Did she want to settle down in one place? Did she not want to travel . . . or want to restrict her travel to civilized areas? Did she want children right away? How many? We had never talked about raising a family. If we spoke frankly, perhaps I could embrace a different way of living. Perhaps. But now? I wanted to wander a bit more, maybe a lot more. I wasn't done exploring the West. Virginia had been saying she wanted the same thing, that this house was only a base for us to return to after our exploits. Was she being truthful?

Durango might make a good hometown. It was small, but developed enough to have fine dining, entertainment, banking, and all of the other services one expected nowadays. The town was out of the way, but I liked that. Besides, with trains we could get just about anywhere in short order. McAllen would stay put because of his daughter and ranch, but what about Sharp? We were business partners, but he had no incentive to hang around Durango, or any other place, for that matter. If I set down roots here, Sharp would surely visit on occasion. I would also need to travel to meet him whenever he found an opportunity to sell Edison's inventions. But to be honest, if I married Virginia, I couldn't continue to ride hither, thither, and yon with him. How would I feel about that? These past couple of years had been the happiest of my life. No . . . the last year with Virginia had been my happiest. Damn. To be honest, I had been happy, or at least content, since I'd left New York, and from the perspective of culture and geography, Durango was as far from New York as I could get. That was a—

"What ya thinkin'?" Sharp asked.

"Nothing," I answered.

"Nothin' appears a deep subject."

"What are your plans?" I asked abruptly.

"Lunch. Built a powerful appetite."

"Joseph did all the work," I said jokingly.

"Yep, saw him makin' friends with his new neighbors."

"Never thought of those men as neighbors, but

I guess you're right." I walked a few paces before adding, "Joseph's never been neighborly."

Sharp laughed. "I'll give 'im some pointers. First rule, don't bash heads."

"Some heads need bashing," I said.

"This is his daughter's home," Sharp said. "Now his and yers too. Best not to make too many enemies."

"Those two men aren't serious threats," I said, referring to the fired teamsters.

"No . . . probably blowhards, but Joseph's gotta get along with these people. He's a tough man. Tough men scare normal folk. He's retired, so he needs to learn to let things be. He doesn't need to fix all that's broken in this town."

I laughed. "May take some time for that to get set in his head."

"Yep, true for sure." He turned to look at me. "Now, Steve, why are ya askin' 'bout my plans?"

"It looks like Virginia wants to set down roots," I answered. "I thought that cottage was a way station, but I suspect that she has more in mind."

Grinning broadly, he asked, "So that's yer deep thoughts?" He laughed out loud. "Hell, Joseph is scarin' townsfolk . . . but yer just plain scared." He slapped me on the shoulder. "Ya got it good, Steve. In fact, ya got it perfect."

"Doesn't feel perfect."

"How 'bout when yer with Virginia?"

I thought about it. "Then it feels perfect. But I

thought she and I agreed to travel and explore, not settle down in a cottage with a white picket fence."

Sharp turned uncharacteristically serious. "Listen to an older man who lived the life you're dreamin' 'bout. It ain't near what it's cracked up to be. Lonely as hell. Sometimes I wish I had married a good woman an' had a family to escort me to old age." He kicked a rock down the street. "Ya got it good, so quit yer bellyachin'."

There was bitterness in Sharp's tone. I assumed it had something to do with Nora West. Watching Virginia and me and then running into an old sweetheart may have made him feel glum. He probably had another fear. McAllen was his longtime friend, and he was intent on putting his traveling days behind him. If both of us plopped down in Durango, I might get between Sharp and McAllen because I lived nearby. I didn't want to make Sharp jealous, because his friendship was important. I liked the man. I had been selfish to worry about him being fancy-free while I got married and settled down. It had never occurred to me that he might miss McAllen's and my friendship as well. I knew it shouldn't have, but the thought made me feel good.

"Steve, listen to me," Sharp said. "Durango may not be yer first choice for a home, but it's where people ya care about are gonna be. The family ya make is far more important than the family ya inherit."

"But you left Nora and all the other women you met," I blurted before thinking. "That seems to go against what you just said."

"I did. Don't make what I said less true."

"I know you don't talk about your personal life, but why'd you never marry?"

"Not your business."

"Help me get over my nerves," I pleaded.

"Some things ya got to figure out for yerself." Sharp kicked another rock. "I can't help ya."

"Did you ever regret not getting married?"

We stopped at the corner of my street.

After a bit, Sharp said, "We all got regrets." He shook his head as if to rid himself of a memory. "But the ones that hurt the deepest are the things we chose to forgo . . . not the things we did."

I nodded. Sharp was telling me I needed to get over my reservations. I had it good. His own quest for a life free of encumbrances had caused regrets. He was telling me to quit waffling and enjoy my good fortune. McAllen had already made a decision to build a ranch and abandon the trail. Sharp was nearing sixty and perhaps wanted to slow down as well. I was the youngest of the three and still had wanderlust, but my friends were moving to another phase in their life, and so should I. At least, that's what I thought Sharp was telling me.

Sharp slapped me on the back and put it much simpler. "Steve, just enjoy life. Quit worrying."

"Except my worry is that my life will change . . . and I like it just the way it is."

"Don't worry 'bout gettin' nailed down in this little mountain town. We'll be back on the trail soon enough. Hell, we still gotta electrify the entire West for Mr. Edison. Lots more adventures in front of us." He smiled encouragingly. "Go on, enjoy yer new home."

Sharp knew the right thing to say, but I felt he had his own internal troubles. That woman, Nora West, had knocked him back on his heels. I saw a path in front of me I knew was going to be great, but I didn't know if it would remain as fun as the last couple of years. On the other hand, I believed Sharp had lost a vision of his future. His friends were deserting him, and a woman from his past reminded him that he could have traveled a completely different path to the here and now. I was worried, but he was scared. I'd better start thinking more about my friends and less about myself.

Chapter 17

a crucial moment

Sharp broke off to walk to his hotel. I sauntered up the short block to my house. I felt less trepidation as I examined the neat cottage sporting a freshly built porch. As I mounted the steps, it occurred to me that I might enjoy whitewashing the raw lumber. I had enjoyed Mark Twain's *The Adventures of Tom Sawyer*, and especially liked the picket fence whitewashing episode. Perhaps I could do a little Tom Sawyering and encourage my neighbors to lend a helping hand. That would be a productive way to meet the people who lived on the street.

Virginia sat in the sitting room, reading a heavy book. She quickly—too quickly—put aside a Montgomery Ward catalog and jumped to her feet.

"Did Joseph get his lumber?"

"Joseph always gets what he wants."

I kissed her. Then I kissed her again, with serious intent.

She gently pushed me away. "Hungry?"

"Are you talking about food . . . or . . .?"

"Food. I've been working all morning and I'm famished. I haven't prepared anything, so what do you want?"

"Let's go out. Henry's?"

She hesitated and then nodded, so we both cleaned up enough to be presentable in refined public. Henry's was a restaurant off Main Avenue, overlooking the Animas River. The food was excellent, and the view from one of the window tables was even better. Since Virginia had cooked supper and breakfast, I thought she would enjoy going out for the midday meal.

As we approached Henry's, Virginia suggested we first walk along the river to build an appetite. After the tense encounter this morning, I didn't need to spark my hunger, but I liked the riverfront and sensed that Virginia had something to say out of the earshot of prying townsfolk.

We crossed over a town bridge to the other side of the Animas. One of the appealing aspects of Durango is that the town had built a pebble pathway along the western edge of the rushing river. It was a perfect day for a stroll. The early autumn sun made the water sparkle as it slid over boulders washed down from the mountain, and the soothing rush of noise made me feel content. Warm weather, a picturesque river, mountains in the background, and autumn-colored trees made everything seem enduring and peaceful.

I was just about to comment on the scenery when Virginia said, "I have an idea. If you don't like it, please say so."

My trepidation instantly returned. "Okay."

"I want to give the cottage to Maggie as a wedding gift."

That startled me. "Maggie's getting married?"

"No, silly, not now, someday. And when that day comes, I want to give her our cottage. The house is temporary. A fun endeavor. We're just fixing it up and taking care of it so we can eventually give it away. Won't that be fun?"

I didn't speak for a long moment. Then I asked, "I'm that obvious, huh?"

She laughed. "I guess I'm the obvious one."

I walked a little further before saying, "Okay, I think this is good. We both understand each other and worry about each other. You saw that the house makes me nervous. I like that you care about me, but you don't have to promise to give it away to make me feel comfortable. I love the house and what you've done with it. I love you, and I want to get married. I just . . . I guess I don't want to get tied down to a single place. At least, not yet."

She smiled. But I felt she was smiling to herself, not me. Like me, she took her time responding.

We walked in silence until a thought struck me. "Are you pregnant?"

"No!" She laughed. Again, this was not a shared laugh. She was laughing at something she internally felt was amusing. Instead of being amused, I was confused.

She stopped walking and took a seat on a rock

along the shore. After I joined her, she spoke softly. "Steve, I want children, but it doesn't need to be right now." She looked at me beside her. "But I can't wait too many years."

I suddenly knew this was a crucial moment. She spoke softly, not for lack of emotion, but to emphasize her words.

"I know," I said. "I want children too. But children move . . . houses don't. Getting stuck in one place is the one thing that frightens me . . . and that may even pass."

"Who told you children move?"

"Maggie went on trips with Joseph . . . all over . . . even to the Arizona Territory. Since I was a little kid, my father and I hunted all over the back country. Pilgrims sailed across the ocean with their children. Pioneers lugged children across the plains in wagons. Abraham Lincoln moved from state to state with his family, and it didn't hurt him. What makes you think children don't move?"

"Those examples are temporary." She seemed frustrated. "Steve, this is serious. I want children . . . and children need a home. I'm not raising vagabonds."

The sharpness of her tone took me aback. We should have discussed this before. Were temporary excursions enough for me? They would need to be. I went west looking for some-thing missing in my life. Now I had found it. I wasn't going to throw it away for wanderlust.

"Temporary will be enough," I said. "As long as we take family trips, I'll be content. More than once a year though, but I promise we'll be home more than away. Hell, with trains, we can go nearly anywhere in a week. We'll bring the whole brood along. How many do you want? Six, seven?"

Now she laughed with me. A good sign.

"Three or four will be plenty, thank you." She gave me a hard look. "Are you sure about this?"

"Absolutely. Let's give the house to Maggie. It'll make a friend of Joseph for life. He'll be thrilled to have her anchored in Durango."

"Steve, I wasn't asking about the house, and you know it. I want to know, are you sure you'll be content with a family and occasional trips?"

"Let me think," I said, dramatically rubbing my chin. "Well, I suppose I can be content if you want only three or four. I'll eventually get used to the idea of a small family."

"Steve! Be serious. Just tell me. Are you okay with children and a permanent home?"

I looked directly into her eyes. "Yes."

She bounced up and down on the rock bench and then kissed me with genuine affection.

After a brief silence, she asked, "If we give this house to Maggie, where do you want to live?"

"Since a private Pullman car probably won't satisfy you, how about San Diego?"

"What do you know about San Diego?"

"I know it's as far as we can get from New York and Philadelphia. No train yet, but passenger ships can get us to the East Coast in comfort. We talked about taking our honeymoon there. Let's take a serious look and see if we like it enough to call it home."

She eyed me askance. "When?"

"When what? Children or permanent home?"

"Okay, I'll play along, Steve. Here's the normal order of things: marriage, honeymoon, and then children. So, my question is, when do we get married?"

I didn't hesitate. "As soon as we close our deals in Silverton."

Chapter 18

that kind of thing goes on

Two weeks later, I answered a fervent knock on the door to find Maggie standing on my freshly painted porch. She appeared anxious and fidgety.

"I need to talk to you," she said.

"Come in. Can I get you a glass of lemonade?"

"No . . . yes, but can I talk while you get it?"

"Sounds important."

She followed me into the kitchen. "It is."

As I opened the icebox, I said, "I thought you were at your aunt's ranch."

"I returned yesterday. School starts soon. Do you know a man named Ben Law?"

That stopped me cold. "Do you?"

"I know about him. He's mean. A killer." She hesitated. "I heard he's on the hunt for you and Mr. Sharp and maybe my pa."

I stopped pouring mid-glass. "Where would you hear such a thing?"

"From Jeremy. His pa works for Law. Jeremy's a bit of a braggart and told me you two would soon get your comeuppance . . . and then he said Law might help his pa take care of my pa."

In the intervening weeks, I had almost forgotten about Law and Phelps. We had been waiting for the rail line to finish so we could hire Werner and a crew to start up again at the Galena Queen. I painted the porch, wrote on my new novel, and enjoyed domestic life with Virginia. A couple of days previously, Sharp had ridden back to Silverton. He had said he wanted to search for additional mining opportunities, but I knew Nora West had something to do with his return. He had sent no telegrams, so I assumed all was well. And as far as I knew, McAllen was still learning to drive a nail with fewer than ten strokes of a hammer.

"Is Sharp in trouble?" I wondered out loud.

"You don't listen. I said Law wants to hurt both of you, maybe all three of you."

"Maggie, your pa and I are here, but Mr. Sharp rode up to Silverton a few days ago. He's the one who could be in danger right now."

"Oh my. You better send a telegram. Maybe ride out and get Pa, and the two of you ride up there. These are bad men."

"Who's Jeremy?"

"Just a boy," she said too quickly. "His father was a teamster. Got fired and now he works for Law. Mean brute . . . son's okay though . . . most of the time."

I handed her a cold glass of lemonade. "Why would he tell you this? Does he know Sharp and I are friends with you?"

"Everybody knows. Ever heard of gossip?

Besides, he wants to bed me. He thinks I'll be beholden to him and swoon if he warns me." She shrugged. "Girls with gutless fathers may fall for that, I guess."

"What?" I was momentarily taken aback.

"Mr. Dancy, you must know that kind of thing goes on. I'm almost grown."

I paced around the kitchen trying to figure out how much to tell Maggie. Jeremy's father held a grudge against her father. If I told her, she would insist on riding out to warn him. If that teamster went to work for Ben Law, then he was in Silverton, meaning that McAllen was safe for the moment. Law had no gripe against McAllen, and it was doubtful he would allow himself to be dragged into another feud. Jeremy probably threw McAllen into the mix to get Maggie's attention. If someone was in danger, it was Sharp. He was the one up in Silverton, wandering around the countryside looking for claims to buy. I decided not to tell Maggie about her father's dispute with these ex-teamsters.

"I need to get to the telegraph office," I said.

"And then ride to help Mr. Sharp," she said. "I'll see Pa and send him to help as well."

"Better leave your pa out of this for the time being. He's busy starting his ranch, and Mr. Sharp and I can handle Law and his bunch. We've done it before."

"Is that why he's after you?"

"We embarrassed him in front of townsfolk. He probably wants his reputation back."

She shook her head. "You need Pa. When Law gets done with you, he'll come after him anyway. He must know Pa wouldn't sit still for your murder. Besides, Jeremy said his pa can't wait for retribution." She had been talking fast and took a break to swallow some lemonade. "Yep, together you got a better chance. That's the way it should be done."

"Maggie, how do you—?" I stopped. "Gossip?"

"Durango's a small town. Did you really believe you could cause a row at the lumber mill and nobody'd notice?"

"We didn't cause the row, your friend's pa did. We just—"

"He's not my friend!" she huffed.

"Poor choice of words," I said, but doubted that it was. "Jeremy's father tried to take advantage of your father, and you know how that works out."

"I do. Mr. Masters made a big mistake, but that doesn't mean a tinker's damn now. Mr. Masters has a grudge, and he'll draw Law into the fight."

"Mr. Masters?"

"Jeremy's pa, Mark Masters."

I shook my head. "Law has never met or even seen your father. I doubt he'll get mixed up in Mr. Master's problems."

"Mr. Dancy, I'm sure he already told Law that the three of you are a gang. Silverton's only fifty

126

miles away. Soon to have a train that can make the distance in hours. Do you think Law wants a Pinkerton around to challenge him . . . or revenge your deaths? An honest-to-goodness bad man is after all three of you. He's got a big gang and he won't go away. You must stop him. Together."

"Okay, I understand. But I'll be the one to ride out to your pa's place."

"I'm going with you . . . to the ranch, that is. I should go to Silverton as well, but you'll have to get along without me." She snapped down her lemonade glass. "How long before we leave? Ma won't let me ride at night."

"I need to send Sharp a telegram, explain to Virginia, and gather up a few things. How about one hour?"

"Forty-five minutes ought to be plenty. I'll meet you at the livery. Don't be late. It's getting dark earlier."

She wheeled around and disappeared out the door.

Damn. I felt sympathy for her future husband. That girl knew her mind and would bend his to her will. Then I thought about the boy, Jeremy. Should I tell McAllen what she'd said? No, not if I ever wanted to have another conversation with Maggie . . . and not if I wanted a peaceful resolution to the next encounter with Law. No sense making McAllen angrier. Besides, McAllen probably didn't need reminding that "that kind of thing goes on."

Chapter 19

short shrift

The ride to McAllen's ranch went fast. Maggie, an exceptional horsewoman, kept a rigorous pace. Like her father, she talked little as she rode, giving me time to worry. Sharp hadn't responded to my telegraphed warning, but only minutes had passed before I'd left to meet up with Maggie at the livery. Sharp knew how to take care of himself, and worrying wouldn't help anyway. Law wanted a fight, so I had to think of a way to stop him. I suspected he was unhinged as well as ruthless. As I thought it through, it seemed that only Phelps might provide an opportunity to avoid bloodshed. If I could discover something about Phelps that would give me leverage, or if I could apply financial pressure to his businesses, perhaps he could be persuaded to call off Law. Maybe. But getting an angle on Phelps may not work. Did Phelps have the wherewithal to dissuade Law?

"That won't work," Maggie said, a bit breathless.

Had she read my mind? "What won't work?"

"If Pa leaves his ranch, Masters will burn everything to the ground: tent, supplies, corral, everything. He's a braggart, not a killer. Instead of a fight, he'd rather sneak out there while Pa's away."

Maggie had evidently been thinking through the problem as well.

"You said Masters was already in Silverton. How could he get leave from Law to come down to raid your father's ranch?"

She threw me an exasperated look. "I never said he had gone to Silverton. I said Masters went to work for Law. His job is to keep an eye on things in Durango and start building a local gang. Of course, Jeremy doesn't call it a gang, but that's what it is. Law made Jeremy's pa boss in Durango and gave him money to hire men. He can't quit talking about how important his pa is now."

"Law gave him money? How much?"

"How would I know? Enough to start a gang, I suppose."

Did Ben Law hire Masters on his own? Without Phelps's approval? That would mean he was more ambitious than I had supposed. If he could take over Phelps's mining operations in Silverton and hold Durango commerce under his thumb, he'd be in control of all mine operations in the San Juan Mountains. Durango was the key to control. The town provided the services and products needed to get ore out of the ground and to market. Done right, Law could be wealthy beyond reckoning. He was ruthless enough. But was he smart enough?

On the other hand, he may have hired Masters under Phelps's direction. In fact, that was more likely, because Law probably didn't have enough money to start an operation down here. Darn. If Phelps had enough money for expansion, then he probably was well fixed, and squeezing his financial position wouldn't be an effective weapon against him.

"We need to handle Masters before going to Silverton," I blurted.

I was talking more to myself than Maggie, but I saw her nod agreement. Masters shouldn't be difficult to handle. He couldn't have assembled a gang in such a short time. What if he did have a few others? We couldn't kill him and any other riffraff he had managed to collect. We needed to figure out a way to put him and his minions in jail. What kind of crime could they have committed?

Before I could figure this out, McAllen's ranch loomed on the horizon like an oasis. A big structure sat atop a knoll, and with nothing else man-made for as far as the eye could see, it looked as imposing as the Inter-Ocean Hotel in Denver. McAllen and Tom had made good progress. As we approached, it became clear that the unfinished structure would eventually become a complex that included a barn, stables, and corrals. Maggie spurred her horse and raced the remaining distance.

By the time I arrived, Maggie had already dismounted and run to hug her father. McAllen looked pleased and a bit puzzled to see his daughter. Tom hung over us, leaning out from a loft in the unfinished barn. He rolled a cigarette, appearing grateful for a respite. I bet McAllen was a hard taskmaster.

"Thanks for bringin' her out, Steve," McAllen said.

"You may not thank me after you hear what she has to say," I answered.

Never one to postpone bad news, McAllen put a hand on each of her shoulders, pushed her to arm's length, and asked, "What is it, girl?"

As she told her story, Tom climbed down from the loft to grab a drink of water from a wooden bucket that sat on a sturdy sawhorse. When he finished, I gulped down several full dippers myself. It was refreshingly cool. The chilled runoff from the mountain snows made the creek a welcome feature of this particular plot of ground.

When she had finished, McAllen asked Tom if he could continue construction by himself. Tom nodded and turned to go back to work. McAllen called him back again.

"Tom, it's possible some men may ride out here to burn everythin' to the ground."

"Ain't my fight," Tom said flatly.

"Agreed. If you see them comin', ride off. If you don't get any forewarnin', don't resist."

"Good plan," Tom said, heading inside the barn.

I doubted that these two men engaged in lively supper conversations. McAllen appeared contemplative. Suddenly he made a decision and trudged over to his tent to pull his things together. I followed him into his makeshift home. The tent had become even more crowded with another cot and additional supplies. I presumed the men merely slept in the tent, because it was no more homey than it had been before.

"I think we should find a way to get Masters arrested," I said as McAllen stuffed belongings into saddlebags.

"Done anything illegal you know 'bout?"

"We could ask around," I offered weakly.

He looked over my shoulder to make sure Maggie was out of earshot. "We'll ask, but if we don't find somethin' right off, I'll break his leg so he stays put. Then we ride up to Silverton and take care of this Ben Law. I want to be back here in well under a week."

He went back to packing.

"Joseph, it's four days of riding back and forth."

"So we make short shrift of Masters and Law. Don't have time to dally with supposed outlaws. Winter's comin'."

Chapter 20

caught with their pants down

A few minutes later, we rode out of McAllen's camp toward town. McAllen and Maggie rode side by side, and I trailed behind. McAllen didn't seem angry or emotional, just determined, and in a hurry. A task needed to be done, and he wanted to do it fast so he could return to building his ranch. I wondered how much Tom could do alone. The two of them working together had made impressive progress in two weeks, but even at the rate they were going, they would never get around to building the house before the first snow. I wondered if McAllen planned to spend the winter in a tent. Then I knew. Of course he did. He would never abandon all his work and materials to the whims of weather or vandals.

Twilight made the lanterns of town a welcome sight. We dropped off Maggie at her mother's house and rode over to mine. After a pleasant supper, McAllen wanted to visit saloons in the hope of finding Masters or information about him. It didn't take long. Masters had been casting around for recruits at places that catered to restless men. If the people we talked to were to be believed, Masters had had little luck. No one knew

133

of any recruits. He evidently had no idea what he was doing. First, he offered too little money for dodgy work, and second, he didn't realize that if these drifters had any ambition, they would be up in Silverton working the mines or stealing from miners. They sure weren't willing to risk injury or jail for a few dollars, especially not from someone as scruffy as Masters. He might appear big and mean, but he was known in these quarters as a hired hand, not a leader. A barkeep told us he and a sidekick had left his saloon to look in the bawdy houses for ready men who needed work.

The whorehouses had been confined to 5th Street, and we found Masters at the second establishment we visited. The madam told us that, finding no takers to join his gang, Masters and Rob had given in to temptation by taking one of her employees to a room. I bet he used the money he had been given to recruit men.

McAllen reached into his pocket and pulled out a handful of coins. The madam gestured for me to do the same. After I complied, she cupped her hands together, signaling that she wanted us to dump every bit of our money there. With a disagreeable grunt, McAllen dropped his money into her grubby hands, and I followed suit. I guessed she held over ten dollars, five times the amount one of her women earned for a tryst. She gave us their room number and allowed us to venture down the long hall.

Considering the frequency of the doors, the cribs must have been no wider than a standard bed. When we burst into the proper room, we saw that Masters and Rob had finished their business and were pulling up their trousers. Both froze in mid-motion at the foot of the bed. They looked like they had been caught with their pants down, which they had. Without hesitation, McAllen stepped over to Masters and slammed him across his knee with his heavy Smith and Wesson .44. After a yelp of pain, Masters dropped, holding his injured knee in a manner that left his uninjured leg exposed. McAllen swung his pistol again, this time at the other leg. Neither rap sounded as if McAllen had broken bones. I had no doubt that, had he intended to, he could have shattered Masters's knee or shin bone. I kept my eye on Rob, but instead of fighting, he tried to scurry around McAllen. After I pointed my gun at him, he quit edging toward the door. His face conveyed pure fright.

McAllen pointed at Rob and said, "Willin' to find other employment?"

"Yep," Rob said, barely audible enough for us to hear.

McAllen waved his pistol at the door, and Rob bounded out of the room. When McAllen gestured at the whore sitting on the bed, she disappeared just as quickly. I ducked into the hall to check for threats and encountered the madam just around the doorjamb, listening to our little drama. Rob and the girl must have nearly knocked her to the floor as they ran out. I waved her inside the room. If she was going to spy, I'd rather have her where I could keep an eye on her. Besides, with her at our side, her enforcers would not come barging in with guns. At least, not unless she screamed.

After I closed the door, McAllen said to Masters, "Do I need to kill you?"

"No, no. I mean you no harm. I got another job now. Better than the mill. Bygones be bygones. Please, forget me cursing you. To tell you the truth, you did me a favor."

"Your new job's the problem. If you continue to do Law's biddin', I need to break your leg . . . or worse."

"Why? Ain't got nothing to do with you." He was puzzled as well as in agony. After a long moment with no response, he added plaintively, "Does it?"

"It does," McAllen said. "Mr. Law is after my friends. I don't allow that."

"I didn't know . . . honest." He rubbed his knees with both hands and looked ready to cry. "I just needed a job. I got family to support."

"If you're so high on your family, what are you doin' in this room? Seems whenever you're in a pickle, you trot out your family like some talisman." He shook his head. "You're not a good man."

While McAllen talked to Masters, I went over to a holster hanging on a chair in the corner. I unloaded the Colt and pocketed the cartridges. The gun was too dirty for a real gunman. I suspected that Masters did his fighting with a heavy piece of wood. When I returned my attention to McAllen, he seemed perplexed.

"You're bothersome," McAllen said. "I don't want to watch my back, so what am I goin' to do with you?"

Masters winced and then said something I never expected. "Hire me."

"What?" McAllen said. "Why should I do that?"

"You got me fired from the mill, now you're telling me I can't work for Law. I heard 'bout you out there working sunup to sunset. Hire me. I'll build you a ranch. Done it twice before. 'Sides, me and Tom been friends since school days."

McAllen actually laughed, something I had seldom witnessed.

"You've given me nothin' but trouble, and now you want me to hire you. Damn, you've got nerve."

"Hell, you don't want to kill me, and I can't get the hang of this damn job. Without money, I'll probably be more troublesome. Hire me. I'll come over to your side and do you right." His expression turned beseeching. "Come on. I'm hotheaded, but I'm a good worker. Ask Mr. Blackman . . . or hey, ask Tom."

"I don't have money for a second hand," McAllen said, but he sounded intrigued.

I knew McAllen would never let me pay the man's salary, so I said, "I'll loan you the money until you sell your first batch of horses. You'll be up and running sooner with a second hand."

"What interest?"

McAllen's response surprised me. First, he'd accepted my offer of Tom's help, and now he appeared ready to accept a loan. And despite rapping Masters across both knees, he did it lightly enough so that the man could walk out of this room. Then he hesitated to take further physical action against him. McAllen took pride in his self-reliance and handled dangerous situations with dispatch and finality. This was not the kind of behavior I had come to expect from him. He must want this ranch badly. Then I realized there was more to it. He wanted a home, a peaceful home that didn't expose his daughter to threats. He wanted to get along with Durango townsfolk, and he was smart enough to know his hardheaded ways of dealing with people would make enemies, not friends. That's why he hadn't actually broken Masters's legs as he had threatened to do. Now he seemed ready to buy Masters. I never would have guessed that this kind of solution would appeal to him.

"Three percent a year," I said.

McAllen looked at Masters. "Will you behave? Remain loyal? Will I have to watch my back?"

"Sir, I'll behave anyway you want. Cause you no problem. I promise."

"Protect my property when I'm gone?"

"Damn right. If I put sweat into your ranch, I sure as hell ain't gonna let somebody wreck it."

"Stay away from whorehouses and take care of your family?"

This time he hesitated a bit before nodding. I didn't believe him about the whorehouses and doubted his commitment to take care of his family. Masters was a ne'er-do-well and probably wouldn't change.

McAllen rubbed his chin. "Why should I believe you?"

He hesitated, then shrugged. "Because my son's sweet on your daughter."

McAllen became so angry, I stiffened.

"Ease off, Joseph," I said. "You can't shoot the father of every boy that finds Maggie attractive."

"The hell, you say." He paced the room so forcefully, the madam stepped out into the hall.

"That's all!" Masters yelled. "I swear. He's just sweet on her! Begged me to get along with you. I promised 'cuz I didn't know you had anything to do with Law. Thought I had it good . . . leastwise I did till I couldn't hire any yahoos onto my crew."

"You thought you had it good? You accepted a job as a ruffian from a notorious gunman."

"Ben said there'd be no rough stuff. Just wanted a show of force. Intimidate lazy businessmen.

139

The worst would be broken windows . . . maybe a beating or two." He realized what he said and looked down, pretending to be ashamed. "I needed work."

McAllen shook his head. "Why in the world should I trust you?"

"Look, if I quit Law, I need a job and a place to lie low until he gets over being mad. I told him about you getting me fired. He'd never look for me at your place."

McAllen surprised me by saying, "Twenty dollars a month plus food and a place to sleep?"

"Ten in advance for my wife to buy food while I'm away?"

"What about the money Law gave you?" I asked.

"Gotta wire it back pronto. Ain't gonna get killed over a couple hundred."

McAllen looked at me and I nodded. It was a good solution for all. As McAllen said, Masters wasn't a good man, but he wasn't the worst sort either. Besides, he had seen McAllen in action, and any sane man would fear his temper.

"Alright. I want you at my ranch first thing tomorrow." He pulled a piece of paper out of his pocket and folded it together with a twenty-dollar bill. He handed them to Masters. "Buy the supplies on this list and give your wife ten dollars. Have the change ready for me when I return to my ranch."

"What should I tell Tom?"

"Show him that note. When he sees it, he'll know you work for me. Tell him we patched up our differences, and you're his new hand. I'm gonna speak with Blackman this afternoon." He pointed at the paper in his hand. "If he speaks ill of you, I'll catch you at the general store, get that back, and put you in the doc's office. You do right by me, and we won't have any further problems, but if you cross me, I'll cripple you for life. Do we have an understandin'?"

Masters nodded. McAllen glared at him until he said out loud, "Yes, sir."

"Now, get outta here."

After he left, McAllen waved the madam in and asked if her girl had been paid. She said her girls were always paid in advance, but she had not received a tip. McAllen gave her a pair of two-bit coins.

"Holding out on me, were you?"

"You got it all now, so quit whinin'," McAllen said. He pointed out the door where Masters had fled. "Do you know that man?"

"Mark? Sure."

"Can I trust him?"

Instead of answering, she jiggled the two quarter-dollar coins. McAllen looked at me, and I pulled out my wallet and gave her a paper dollar. She was having a profitable afternoon.

She stuffed the money in a place men no longer

141

paid to see. "He pays . . . and he tips better than you." She shrugged. "I like Mark. He busted some heads here once that needed busting. Helped me when he didn't need to. You could do worse."

"Tell your girl we apologize if we scared her," I said.

She gave me a blank stare and jiggled the coins again. I sighed and gave her another dollar.

"Split that three ways. I'm sure you can do the arithmetic."

"I can . . . and apology accepted. Now, can I bring you gentlemen some entertainment?"

McAllen said, "Not my style . . . and my young friend here has a fiancée waiting for him." He tipped his hat. "We'll be takin' your leave."

When we stepped outside, I said, "Well you made short shrift of Masters."

"I did." He sounded pleased with himself.

"Law may not be so quick."

"Get a good night's sleep, Steve. Tomorrow we ride hell-bent for Silverton. I want to be done with Ben Law fast and permanent."

Chapter 21

don't feel kindly

McAllen and I caught up to the construction of the Denver & Rio Grande only five miles outside of Silverton. Since nary a cloud was in sight, Karl Werner would likely make good on his promise to complete the line before the first snow. As we approached, we found Werner with James Merck at the head of the rail line, examining the terrain ahead. Merck was superintendent over all construction, which made him Werner's boss. I had met and eaten meals with him on our first trip to Silverton. We got along well, so his first words surprised me.

"Mr. Dancy, I suggest you and your friend ride on," Merck sternly ordered. "Silverton's only five miles down the trail."

"I have something to discuss," I said.

"I don't . . . nor do I have time for idle banter."

He turned his back on us.

"I thought you were going to run the Denver & Rio Grande operations in this area after completion of the line," I said.

Without turning around, he said, "I will. Now, if you'll move along, I'll finish building my railroad."

Werner had ignored McAllen and me since we'd ridden up. Not a proper way for him to greet his new employer. Actually, because our agreement would make Werner a junior partner in our electrification enterprise, I found his behavior extremely odd. He must have told Merck about our offer, and Merck objected. I had assumed Merck wouldn't care, because he planned to remain in the Silverton-Durango area, running the line. The two men got along well, so I thought Merck would be pleased that a friend would remain in the area for a spell and return on a regular basis. But I had mishandled the situation. Common courtesy required me to inform Merck of our arrangement. I had been impolite, but that didn't mean I could be put off easily.

"Mr. Merck, to a great extent, you are building my railroad, not yours. As a major shareholder, I expect a friendlier reception."

He turned slowly to meet my gaze.

"Mr. Dancy, I have wired Denver and informed them that you were interfering with the profitability of this line. They directed me to treat you with deference no longer. You'll find a letter from our attorney waiting for you in Silverton. It will explain everything. Now, please ride on before I lose my temper."

Before I could grasp what he'd said, McAllen asked flatly, "And what might that entail?"

Merck seemed to notice McAllen for the first time. "Who the hell are you?"

"A friend of Mr. Dancy," McAllen answered. "I just want to know if that was a threat. I don't take kindly to threats."

"Why the hell should I care? I don't feel kindly." Merck waved his arm around. "If I yell, all these men will come running to help me tear you apart limb from limb." He took on what he probably assumed was a hard glare. "I don't want you to fret about my meaning, so let me make this *very* clear . . . that *was* a threat."

I expected McAllen to explode, but instead he looked blank. He examined Merck as if he were some kind of specimen on a lab table. Then he scanned the men, who ignored us and continued to work.

"We don't want to interfere with you buildin' your railroad," McAllen said. "Why don't you just tell us what got your hackles up? If we can fix it, we will, and if we can't, we'll ride on and disrupt your day no further."

McAllen sat in his saddle as still as a bronze statue. All he needed was a raised sword to resemble a perfect monument to a long-forgotten general.

Merck relaxed. "Mr. Dancy appears to have angered Mr. Phelps, the largest mine operator in Silverton. He demands that we separate all business connections with you and Mr. Sharp."

145

He looked pointedly at me. "No transporting your ore, your person, or your supplies on this train. I don't know what your dispute's about, but Mr. Phelps managed to convince the other mine owners to join in boycotting the D&RG. If I may remind you, we need ore shipments to pay for this line. Otherwise, we've wasted a lot of money, and some of it was apparently yours."

"He can't hold out long," I said. "You're far cheaper and way faster. He has to be holding more over you than a brief boycott."

His back stiffened. "I can't say anything further."

"Yes, you can," I said. "Or I'll get you shipped off to Alaska."

"I've already gotten a judge to declare your actions tortious interference. You'll find a copy of the judge's order with Mr. Sharp."

"I assume that was a Silverton judge on Phelps's payroll. I don't care what you told Denver, money talks, and I have enough to speak loudly. I bet your head office didn't take into account Mr. Sharp's or Thomas Edison's holdings either. The right rumors spread around Wall Street while we noisily dump our stock would put enormous strain on the Denver & Rio Grande." I let him consider what I'd said before demanding, "What else is Phelps threatening?"

Surveying both of us, Merck seemed resigned. He pointed behind him. "He owns that mountain.

We can't get the last five miles without a right-of-way, which he'll withdraw if we do any business with you. If he even finds out I told you, he'll refuse us right-of-way." He looked pleadingly at us. "At this late date, eminent domain will take far too long. I'm forced to trust your discretion on this matter. May I remind you, a bad outcome will cost you a lot of money?"

"May we dismount?" I asked.

He nodded and beckoned a man over to take our horses away, hopefully to be groomed and fed. The four of us stood in a small circle, frenzied activity all around us. I could see that the proximity of so many people moving frantically made McAllen nervous. I had noticed his fear of crowds in New York but never expected him to feel hemmed in after we returned west. I motioned everyone toward a quiet spot behind a massive stack of railroad ties.

When we were a bit more secluded, I said, "You can count on our discretion. We're riding to Silverton to resolve our issues with Phelps. Don't worry. We won't involve you or put your progress in jeopardy. Do you have right-of-way at the moment?"

"We do. We wouldn't have started construction without it."

"Then we'll make sure you keep it. I will lose money if this line doesn't get completed or run profitably."

He nodded in relief. Then I looked purposefully at Werner.

Werner nodded his head toward Mercer. "He knows about the job offer."

"That wasn't merely an offer," I said. "You accepted."

"I accepted based on completion of this rail line," Werner said. "If we can't reach Silverton—" He threw both palms up in a sign of helplessness.

His gesture irritated me. "You'll finish . . . and Phelps will no longer be bothersome."

"In that event, we'll still have a deal."

I was about to argue further but thought better of it. If we succeeded in taming Phelps, Werner would accept our offer, and if we weren't successful, then the Denver & Rio Grande would suffer a severe setback. I decided to withhold final judgment until I could measure Werner's actions over the next few days or weeks. If he crossed us or provided scant support, I'd withdraw my offer.

I turned to McAllen. "Let's go find Jeff."

Without a word, McAllen walked off in the direction they had led our horses. We found them still saddled and corralled with the line's working stock. A liveryman led them out of the pen for us, and we swung into our saddles. After we had weaved our way past the construction, I pulled up to examine the mountain blocking the progress of the rail line.

"Don't see any mining," McAllen said.

"You would buy this mountain only if you wanted leverage against the D&RG. And Phelps didn't buy it yesterday."

"Meaning?"

"They said he previously gave them right-of-way. That means he owned it before they committed to build this line. He always intended to withdraw it at the last moment. Probably wanted to use his leverage with the line to solidify his control over the region. He just used us as a handy excuse."

"Does that change anything?" McAllen asked.

I shrugged. "Probably not." Then I mused, "Maybe he doesn't have clear title."

"What do you mean?"

"He ordered Merck to keep quiet about his threat. If he had clear title, he'd rub our noses in it. The man loves to flaunt his wins."

"Who else could have a claim on this land?" McAllen asked.

"That is what we'd better find out . . . and fast."

Chapter 22

sordid details

We found Sharp at the Silver Plate. He wasn't alone. Nora West sat opposite him at a table for two. Sharp didn't notice us, so we took seats at another table. After perusing the blackboard, we ordered steaks with all the fixings. Two days on the trail had made us hungry for a real meal, and I planned to follow up with apple pie for dessert.

"Who's the woman with Jeff?" McAllen asked.

I explained all the sordid details.

McAllen glared momentarily at Sharp and then said, "That's *his* problem."

About halfway through our meal, Sharp must have recognized our voices and glanced over at us. We nodded and returned to our supper. McAllen asked how the title to the mountain could be muddled up. I explained that it was probably not muddled, but that Phelps may not have completed all the payments, or he had an unreliable partner, or he had sold the land since issuing the original right-of-way. McAllen's question helped clarify my thoughts. If Phelps had sold the land, then his threat was a bluff, and a poor one at that. A quick check at the courthouse would wreak havoc with his blackmail scheme. I also doubted Phelps would take on a partner he wouldn't trust to back him up. I was left hoping that he had borrowed money to buy the mountain and fell behind in the payments, like another mine owner in my past who had gotten too ambitious for his pocketbook. I had purchased a small bank so I could foreclose his mortgages. Unfortunately, I'd only escalated our feud instead of ending it, and my disagreements with Sean Washburn had ended in bloodshed. Although far from timid, Phelps seemed not nearly as ruthless as Washburn, so I hoped our dispute could be resolved amicably. It was probably a false hope, but I needed something I could use against Phelps that would force him to restrain Ben Law.

Sharp and Mrs. West came over to our table after finishing their meal.

"I thought you left town," I said to Mrs. West.

"Jeff sent me a telegram and asked me to wait until he returned so we could talk."

I smiled at Sharp. "And here I thought you came here searching for mining opportunities we could add to our Galena Queen claim."

"I did and I have," Sharp said. "We'll talk in the morning."

"Yes," McAllen said. "We have a number of subjects to get settled. Seven o'clock."

Sharp laughed. "We have a big night planned. Big Mike is hosting us for a new burlesque musical. We expect to be late. Nine?"

"Eight," McAllen said gruffly.

Sharp started to argue, and then I could almost see him decide to show up whenever he rolled out of bed. He gave us a sociable wave and walked out arm in arm with his old/new sweetheart. I turned to face an unhappy McAllen.

"Damn it, he'll come traipsing in late wearing a damned silly grin."

"He will," I said. "I'm anxious to see the bankers in town. If he's too late, can you explain things while I investigate the title to that mountain?"

"I'm here to settle with Ben Law, not build a railroad, buy claims, or accommodate Jeff's love life. If you're not back by mid-morning, I'll go shoot Law so I can get back to my ranch."

"I'll hurry," I said with a smile.

Chapter 23

a master gunman

The next morning, McAllen and I ate breakfast by ourselves. Sharp did not show up at eight nor even by nine o'clock. Although McAllen's mood had improved after a night's rest and a couple of meals, I didn't expect him to continue his amicable ways once Sharp arrived.

"Who's your friend?"

I recognized Ben Law's voice. He stood behind me, but instead of turning in my seat, I looked at McAllen to gauge his reaction. McAllen had turned hard and appraising.

McAllen said, "Only weak men surround themselves with bodyguards."

I took that to mean that Law had two or more of his ruffians in tow.

"These are my associates. We came in to eat breakfast. I'd introduce you, but I don't know your name."

Now I scooted my chair around so I could see Law and have easier access to my Colt. Law looked exceptionally pleased with himself and glanced conspiringly between his two companions as if sharing an amusing story only they would understand. McAllen had decades of experience handling gunmen, so I let him take the lead.

"That the way you usually make introductions? Most men offer their hand and name together. You hang your hand alongside your pistol."

"You're Joseph McAllen, late of the Pinkertons," Law said without offering hand or name.

"And you're Ben Law, lackey of Mr. Phelps," McAllen said.

Law visibly bristled. "You son of a bitch, I'm no lackey."

Instead of taking offense, McAllen laughed lightly. "Now that we've completed our introductions, go eat your breakfast. We'll settle grievances later in the day."

"Is that a threat? You think you're some type of bad man? As a youngster barely out of knee britches, I dealt with men tougher than you."

"Then dismiss your men, and we'll see how I fare against a master gunman such as yourself."

McAllen conveyed indifference with his matter-of-fact tone. I saw confusion register on Law's face. My guess was that he seldom encountered anyone who sloughed off his threats. He certainly wasn't going to dismiss his men—he wore them like clothing—but if he backed down, others might lose their fear of what he might do to them. I waited to see what he'd decide to do. In the end, he did what all minor martinets do when confronted with a plausible challenge to their

154

authority. He made an excuse to escape a fight.

"Tell you what, let's wait until your trail partner shows up, and then we can settle our so-called grievances all at once."

"Hell, I'm right here," Sharp said from the doorway. "Looks like the numbers line up even-like. If ya'll excuse me for a moment, I'll run upstairs an' get my gun."

Sharp turned toward the stairs, but before he could depart, Law said, "No need. We don't want bloodshed on this fine mornin'. We came for breakfast, not a killin'. We'll see you gentlemen at a later date." After a meaningful pause, he added, "You can bet on it."

"At a later hour, you mean," McAllen said. "I don't have time for dawdlers. I hear you want a fight. If so, it happens today. I won't hang around Silverton waitin' for you to build up your courage. No ambush. No catchin' us unaware. No back shootin'." McAllen stood to his full height and squared on the men. "Fight straight up or get out of town."

Law feigned disappointment. "Damn. I'd like nothin' better than to oblige you, but my employer has given me clear orders. I'm not to fight anyone except at his direction . . . and, at the moment, he doesn't care about you upstarts. So . . ." He threw his arms wide palms up as if it were all out of his control.

From behind, Sharp harrumphed. "That's easy

155

to remedy. Hell, I'll get yer boss's dander up before the noonday meal."

Law gave Sharp a hard look, turned his back on us, and walked over to another table.

After Sharp took a seat at our table, McAllen said, "Nice of you to join us . . . we've eaten."

"Then ya can watch me eat," Sharp said with a smile. "Barely after nine o'clock, just when I said I'd arrive."

"I said eight," McAllen snapped.

"So you did." Sharp grinned. "Otherwise occupied."

"Well, I'm not goin' to sit here and watch you eat. I got things to do."

"What?" I asked, surprised that McAllen had things to do in Silverton.

McAllen, flustered for a moment, blurted, "Maybe I'll go to the bank with you."

I laughed. "No, Joseph, you'd better stay with Jeff. But please don't kill those men over there. These fine people are eating their morning meal. Loud noise and blood ruins the appetite."

As I scooted my chair away from the table, McAllen said, "Steve, don't take long. Despite your tomfoolery, we need to deal with these men."

Chapter 24

need to protect

I plopped heavily into a chair. I had found McAllen and Sharp in the small hotel lobby, trading heated looks. Good friends can exasperate each other. For one thing, they know each other's foibles and have already heard all of their rationalizations for bad behavior. Excuses that may have worked in the beginning grow thin over time. I stopped that line of thought when I realized that my shortcomings were no doubt equally transparent to them.

"Phelps has things tied up better than I had expected. He owns that mountain clear. Paid off the mortgage a few days ago." I shook my head. "Phelps is clever. He guessed I'd probe for any ownership issues."

"Maybe it's not you he's worried about," Sharp said. "Phelps didn't want to tie up his money on a worthless mountain until he needed to use it as a bludgeon. As soon as he issued his threat against the D&RG, he knew the railroad would check the ownership." Sharp laughed. "Phelps ain't dumb like Washburn. Ya really think ya could just buy a bank an' foreclose on past-due mortgages like ya did in Nevada?"

"Worth a try," I said weakly.

" 'Nother problem," Sharp said. "I discovered Phelps an' Law are related somehow, cousins I think. Probably why Law feels he can push Phelps."

"Related?" I said, shaking my head. "Well, hell, Cain killed Abel . . . so maybe we can still get them at each other's throats."

"If I remember my Sunday bible lessons, envy drove Cain," Sharp said. "Can we make Law even more jealous of his younger cousin?"

"To hell with that," McAllen said. "We shoot Law and let Phelps run his little empire. Who cares what Phelps does up here? Our real problem is that Law isn't really spoiling for a fight. He talks big, acts small. He's gonna sidestep us unless we find a way to rile him good."

"Jeff and I care about Phelps's *little* empire," I said. "He used his control of miners to keep us from working our claim. Now he's threatening to halt progress on the D&RG. We'll never be able to ship ore by rail as long as Phelps runs things around here."

McAllen looked uncomfortable, but attentive, so I kept going. "Joseph, Law knows you'll come after him if he kills us. He also suspects you'll interfere with his plan to become the high and mighty grand lord of Durango. That makes you a target too. We need to take care of Law and Phelps. I'm sorry you got dragged into this, but there's no simple answer. Any half solution will only bite us later."

Instead of getting angry, McAllen appeared to calmly think about what I had said. He stood and paced the lobby. Sharp and I let him think.

"You're right, Steve," he said after retaking his seat. "I thought when I quit Pinkertons, I was done with this type of work. Foolish of me. Before I protected other people's property or person, but now I need to protect my own property and family. I've known lots of men like Law and Phelps. If I want peace, they need to go to jail or deep into the ground."

"We can't just shoot Law, so what'll we do?" I asked.

Sharp laughed. "Hell, I'll put the word around town that he's a swindler an' a coward an' a liar an' worse. I'll insult his manhood, his looks, his dreadful smell. His sissy bandanna. I'll tell everyone he's loco. When it all gets back to him, he'll come find us."

"Damn it, Jeff, that could take days, even weeks," McAllen said. "I got a ranch to build, and the almanac says bad weather's comin' early this year."

Sharp jumped out of his chair and replaced McAllen in pacing around. After a couple of laps, he said, "Big Mike hates Phelps, but Law keeps Big Mike from takin' care of that preenin' peacock. He's ready to set up that meetin' with the other mine owners. Thinks we can unify 'em against Phelps an' his crew." He shook his head. "I don't think it's a good idea. Not yet. It'd be like a declaration of war. Let's try everythin' else before we turn the Animas red." He stopped pacing and looked at us. "Hey, listen, we're not in a big hurry. I'll start the rumors an' ask Mike to keep 'em goin'. He'll say I got drunk in his place an' yelled blasphemous insults at Ben Law. Instead of hangin' around, the three of us ride back to yer ranch. He'll come after us, don't ya worry. Open defiance threatens his hold on Silverton an' his plans for Durango. We go down south an' wait for his lordship to show up, an' in the meantime, we build yer ranch. We can even prepare a few surprises for 'em. What do ya think?"

"What about those new claims you bought?" I asked. "Can we shut them down in a couple of hours?"

"Yep," Sharp replied. "Easy. Law already told the miners they can't work for us. There's a shed on one of the properties we can use to lock away the tools. Phelps wants those claims, so he's already mad as a hornet. He'll just get madder every time he rides by 'em. Hell, if Law won't come on his own to settle the score, Phelps may very well send him."

Sharp looked directly at McAllen. "Joseph, what do ya think? Gits yer ranch built, an' we fight on our soil."

"Six," McAllen said, sounding distracted.

"Six? Six what?" I asked.

"Six workers at the ranch. I hired Steve's carpenter, a man named Tom, to help with the buildin'. Before I left, I sent Mark Masters to the ranch as well. With the three of us and Maggie, that makes six hands." He smiled with closed lips. "We'll get the damn thing built in no time."

"Sure you want Maggie out there?" I asked. "There'll probably be gunplay at some point. Also, you need to let Tom and Mark know the danger . . . and when you do, they may skedaddle."

"I had been thinkin' that the only sure way to keep Maggie safe was to stay right here in Silverton until Law is dead, but if Law's smart, he'll send a few men down to snatch her. That'll put me at their mercy. I need to be down there to protect her, and if I return, she won't stay away from the ranch. In case you haven't noticed, Maggie's headstrong."

Sharp nodded slowly. "Law probably won't think of it, but Phelps sure as hell will. Yer right. Maggie's our Achilles heel."

"Then I'd rather she remains in my shadow . . . even if there's some risk. I've had her snatched before to get at me. I don't want to repeat the experience." McAllen remained quiet for a moment. "Listen, if we run Phelps out of Silverton, you and Jeff will get even richer, so how 'bout hirin' some of my old team to create a picket line around the ranch? We can work out the details later, but a four-man team ought to do the job."

I looked at Sharp and he nodded. "Eight," I said. "We'll need around-the-clock sentries. Four on, four off. Plus, eight Pinks will make Tom and Mark feel safer. Maybe they'll stay on. I'll send a telegram to the Pinkerton office while Jeff spreads ugly rumors belittling Mr. Law's sanity and manliness. Then the three of us can get everything valuable into that shed. We ride out in a few hours."

We all traded glances. Everyone nodded.

McAllen stood. "Let's get this done and get the hell off this mountain."

Chapter 25

tread with care

After two long days of riding, we arrived back in Durango. McAllen left us on the outskirts of town to pick up Maggie and ride directly to his ranch. Sharp had brought Nora West down from Silverton, so the two of them rode to his hotel. I had apprehensions about bringing her along at first, but she proved sturdier than she appeared and rode nearly every daylight hour without complaint. After I stabled my horse at the livery and walked to my cottage, I discovered further surprises at home. Virginia had been busy, but before I could admire her handiwork, she hauled me out to the front porch and sat me down without kiss, food, or drink. I braced for something serious.

"Steve, I want to know right now . . . what are your intentions?"

She sounded miffed, so I couldn't claim not to have received appropriate forewarning to tread with care. Instead, I responded with all the subtlety of a schoolboy presented with pigtails and an ink bottle.

"Supper."

"Damn it, Steve, do you ever think beyond the moment?" She sounded abnormally cross. She folded her arms close against her breasts. "Okay, what about after supper?"

"I've been gone nearly a week. Do I need to explain my intentions after we eat?"

"You do unless you want to sleep in the guest room."

"Wait a minute, are we having different conversations?"

"And here I thought you might have gone dull."

"Please," I pleaded, "what are you talking about?"

After a heavy sigh, she said, "We came to Durango to get married. I thought that's what we agreed to. Since we've arrived, you've never brought the subject up. Not once. I'm the one who brings it up. You keep leaving . . . with your men friends. You leave me alone in this house with no friends or family. So . . . once more, what are your intentions? Are we getting married, or are we just living together . . . on occasion?"

"We're getting married. I thought we settled this the other day. The day we ate lunch at Henry's. We get married and start a family."

"That was a pleasant afternoon by the river, but saying it's so doesn't make it so. You have to stay put long enough for a ceremony, you know."

"I presumed you were planning the ceremony. Was I wrong? When I get home, all I see is new paint, a new porch, new furniture, a new garden, and—like this time—a new buggy in the side yard. From what I see, a wedding would distract you from all of your nesting."

Rage flared in her eyes. For a moment, I thought she might slap me, or worse. Instead, she closed her eyes and took several deep breaths. When she opened them, she no longer looked like she wanted to kill me, but she appeared annoyed that I remained within sight.

After another heavy sigh, she said, "Let's talk about the get home part. You keep running off. I have nothing to do when you're away, so I work on our house. I'd call it *our home,* by the way, but you're gone so much it doesn't feel like either word is appropriate. So, let's start with why you leave all the time."

"I told you. I go to Silverton to sell Edison's inventions and invest in mining claims. I rode out to McAllen's ranch one day." I shifted uncomfortably in my seat. "I tell you every place I go. What do you think—I have another woman somewhere? Is that why you're angry?"

"Actually, that thought never occurred to me. Do you?"

"No."

"I didn't think so." She gave me an exasperated look. "What I suspect is that you're getting cold feet, and you gallivant around with your male friends as a way to avoid marrying me."

"I'm not avoiding anything. I want to get married." I realized I needed to make it more personal, so I quickly revised. "I want to marry *you* . . . but I have a problem." From her expression, I could tell I had blundered badly. "Not with the marriage, but with some men. It's a long story, but Jeff and I ran into trouble in Silverton." She gave me another exasperated look, but I plunged ahead anyway. "In an unrelated matter, McAllen made the same people angry. That's not quite accurate, but the result is the same. He got some men fired, and as a result, they held a grudge against him. They ended up going to work for the same men Jeff and I had trouble with in Silverton."

"You, Sharp, and McAllen are in yet another feud? Oh, Steve, how does this keep happening? Normal people don't get into a fight every time they ride into a new town." She appeared beyond exasperation now. "Damn it, Steve, when are you going to grow up?"

"You can't believe I went looking for this."

"I don't know . . . perhaps you did. It keeps happening." When I didn't respond, she added, "You said it was a long story. Let's hear it. All of it."

I explained what had happened over the last month. She didn't interrupt, and her expression remained neutral. I told her everything, including Sharp's involvement with Nora West, our new mines, our chance to illuminate the entire town, and McAllen's impatience to be done with Law so he could build his ranch.

When I finished, she sat only a moment before saying, "Do you understand why you keep getting into these types of situations?"

"Virginia, we deal with miners and mining camps. Miners dig money out of dirt. Money attracts ambitious men . . . and huge amounts of money will attract ruthless, ambitious men. I'm just coming to this realization: It's the nature of our work. Jeff and I go into situations where hard men hold power and accumulate wealth, and they're willing to do anything to hold onto it."

"I see one in front of me."

"I have all the money I want."

"Then why are you peddling another man's inventions?"

That gave me pause. Introspection was not one of my strong suits. Finally, I said, "I think it's because I like to make things happen. I like the game. Money's not important, it's just the score."

"So you see one of these ruthless, ambitious men and feel a need to challenge him in some kind of contest, a contest in which someone frequently ends up dead. Steve, that kind of behavior will get you killed one day. It's crazy. You told me you don't think Law is completely sane, but what about you? Do you think it's sane to get into gunfight after gunfight until you finally lose?"

I got up and paced the porch. She had a point. I kept running into deadly duels because I kept thrusting myself into situations controlled by men who had acquired power through violence. When I challenged their position, they responded with the same tactics that had made them successful in the first place. Competitiveness was my nature, so I probably would keep repeating the same behavior. Which left me with a quandary. Either I return to New York, where business could be even more ruthless but seldom lethal, or quit all of my business endeavors.

In the West, the pecking order was determined by strength and willingness to use force. The strong prospered by taking from the weak. In the East, police and courts maintained a façade of civilization, but the process was the same . . . except the smart took from the less smart. In New York, I enjoyed defeating the smart set who had tilted the table in their favor. In the West, I liked out-gunning the strong. Why? Guilt over my family's business transgressions? Some perverse sense of righteousness? It wasn't merely the thrill of a contest, because I didn't challenge people like Sharp who had built their wealth honestly. I had never put it into words, but now I knew I despised cheaters and wanted to see them lose. I had the wherewithal to defeat them, and I enjoyed their defeat. Worse, I enjoyed it more in the West. The rules were clear, the resolution final.

"Yes."

"Yes what?" Virginia asked in an unemotional tone that let me know she had vented her anger.

168

"Yes, I believe when I see one of these ruthless, ambitious men, I feel an inborn need to challenge them. It's not something I control . . . it controls me."

"Because?"

"Because I enjoy defeating them. I can't explain it, but I know it's true."

Instead of appearing angry, she looked pleased. "Well, I can live with that. I just can't live with self-deception. If we can be honest with ourselves and each other, we can have a successful marriage."

"You're not asking me to change?"

She laughed. "Impossible. Some fiancées think they can change a man after marriage, but it's a fool's errand."

"And you're not foolish?"

"I don't tilt at windmills."

"Okay." I quit my pacing and sat back down, taking both of her hands in mine. "You say you can't live with self-deception. What about you? I'm not the only one who has trouble with introspection."

"What are you talking about?"

"When I got home, you were heated. You were worried that day we ate at Henry's too. It's not all me. You have doubts . . . and you suppose that I have them as well. What's got you so concerned?"

She pulled her hands away, stood, and took a

turn at pacing. Finally, she faced me and said, "You're right. In truth, I liked our adventures. I even enjoyed the street fight in New York . . . at least the aftermath. I like traveling in luxury, with a tinge of danger. So in that, I'm somewhat like you, but not as extreme. Yes . . . there's a concern that once we marry, we'll become another boring couple. But that's a concern, not a fear."

I didn't want to ask, but I did anyway. "What do you fear?"

"That I'll lose you . . . like I lost my first husband."

That hit me between the eyes. What a quandary for her. She enjoyed the element of danger in our relationship, but her first husband's death haunted her. She was worried that like me, she was repeating the same behaviors: marrying someone who needed to travel and did dangerous work. Her first husband was a mining engineer who took her west. It was a thrilling adventure for both of them, but he was the only one who faced real peril. When the day came that tons of rock collapsed on him, Virginia suddenly learned that risks on the frontier could instantly turn life threatening.

Suddenly, I started laughing. She immediately grew cross, and I pulled her down into the seat beside me.

"I'm not laughing at your fear," I said. "I'm laughing at us. What a pair we make. We love each other, and we love the type of life we live together, but we're a couple of worriers. We have everything we need to make us happy . . . until we don't. But hell, it makes no sense to deny doing what makes us happy just because it will end one day. Then we'd be like Jeff, who ran away from what would make him happy and now regrets seven lost years he could have spent with the woman he loves. I laughed because we're being foolish, worrying the future when we ought to be enjoying the present."

Instead of answering, she kissed me. A bit too passionately for sitting out in public, but when we broke, I didn't spot any neighbors spying on us.

I smiled. "So, does that mean we're still getting married?"

"Yes. Soon. But when we marry, I want to take off for San Diego right away, so all these Silverton troubles need to be settled. I wouldn't even think of asking you to drop it all and go now. You won't abandon your friends. So . . . you explained how this mess got started, now tell me how you're going to get out of it."

"What makes you think we have a plan?"

"Steve, you always have a plan. And if you don't, Joseph does." She gave me a long, hard look before adding, "So?"

"Jeff and I need to head out to McAllen's ranch for a week. Maybe a little longer. We're going to help him build his place before he freezes to death in that tent of his."

Her face scrunched into a frown. Before she could rebuke me, I added, "We do have a plan. If it works, Phelps and Law will come to us out at the ranch. We left bait in Silverton that should draw them to us instead of us chasing them. Before you get overly worried, I've hired a Pinkerton team that should arrive in a day or two, so we won't be alone out there. McAllen handpicked the team, so once they arrive, we'll have the upper hand."

"Then I'll join you. Joseph will need help setting up house and home." She waved her arm around to encompass our new cottage. "As you can see, I'm an accomplished home builder."

"Virginia, there's no place for you to stay. We'll be sleeping on the ground in bedrolls."

"I've slept on the ground before. Besides, it's only a three-hour ride. Joseph will need supplies and furnishings, so we can sleep in our own bed when we make shopping trips back to town."

I didn't like the idea. Virginia would be put in danger, and escorting her into town would mean I might be away from the ranch when Law attacked. After our previous conversation, I knew there would be hell to pay if I objected, so I simply said we would leave at daybreak.

"You're not going to try to talk me out of it?" she teased.

"Me? Never. I don't tilt at windmills. Besides, I've been in gunfights with you. You're handy to have around."

Chapter 26

little else to contemplate

Virginia and I rose at daybreak and packed our saddlebags and bedrolls. While she prepared a quick breakfast, I went down to the livery and brought back our horses, which by prearrangement had already been saddled by the liveryman. With a larger crew, McAllen and Sharp had put together a long list of needed supplies, so I also rented a packhorse. After I threw the saddlebags and bedrolls onto our horses, Virginia and I sat on the new porch eating bacon and biscuits and sipping piping hot coffee. I kiddingly told Virginia her sole duty at the ranch was to make the coffee before McAllen got anywhere near the stove. We laughed and enjoyed the crisp, clear morning air and watched the nascent light turn into day.

I had arranged to meet Sharp at the general store at seven o'clock. When we rode up trailing a packhorse, Sharp didn't seem surprised to see Virginia riding alongside me. Nora West was nowhere to be seen, however. The shopkeeper was still hauling goods out of the store to display on the boardwalk. I'd never understood shopkeepers who thought a barrel of brooms and a couple of dresses hung outside on hooks would entice shoppers into the store. The only outdoor display at our Leadville shop had been a cigar store Indian. He'd never told me if he'd sold a cigar or lured even a single shopper inside.

With Virginia's help with shopping, it quickly became a two-packhorse trip. For a moment, I considered a buckboard, but horseback would be faster, so I returned to the livery and rented another packhorse. After we distributed the loads properly in the panniers, Sharp asked if he could ride on ahead. Leading packhorses would be slow going, and he wanted to hurry out to the ranch. Since we preferred to ride together anyway, we sent him on his way.

Virginia was a fine horsewoman, riding with easy grace. She seemed thrilled to be out of town and on the open trail. All my reservations and second thoughts vanished. From the moment she woke, she was excited by our impending adventure. Despite her cheerfulness, there was no idle chatter. She rode easy, with a thin smile, but lost in her own thoughts. I might as well have been riding with McAllen.

She had brought her handgun and a rifle. She had also brought the special purse she had picked up in New York City. It looked like an ordinary handbag, but the colorful beading on the outside hid a heavy sailcloth lining that held over a pound of lead shot. It was basically an enormous sap with a handle long enough to hit an assailant several feet away. A female Pinkerton agent had taught Virginia how to wield it with devastating force. I started to tell her the weapon would be useless in this situation, but held my tongue because the handbag made her feel more secure. And I didn't want her swinging it at me.

During the ride, I kept a sharp eye on the horizon in every direction. I saw nothing untoward and hoped Phelps and Law would react slowly to our bait. They would need to be away from Silverton for at least a week, so it would take some time to ensure that operations continued in their absence. I hoped putting their business in order would take a day or two. Mines and saloons didn't run themselves. They would also need to muster men and gather supplies. As they pass the D&RG rail construction, they would talk to Merck and make sure he stayed in line. I knew I was simply rationalizing. I wanted the Pinkertons to arrive before our attackers, so I mentally threw all kinds of obstacles in Phelps's path to the McAllen ranch. Wishful thinking. McAllen or Sharp would have pulled up stakes and charged out to achieve surprise. If Phelps and Law did the same, they could be here as early as this afternoon.

How would the attack come? Trying to hold our ground at the ranch would be more like a military battle. I had never been in the military, and to my knowledge neither had McAllen or Sharp, but I had studied battles in college. I knew the characteristics. We held a defensive position sitting on high ground. Not seriously high, but with flat plains all around us, enough of an incline to encumber an attacker. The size of the opposing force was uncertain, but no doubt would be larger than ours. Our reinforcements might not arrive in time. Defenders of a stronghold held an advantage unless the attackers outnumbered them. I thought about that. Law would bring enough men—even if he didn't know the terrain. In every one of our encounters, he had always shown up with more men than the situation called for.

We needed to emphasize our natural advantages. If Law didn't know we were encamped on a knoll, he might ride up unawares, so we would spot him from afar. He might not even realize that we saw him until he came within range. Not likely. With flat plains all around, the barn stood out like a wart on the end of a nose. No, if he's cautious, he'll sneak up at night. I automatically looked at the brightly lit sky. Not being an outdoorsman, I didn't keep track of the moon. Was it new, or full, or something in between?

"Virginia, do you know the phase of the moon?"

She answered quickly and with certainty. "The new moon was three days ago. When you're away, there's little else to contemplate at night."

Her laughter didn't take all the sting out of her quip.

Did she remain miffed about my absences? After a night's sleep, she probably wondered if she had inadvertently facilitated another delay in our marriage. I decided not to pick at the scab.

Her answer about the phase of the moon made me even more anxious for the Pinkertons to arrive, because each day would bring additional moonlight.

Now Virginia interrupted my thoughts.

"What if those Silverton men have already attacked McAllen's ranch?" she asked.

"We rode down the mountain hard and arrived only last night. Law doesn't know exactly where the ranch is, so we'll arrive in time for the festivities."

"And if he never comes? What if he smells a trap and decides to wait for you in Silverton?"

"Then our plan is shot to hell." I smiled. "But we'll have built Joseph's ranch."

After a long moment, she asked, "How long will you keep the Pinkertons?"

"As long as it takes."

"That may be a long time. From what you've told me, Ben Law likes to fight on his own terms. He doesn't sound like the kind of man who will be goaded into charging blindly into territory he doesn't know."

I didn't answer right away because she was right. Sharp's insults might be of little consequence. Had we anticipated that our taunts would work just so we could go home? Probably. McAllen wanted to return to his ranch, and I didn't want to provoke a fight that might get us arrested or worse. Our provocations could easily have gone too far. The more I thought about it, the more I became convinced that Law wouldn't come off his mountain to attack us. I felt better. No attack meant that Virginia would remain safe.

The sight of McAllen's ranch answered Virginia's first question. The attack had not yet occurred. In fact, I could hear hammering even before I could see the ranch. I'd better let McAllen know how far sound traveled on the plains.

I laughed.

"What's funny?" Virginia asked.

"Sharp didn't want to dillydally with us, so he rode ahead. I bet McAllen put him to work the moment he arrived. Serves him right."

As we approached the ranch, my suspicions were confirmed, but it didn't look as if Sharp objected. I spotted him on the roof of the barn, skillfully swinging his hammer to the rhythm of a song he sang with far less skill than enthusiasm.

To my astonishment, Virginia joined in with him, and soon the two were singing away at the top of their lungs, Sharp with gusto and Virginia with a melodious voice I didn't know she possessed.

The duo's timing was perfect. As we pulled up in front of the barn, Virginia and Sharp finished the last refrain of their song. Everyone laughed. Well, not everyone. McAllen obviously disapproved of this interruption.

"Sharp, stop singin'!" he barked. "You do it wrong."

Then he removed his hat and swung it across his waist as he bowed. "Mrs. Baker, you, on the other hand, may sing to your heart's content."

Then he snugged his hat back onto his head and purposefully surveyed the men who had been idled by this merry demonstration.

"Now, everyone, back to work!"

Chapter 27

we need a plan

As we dismounted, McAllen made additional perfunctory greetings, but his attention was on the packhorses. Hurrying over, he untied the restraining rope, and all kinds of goods clattered to the ground. All four horses bucked to one degree or another, but luckily, the second load remained secure. McAllen gave me a disapproving look and said that he'd show me how to tie down a load properly. I ignored his rebuke. If he hadn't been so impatient, I could have assisted him, and nothing would have fallen. McAllen, Virginia, and I picked up the supplies, dusted them off, and arranged everything on a rough-hewn table that must have been used for meals. Then we unloaded the second packhorse. This time we didn't bruise the earth or frighten the horses.

After we had groomed and fed the horses, I walked under the eave of the barn and yelled to get Sharp's attention. He took a break from hammering and shuffled down the roof slope on his butt until he could see me. He squatted with arms around his knees about two feet back from the eave, smiling around nails held between his teeth.

He spit the nails at me.

"Are you always full of good cheer?" I asked sarcastically.

He looked contemplative, as if I had asked a serious question.

"Not sure," he finally responded, "but certainly full of vinegar since I took up with Nora again."

He grinned unashamedly and I felt happy for him.

"How far can you see from up there?" I asked.

"Whole valley. Good lookout point."

"How thick is the wood?"

"Thought of that. A rifle bullet would pass right through one side of the roof an' on through the other. Not much of a shield against lead."

"Betcha done more thinkin'," I said, imitating Sharp's twang.

"Yep. After I'm done here, I'm gonna go inside an' nail hardwood planks up against the roof peak."

"Both sides?"

"Yep. Thicker, the better. Maybe even get some tin sheets next time we're in town."

I nodded. "I'll start carrying lumber into the barn."

"Before ya do, throw up some small pieces of wood. I want to nail 'em to the roof as a boot hold. A lookout's gonna need somethin' to brace against. Hard to hold on to the peak an' spy through a lookin' glass without somethin' to stand on."

"Got one of those?" I asked.

"Joseph does, but ya need to hold it to yer eye with both hands, or it bounces like a two-dollar whore. A foot brace should allow ya to lie against the roof without holdin' on. Throw me up at least six pieces of wood. I'll nail 'em at different heights. That way each of us can pick a set that will expose only our heads."

Virginia had walked up beside me. She yelled up, "Make one high enough for the women. We can take our turns as lookouts."

Having overheard, Maggie yelled that she would take her turn as well. Then she volunteered to get Sharp the pieces of wood while I sorted out solid planks for use inside the barn. I decided I would test Sharp's idea by firing a rifle at a double thickness of hardwood. If someone was going to be on the barn roof when the fighting started, I wanted to make sure they were well shielded.

As I carried two planks past the barn in order to shoot away from people, I saw Maggie purposely toss wood blocks at Sharp so hard that he had to duck instead of catching them. Both of them laughed like a couple of kids. I hoped the mood remained joyful. Someone shooting at you had a way of ruining an otherwise good time.

As I lined up the wood for a test shot, McAllen came over. "I overheard your conversation. I bought this lumber for the floor in my house."

He took off his hat and wiped his brow with a shirtsleeve. "I guess it's okay. I don't want bullet holes causing leaks in my barn."

"We were worried about bullets causing leaks in our bodies," I said, a bit put out.

McAllen's closed-mouth smile told me he was joking. I knew it for sure when he simply walked away without another word.

I nailed two mountain ash planks together, wedged them between two rocks, and walked fifty feet away. If Law or his men were close, they would ride around the barn and shoot us from behind. From further away, their bullets would have less power than my test shot. I had borrowed a Winchester '73 because it carried less power than my model '76. I thought it was still a legitimate test, because few men in the West carried the higher-powered rifle. I yelled a warning before I put two bullets into the planks. Seeing what I was doing, Sharp had climbed down. We walked over to examine the damage. Both bullets had penetrated all the way through.

"Well, crap," Sharp said.

"You also have the roof planks and shingling," I joked.

Sharp rubbed his chin. "What if you hit the wood with a glancing blow?"

"Good thought," I said.

We both walked back to my original shooting position and then to the side about twenty feet. I fired twice more. We liked the results better. Hit at an angle, the wood provided good protection. Since it was unlikely the attackers would come at the barn straight on, the planks would help whoever was on the roof.

Around noon, we took a break. Seven of us sat around a dead campfire in the central living area. I called it a living area because, although it was outdoors, McAllen had circled rocks from the creek for a fire pit, arranged camp chairs, and to the side of his cooking stove, he had placed a crude table slammed together by Tom. The seven included McAllen, Sharp, Maggie, Virginia, Tom the carpenter, Mark Masters, and me. We chewed rock-hard biscuits, tough jerky, and raisins while McAllen explained the situation. He described all of the events that had ignited the feud, said that help was on the way in the form of Pinkertons, told Mark and Tom about Phelps and Law, and explained that we had started vile rumors to entice them to the ranch. There were a few flinches when the realization struck that we had invited an attack.

McAllen spoke directly to Tom and Mark. "This ain't what you signed up for. If you want to leave, there won't be any hard feelings."

At first, the two men looked at the ground in front of their feet. I understood their trepidation. This was not their feud and they barely knew us. Why should they get involved?

After a while, Masters lifted his head and studied Maggie. Then he looked at McAllen and nodded that he would join our cause. I suspected he hadn't done much for his family, but if he could stand with us, it would please his son and give him a chance with the girl he favored. The manly action befitted western culture, but Masters ruined it by prattling on about his promise to remain loyal and protect the ranch no matter what. He sounded like he wanted hero status before the first shot was fired. On second thought, perhaps he did deserve accolades merely for staying. The dangers had been clearly defined. He finally got weary of talking or possibly noticed that people had quit paying attention.

When Masters fell silent, Tom said, "I'll stay till my work's done."

In my mind, that meant Tom had committed for the duration. The corrals and barn were close to being finished, but the house hadn't yet been fully framed. Even with all the help, it would be a race to beat the first heavy snow, assuming that flying lead didn't distract us for an extended period.

I wondered about Tom's motivation. I had heard somewhere that he had a sister with kids in town, but to my knowledge, none were enamored of Maggie. It could be pride in his work, but someone with his skills could certainly find other jobs he could work to completion without dodging lead. I glanced at McAllen. The two men had worked and lived together for a long enough period that they'd gotten to know each other. No, it wasn't pride in his work that induced him to stay. It was loyalty to Joseph McAllen. In the past, I had also followed McAllen into dangerous situations. The man encouraged loyalty without ever asking for it, and he had a knack for drawing out the best in people.

McAllen asked Sharp to describe what he was doing to the barn. Sharp explained that after he finished, the roof should stop a rifle bullet if the lookout remained directly above the foot braces. He asked everyone after we broke up to test their positioning on the braces to make sure they could stand comfortably with their hands free.

At this point, McAllen took over again. "From now on, someone must always be on the roof . . . with this." He held up a brass telescope. "Two-hour shifts?"

Everyone nodded, including the women.

McAllen nodded, as well. "Okay, we need a plan. Anyone got one?"

It was so quiet, I heard water in the creek burble over rocks.

Chapter 28

lookin' for blood

Getting no response, McAllen said, "The roof's our best vantage point and shootin' position. As soon as we spot 'em, two people go up top . . . our best shots . . . that'd be Jeff and Steve. That leaves five of us on the ground."

That wasn't exactly a plan, but at least it was an action. Perhaps if we put several actions together, we could approximate a plan.

"From what direction do you think they'll come?" I asked.

Masters eagerly jumped in. "From Silverton, they gotta come down along the rail line and straight into Durango. They'll go into town because they'll need directions to this ranch.

"If Law's clever, only a couple of riders will go into town so as to not raise a ruckus," I added.

Masters literally puffed up with pride. "I worked for Law and got to know him a bit. He's careless. I bet they all ride into town throwing up a big cloud of dust. He likes a big show. No matter what time they arrive, they won't hang around town. Not Law. No, sir. They'll race out here right off. The man's impatient as hell." He pointed toward Durango. "That means they'll come from that direction. They'll charge ahead until they see the ranch. I was a teamster, and I can tell you, we won't be hard to find, 'cuz those heavy wagons have carved ruts between town and here. Almost a regular trail by now. And they'll see the ranch from afar 'cuz the barn sticks up like a big windmill on this-here hill. When they spot the ranch, they won't hesitate a second—just charge right in. They're too dumb to guess we got lookouts or that we'll be ready for 'em."

I was surprised to hear McAllen say, "Sounds about right."

Awarded approval, Masters continued to hold forth like a seasoned army scout. "He could circle part of his men around and attack from two sides. Or he might ride direct on up to the barn friendly like . . . leastwise till the shooting starts. If he thinks we didn't spot him, he might hunker down and wait for nightfall, then sneak in close and try to take us by surprise. Or he could camp between us and Durango and dare us to try escaping into town."

"A siege?" I asked skeptically.

"Yep, situated up on this hill, it would be the smart move, especially with seven of us."

McAllen harrumphed. "Not likely. Take too long, and they got business back up the hill. Besides, they don't know we have seven shooters."

The praise from McAllen had vanished in a

heartbeat, and Masters looked crestfallen. "I already said he ain't smart. Just threw that out so we consider every angle."

McAllen spoke with finality. "One of Mark's scenarios has it about right. He'll ride right up into our faces. Law likes to intimidate and thump his chest."

"Have you ever met Ben Law?" Masters asked defensively.

"We met. Briefly. A coward," McAllen answered. "Only fights when he's got a strong advantage. He relies on his victims givin' him the upper hand because they don't believe he actually means to kill 'em. But he will. And he'll come at us lookin' for blood . . . no doubt about it. Probably believes there are only two or maybe three of us out here. Still, he likes the odds in his favor, so he'll bring lots of men."

"You got all this from a brief meet," Masters said. "Hell, I was with him for days. Saw how he thinks. And I'll tell you, he ain't no coward. He likes killing. Good at it too."

From the look on McAllen's face, I knew Masters had compounded his error. McAllen had been about as accommodating as his nature allowed. When he was a Pinkerton, only those who had earned his respect in deadly situations could challenge him or his plans. I thought he was going to verbally cut down Masters, but instead his expression relaxed, and he almost smiled.

"For a moment, let's pretend I have years of experience facing outlaws who thought they were good at killin'. Let's assume further that I wouldn't be here if I didn't know how to read a man and his intentions. Is that okay with you, Mark?"

Maggie opened her mouth to back up her father but shut it when he placed a firm hand on her knee.

Masters started to say something, thought better of it, and just nodded. He was learning.

"Okay, here's how I see it," McAllen said. "Law's not goin' to get fancy. He'll ride straight in with superior force, say howdy, and then start shootin'. He'll have the sheriff or someone else with him to testify that we started shootin' first."

"The sheriff?" I blurted.

"He can't leave a pile of corpses out here with no alibi. He'll bring along an officer of the court to say we started the fight."

"The sheriff or a marshal or a lawyer," Sharp mused. "Yep, whoever he can buy."

"Mark?" McAllen asked.

Masters was surprised that McAllen asked his opinion, but now that McAllen had taught the man a lesson, he wanted him back in the fold.

"The sheriff can't be bought . . . good man . . . but the local marshal would provide an alibi for a few bottles of whiskey. He's a lush and straight as a dog's hind leg."

With the mode of attack settled, we traded

glances until I asked, "So how do we defend against a close-quarters attack?"

"Depends," McAllen responded. "If we want him to go away, we show our strength. Not two or three shooters, but seven. I guess he'll bring a dozen or fewer men with him. He'll turn tail if we're behind cover and they're mounted. If we want to end this right here and now, we hide our strength until the shootin' starts."

Sharp rubbed his chin. "Can I guess which ya prefer, Joseph?"

"We didn't lure him down here to chase him away," McAllen said.

Everybody nodded, so he continued. "When the lookout spots his party approachin', Virginia and Maggie go to the creek bed and keep an eye on things through the grass. Be careful to keep your heads below the grass. Steve and Jeff remain on the opposite slope of the roof. That leaves Tom, Mark, and me in the open. How are you boys with that?"

Masters looked uneasy. "You know, he might shoot me on the spot as a deserter. I ain't no coward, but I'd prefer a fighting chance."

Tom said, "Got no problem with standing in the open, but I gotta be holding my shotgun. As for Mark, he's a provocation. Better keep him out of sight if we're aiming for surprise."

"I want you holdin' that shotgun as well," McAllen said. "As for Mark . . . you're right, if

Law sees him, he may go berserk, and we'll lose control of the situation." He looked at Masters. "Stay behind cover."

"Where?" Masters asked, obviously relieved.

McAllen answered immediately. He looked around before saying, "We want a cross fire. If Tom and I meet them in front of the house, the women shoot from the creek, and Steve and Jeff are on the barn roof, then I want someone shootin' from behind them." He gestured toward the trail. "Over there somewhere. They'll be trapped in a circle of fire. No escape."

"That means they gotta ride right by me," Masters said. He gestured as well. "There ain't no cover over there at all."

"I'll build an outhouse," Tom said immediately. "Need one anyway. Gotta be hardwood so it's sturdy enough to deflect a shot. Double thick with a flap door on it fer shooting out." Tom suddenly seemed amused. "You can throw crap at 'em all day long."

"I hate outhouses," Masters said.

"We won't use it until after the fight," McAllen said firmly.

"Much obliged," Mark said. "But I may use it when the shooting starts."

Everyone laughed except McAllen.

Virginia spoke for the first time. "Can we put a chamber pot in there? Sure would enjoy the privacy. We'll empty it each time."

"As soon as we can get to town to buy one," McAllen said dismissively, and then he stood. "Let's get to it. This ranch won't build itself. Maggie, how 'bout you take the first watch?"

She immediately picked up the spyglass, shouldered her rifle, and headed toward the ladder lying against the front of the barn. Sharp jumped up, ran ahead of her, and moved the ladder to the other side, where it wouldn't be seen by anyone approaching from our wagon-rut trail.

When he returned to our group, Sharp asked, "Tom, ya got any more of them nail sacks?"

He meant the aprons he wore on the roof to nail shingles. Without a word, Tom went to his wagon and came back with two heavy canvas aprons.

"Ammunition?" McAllen asked.

"Yep," Sharp said. "One on the roof and another in the creek bed. We can store boxed ammunition in the outhouse once it's built." Then he laughed. "Ya men in the open . . . well, hell, ya'll probably be dead before either of ya need to reload."

His grin was not returned by either man.

McAllen said, "Tom, put a partial wall on the house. Only waist high, thick as you can make it. When you fire your shotgun, the horses will buck, and that's when we leap behind the wall. I'll kill Law outright and hightail it with you." He gazed before him, as if envisioning the fight. "On second thought, blast the horses with your shotgun. Ought to throw everything and everybody off balance."

Tom seemed to envision the fight as well. "Law's horse?"

"Not Law's. I'll take care of him. I want his horse to have all four hooves set solid on the ground."

Tom nodded. "We may come out of this."

"Might," McAllen said, "but I ain't seen a plan that worked right yet."

Chapter 29

last of the whiskey

By the next afternoon, we had nailed wooden shields to the inside of the barn walls, built a spanking new outhouse with extra-thick walls, installed a sturdy short wall along the front of the house, and distributed ammunition to our four shooting locations. We provisioned the creek bed with rifles, ammunition, and hardtack. The site had its own supply of water, so no canteens were needed. Since the creek lay below the knoll, the women would be shooting uphill, but because the slope was slight, the sightline should remain clear unless our attackers retreated toward town. Masters, shooting from the outhouse, would give them second thoughts about going in that direction. Sharp had driven huge nails into the barn roof so we could mount our rifles up there, and they would be waiting for us when we climbed into position. We used other nails on the roof to support canteens and canvas aprons full of ammunition. After my first stint of guard duty, I hauled up horse blankets to spread against the rough shingles.

Maggie had suggested that we picket the horses out of harm's way, so we staked them well out of the line of fire in the creek bed north of the ranch. They had plenty of grass and water, but if our vigil lasted more than a day, we would need to move the horses progressively further away from the ranch.

We were ready.

Except, nothing happened.

For days.

With so many workers, we made fast progress building the ranch. After four days, the barn, stables, and corrals were finished, and the ranch house framed, roofed, and fronted by a covered porch. In those four days, the seven of us had also consumed most of McAllen's provisions and used up the building supplies. The Pinkerton team could arrive at any moment, and we would need vast quantities of food and drink to support fifteen of us. We needed to take one or two wagons into town for food, lumber, hardware, and furnishings, or we'd soon be sitting on our rumps.

McAllen had directed us to build a deep porch extending the entire width of the house before we constructed the interior walls, floors, and ceilings. Tom, Masters, Sharp, and I finished the porch in a day, and it became the center of our community. We ate meals there, and it provided a shady place to rest during breaks in our work. We also gathered on the porch in the evening to watch the sunset. One of us always served guard duty, so the remaining six fit comfortably on the veranda to salute a good day's work behind us. McAllen set a rule that the stopper on the whiskey bottle must stay in place until the sun began to set. As soon as the bottom of the sun touched the distant horizon, we poured everyone a tin cup of Jameson's. Our little ceremony included Maggie, although McAllen diluted her drink with a generous amount of water. With drinks in hand, we sat with our backs against the house on benches Tom had cobbled together from odd pieces of lumber. Our nightly ritual included ribbing McAllen about his lack of building skills.

This evening, however, we didn't tease McAllen. Construction had stopped. Planking bought for the main house had been reassigned to an outhouse. The hardwood for the floors had been used to reinforce the barn, outhouse, and front exterior wall of the house. Building materials weren't the only thing in short supply. Our labors increased our appetites, and we had eaten most of the food. Even the last remaining whiskey bottle wouldn't survive the night.

Tom searched the sky for clouds. "Mr. McAllen, we need paint before it rains or snows; otherwise, our work will warp."

"We need more than paint," Sharp sniffed. "Just poured the last of the whiskey." He shook his head. "Maggie sure developed a taste for prairie dew."

We all laughed. McAllen carefully rationed his

daughter's whiskey, while Sharp and Masters stayed up late bragging about their numerous exploits. Their stories became increasingly outlandish with each sip of so-called prairie dew.

When the laughter faded, McAllen said, "Been thinkin' on it. In the mornin', we'll split ranks. Some of us go into town. I suggest—"

Everyone laughed again when Virginia leaped to her feet and threw up her hand. "I'll go. Heaven knows you boys will appreciate me getting a bath."

Then Maggie blurted, "I'm staying with you, Pa."

"Glad to hear it, 'cuz you don't have a choice," McAllen said. "But your ma needs to see you're still in one piece, so we'll join Mrs. Baker on the trip into town. That leaves a question. Should three go and four stay, or the other way around?"

"If Law comes, he'll approach by the wagon trail," I said. "The party going to town may run right into them. I'm uncomfortable with the women going. Can't we get by until the Pinkertons show up? Stay together until then? Can't be more than a day or two."

I knew the futility of my argument. McAllen had already determined the answer to his question. He would take four to town so he had two men to drive wagons. But if they met trouble on the trail, four would not be enough.

McAllen gazed off into the sunset. "Law's not coming. Hell, if we run into anyone on the trail, it'll be Pinkertons. Our plan didn't work. Let's at least get this ranch built."

"Another day won't matter," I said weakly.

"It will," McAllen said. "With this crew, one calendar day is seven days of work lost." McAllen leaned over and snapped his empty tin cup on the floor. "We leave first light. Tom comes with us."

"Wait a minute," I said. "I should go with you."

McAllen shook his head. "Tom knows the remaining work to be done and what supplies we need to get it done. You and Sharp are the best shots to protect the ranch."

"I want to protect Virginia," I blurted.

"I'll take care of her and Maggie. I need Tom's help at the mill and general store. I don't want to run short again."

I looked at Virginia and knew instantly that she was going into town. She was a hardy woman, but she needed a break from camping with a bunch of men. Besides, Virginia also felt a need to protect Maggie. She would go where Maggie went, and Maggie would go where her pa went. McAllen was right. If Law had intended to come down, he would have made the journey by now. I reluctantly nodded assent, and Virginia rewarded me with a smile that said she appreciated the absence of an argument.

"Both wagons," McAllen said. "We'll get enough supplies to finish the house and a few furnishin's. I figure a stove for heat and coffee, blankets, a mattress, cookin' pots and such, and enough provisions to get me through winter."

I doubted all that would fit into two buckboards. It represented a good list of what McAllen needed, but he was fooling himself if he thought this would be the last trip before winter. Other than building tools, buckets, and brushes to groom horses, the ranch had no furnishings at all. In fact, McAllen had only one lantern, which might have been fine if he were alone, but was insufficient for seven of us. We were even down to less than a half box of matches. Virginia had been promised a chamber pot, which she reminded me about whenever she had to go behind the house. Another McAllen rule stipulated that we had to go a hundred feet from the house, so the women insisted on taking our sole lantern after dark.

"After we finish buildin'," McAllen said, "the question I got rumblin' 'round my head is, do we head back up to Silverton or wait for spring?"

Sharp answered. "If they didn't come down after what I said, then Law's just spewin' a bunch of empty threats." He shrugged. "Perhaps we leave it be."

"We can't leave it be," I said. "What about the Galena Queen? Our deal with Big Mike? Partnering with Karl Werner?"

"Let's go elsewhere," Sharp said. "There are other mines, other saloons, other superintendents

200

we can hire . . . if we still want to sell Edison's inventions."

I was startled by the comment. "You want out?"

He gave me a direct look. "Steve, yer gettin' married. Findin' Nora has changed my mind 'bout things. Joseph's got a ranch to run. I say, let all that other stuff go."

"Will Law let us go?" I said this more to myself than to anyone in particular.

"I suspect he already has," Sharp said.

"Riders!" Masters yelled from the barn roof.

We all turned in unison to stare dumbly down the wagon trail. We could see nothing in the fading light, but that's why we kept a lookout on the barn. Everyone sprang into action. The two women raced to the creek bed while Masters scurried down the ladder to take his position in the outhouse. McAllen grabbed his rifle and Tom his shotgun, which had both been leaning against the house half wall. Sharp and I ran to the ladder and climbed as fast as we could.

Once I was in position, I still couldn't see any riders. Then I spotted a far-off dust cloud that must have alerted Masters. They were still over a mile out, but closing fast. Whoever was coming, they were riding hard. With the spyglass, I made out men galloping two abreast and several rows deep.

Damn.

We would face bloody hell in a few short minutes.

Chapter 30

two shakes of a lamb's tail

The fading light of dusk made it difficult to see. I handed the spyglass to Sharp and reached for my rifle that was hanging from a nail next to my assigned station on the roof. I worked the lever on my Winchester '76 and then inserted another 45-75 cartridge into the loading gate.

After another glance at the approaching riders, I looked behind me to see if I could spot Virginia and Maggie in the creek bed, relieved that they were well hidden. Masters had made it to the outhouse, and McAllen and Tom sat casually on the porch with their weapons across their laps. Everyone was in position. I hoped to hell this plan worked.

I took another look at the approaching cloud of dust. Sharp and I were supposed to keep our heads below the roof peak, but if I could barely make out the riders, surely they couldn't see us. A moment later, I ducked down below the peak and rolled onto my back. I still could not make out Maggie and Virginia. Everything seemed ready, but I started having misgivings. From our elevated perch, it was obvious that the women were too far away. Maggie was a good shot, but

Virginia's poor shooting skill with a pistol was only somewhat improved with a rifle. If the riders came all the way forward to the ranch house, the women would be shooting from about forty yards and slightly uphill in waning twilight. I bet they could barely discern targets when silhouetted against a dark eastern sky. I glanced to where the moon would rise, even though I knew it wouldn't peek over the horizon for an hour yet. I also worried that the small flap window Tom had built into the outhouse door would limit Master's peripheral vision. They could come at him from the side, and he would never see them. If we lived through this encounter, we would need a better plan for next time. Then I realized there would be no next time. This was it. This time, we would be fighting for all of the marbles.

"Pinkertons," Sharp whispered urgently as he thrust the spyglass at me.

My relief surprised me. The riders weren't a threat; they were our guardians. I had been engaged in several gunfights since coming west, but none had made me as nervous as this one. Too many people I cared about were at risk. Sharp looked as if he were about to shout the good news, but I put a finger to my lips and put the spyglass up to my eye. I wanted to see for myself before we alerted everyone within a mile. When I lowered the spyglass, I felt like a school kid on Christmas morning. I nodded, and Sharp let out a whoop that told our compatriots that the riders were not Phelps and his gang.

Then Sharp yelled down toward the creek, "Maggie, bring a bucket of cool water for our Pinkerton friends. They'll be thirsty as hell. An' hurry up, girl, they'll be here in two shakes of a lamb's tail."

With that, there were whoops and shouts all around.

In a very short time, the Pinkertons rode up to the ranch and brought their horses to a halt in front of McAllen and Tom on the porch. As we scrambled down the ladder, Maggie and Virginia scurried forward, each gripping the handle of a bucket that splashed water along the ground as they ran. Masters emerged last, tentatively opening the outhouse door.

The team leader gave Masters the once-over, and then said, "Don't let us interrupt you."

Unlike McAllen, this Pinkerton was not humorless.

McAllen said, "How do you do, Pete. Pleasant ride?"

"Tolerable." Pete looked around. "This the ranch you been bragging about? Looks thin of horses."

"Means lots of room for your mounts. Put them in the corral or stables. Brushes inside the barn door. Climb on down. My daughter Maggie brought you water. It's mountain runoff, so it's cool."

The Pinkertons dismounted, and some introductions were made. Their leader, Peter Lawson, had assumed McAllen's old position as head of the Denver office. The rest of the Pinkertons remained nameless. Lawson had evidently picked up McAllen's old habits. When I'd first met McAllen, he led a team hired to protect me from a notorious mining tycoon in Nevada. He had explained that he did not introduce his team because he didn't want any personal connection between the client and his men. Despite his precautions, I became friends with Sam, who had been killed trying to protect me. The pain I felt then helped me to understand why McAllen kept an emotional distance between his team and the client.

After gulping down a couple of ladles of water, Lawson said, "That was refreshing after a dusty ride, but by any chance, do you have beer cooling in that creek?"

Sharp answered. " 'Fraid not. Nor do we have any whiskey. Some scoundrel drank the last of it not less than twenty minutes ago."

"Unless that situation can be rectified, my fee just went up."

Sharp smiled. "Ya interrupted our meetin' 'bout goin' to town tomorrow for that very purpose."

Lawson examined our motley crew. "Meeting to figure out who goes for supplies and who remains with the fort?"

"Yep," McAllen said. "Now we gotta look at it

anew." He turned to Masters. "Mark, back on the roof. Your two hours ain't up."

"Thought that's why we hired these men," Masters said.

"They're gonna set up down the trail so they can intercept trouble before it gets here. First, Mr. Lawson and I need to split his team in two groups and figure out where his men are gonna be stationed." He looked the Pinkertons over. "Anybody got a harmonica?"

One of the Pinkertons held out a mouth organ. He didn't look enthusiastic about giving it up.

McAllen took it and handed it to Masters. "Blow this if you see anything. Same note. Right in the middle. Don't get fancy. Pass it on when your spell is up. Now climb that ladder."

"Why don't I just shout out?" Masters asked.

"Mark, do as you're told. I don't want any yellin' that alerts Law."

Masters reluctantly climbed back to his guard position. The Pinkertons led their horses to the barn. Maggie ran for another bucket of water. Virginia put a pot of coffee on the fire. Everyone seemed to have something to do except me. I picked up the whiskey bottle and stowed it with our collection of empties at the side of the house. The stack looked big enough for some serious shooting practice.

"Looks like now we'll have to do our planning over coffee instead of prairie dew," I said.

McAllen ignored my comment and watched the Pinkertons walk their horses into the stables.

"Their arrival changes things," I offered.

As he spoke, McAllen kept his eye on the Pinkertons' backsides. "Their arrival changes everything."

Chapter 31

cut it all loose

After we'd regathered, McAllen told us he wanted to wait until morning to set new plans. He suggested we spend the evening celebrating our good fortune. Since we would soon resupply, we went all out for supper. We fried the remaining bacon, baked fresh biscuits, heated several cans of beans, and served canned peaches for dessert.

After supper, we sat around telling tall tales until the Pinkerton with the harmonica played a few soulful tunes. It didn't feel celebratory, but we had a pleasant evening, and I gathered some fascinating material for my next book.

By the time everyone meandered off to bed, the moon had risen enough to make the prairie glow agreeably. I took Virginia by the elbow and led her away from the porch. When we were out of earshot, I suggested a walk to set our own plans. It was a warm autumn evening, and Virginia and I had had no private time since arriving at the ranch. She seemed perplexed, so I reminded her that Sharp had suggested a fresh start. She was relieved to discover I didn't want to rehash our plans for a wedding or family.

I grabbed my rifle as we set off on foot. Law

didn't worry me because Lawson had already dispatched men well out on the periphery of the ranch, but if trouble came, I didn't want to be caught with only a pistol.

To keep from stepping in a prairie dog hole, we walked along the wagon wheel ruts. The canopy of stars and the still, warm night made me feel content. I could hardly believe there was trouble anywhere in this world.

After we had strolled about five minutes, I asked, "What do you think?"

"I think this conversation could get me in trouble. Tell me what you think first."

"I think Jeff makes sense. Look at us. We're trying to build a ranch with one eye on the horizon. We're in danger. Why? For what? Let's cut it all loose. Like Jeff said, all of us are ready to start a new life. Let's go live the way we want. To hell with Phelps, Law, and all the rest of them."

"Won't you lose a lot of money?"

"Depends on how you define a lot. I have more than we need. Besides, if I manage it right, I can get out of the Edison contract without too much damage. He'll buy back the inventory we have in Denver because he can't abide his inventions being controlled by someone he doesn't know. Probably at a discount, but it won't be too much of a loss. Barney Ford can sublease the warehouse for a fee. A feud's not in Phelps's interests, so we'll offer a truce if he'll give us a reasonable price for the Galena Queen and our other Silverton claims." I walked on a few paces. "Big Mike's more difficult. If he feels cheated, he could mess things up for us in Menlo Park, so I need to make an arrangement that will satisfy him." I stopped and looked directly at Virginia. "All of our business ties can go away. I want something else now. I want you."

Virginia resumed walking again, placing one foot directly in front of the other to stay in the wagon rut. She remained silent for a long moment.

"And you want to know what I think?"

"I do."

She laughed. "Hold that phrase. You'll need it later."

I was too uneasy to find her comment amusing. She was stalling. Why? I thought my suggestions would make her happy.

"What will you do?" she asked.

"Something else. Write another book. Travel with you. Start a family. Who knows?"

"I know. I know you can't be idle. I know you'll always be alert to ways to make money. I know you'll be a miserable man to live with if you belie your nature."

"I like writing," I said weakly.

"As a break between adventures, not as a daily endeavor. Besides, you need adventures to write about. Nothing in your first book was a complete flight of fancy."

"You think I should keep all my ventures . . . including those that have caused us to hire guards?"

"No."

"Then what?"

"I like the idea of a fresh start. It's why I came west. Out here, you can start a new life." She waved her arm to encompass everything about her. "Most of the people who come here want to leave their past far behind. For us, it was our families. Others want to escape a future with no hope. They might want to escape poverty, or a crime they committed, or shame for violating some convention or other, or they may be running away from an abusive relationship, or possibly even responsibilities they can no longer endure. The one thing they all have in common is a desire for a clean slate, a fresh start. None of them realizes that the slate quickly fills back up with the same old story. We make our own bed—and it doesn't matter if it's in New York or Philadelphia or Durango—we seem to repeat the same mistakes, live the same cycles, and encounter the same fears. We learn too late that geography doesn't matter."

I went from ill at ease to frightened. "What are you saying?"

"I just said it."

"Well, it confused me. Are you saying you don't like the kind of person I am?"

"No, no. I love the person you are. I'm concerned that maybe you don't know who that person is."

I stopped walking. Despite the light from the half-moon, the clear night blazed with stars. The temperature held a slight nip but felt perfect for a walk, and our moving presence muted any nearby sounds. I could hear talking in the distance and realized we had ventured far away from the ranch. I took Virginia's hand and turned us around.

"You think if we wipe the slate clean, we'll soon be in another mess. One that I, or possibly we, make for ourselves."

"Now, aren't you the bright young man?"

In the dark, I knew she was smiling. I understood better than she thought I did. I wouldn't find myself in these situations unless something in my nature drew me into them. But that didn't answer my question.

"Suppose in the future we find ourselves in another dispute with crooks, outlaws, killers, swindlers, or whatever, does that mean we need to challenge this particular set of bad men? Even if the future holds the exact same scenario, do Phelps and Law deserve our attention? Do we follow Sharp's suggestion and let them brew in their own stew?" I let that sink in a bit before adding, "That *was* my question."

She answered by saying, "The D&RG is almost complete."

"Meaning?"

"Meaning Durango and Silverton will be two hours apart," she answered.

I thought about that, then said, "Okay, I understand. Our home and the home of the only people we care about will be in Durango. McAllen can't pull up his ranch. Maggie's parents are town principals. Her aunt lives a few hours' ride away. Sharp will likely live here or visit often. And Law already tried to put Durango under his thumb by hiring Mark to recruit a gang of enforcers. By skedaddling, we leave our friends in danger. Phelps and Law won't just leave them be. On the other hand, what if we can settle things amicably with Phelps, including an agreement to restrain his activities to Silverton? We can still—"

"Steve, where are you going with this?" Now she was the one who sounded wary.

"Who cares if we fill up the slate again? Right now, at this moment, I want a clean slate. I think I can manage it so everyone gets what he wants. Our friends will be fine."

"Oh my, I need to be more forthright. Steve, the truth is I don't give a hoot for Phelps or Law . . . I like the Edisons and enjoy being part of their world. I want to visit Menlo Park again. You know I like inventions and engineering."

She looked at me with pleading eyes. "Are you sure you need to cancel the license?"

Dunderhead. Now I finally saw the real issue. I pondered her question. Trying to sell Edison's electricity to miners would keep me in mining camps and dealing with men who used any means necessary to become king of their particular hill. Sharp had made me realize how Edison's inventions could improve the life of miners and increase profits for owners, but it occurred to me that if I had never met Sharp, I would concentrate on electrifying cities. Could that work? Possibly, but then I would be dealing with politicians, who I disliked even more than winner-take-all mine owners.

"Virginia, if we abandon electrification for Silverton, we don't have another prospect. To be fair, we need to level with Tom. He's demanding a big sale soon, or he'll be the one to cancel our license. We need to wipe the slate completely . . . or continue along this same road."

"I know. I just wish there was a way to keep what I like and discard the refuse." She took about three more steps before adding, "If those are the only two choices, then let's begin our married life without any baggage. None at all."

I squeezed her hand. "Let's talk to Jeff together."

"What will we do after our honeymoon?"

"I don't know." Then I smiled to myself. "And not knowing is exciting."

Chapter 32

shoot the bastard

The next morning, McAllen pulled us together. Instead of having a discussion, he told us what to do. Everyone would return to Durango, with two Pinkertons for protection. The other six Pinkertons, including Lawson, would remain to guard the ranch. We would all spend the night in Durango and return the following afternoon in a group. Per McAllen, one afternoon and a morning in Durango would give us an adequate respite from ranch work and the nerve-racking vigilance we'd had to maintain. Tom would shop for supplies with McAllen but would also be given time to visit his sister and her family. Masters could spend the day with his family and hopefully avoid the bawdy neighborhoods. McAllen planned to drop off Maggie at her home, and it would be up to her mother and stepfather whether she returned to the ranch.

Since we received no instructions, Virginia and I intended to enjoy a bath, fresh clothes, a decent meal, and our own bed. Sharp, also free as the wind, undoubtedly intended a tryst with Nora West.

We left immediately after a sparse breakfast. McAllen wanted to save whatever food stock remained for the Pinkertons. Sharp, Virginia, and I rode in one buckboard, while Masters and Maggie drove the second. McAllen and Tom, both on horseback, rode alongside the wagons, and the two Pinkertons scouted ahead for trouble. Sharp drove the team, and Virginia sat between us. It was a tight fit. As the buckboard bounced and swayed, Virginia rubbed against me, and I knew the same thing was happening on her other side. I felt a twinge of jealousy, knowing that Sharp at one time had been enamored of Virginia. It was a silly thought. Sharp no longer had an interest in her, especially since he had rekindled his affair with Nora.

We took the opportunity of the long ride to explain our plans from the previous night. Sharp was pleased as hell. Whenever he got bored with life, he moved to another occupation, and he was done with mining. I should have guessed earlier. Sharp had done all kinds of work before building a mining empire and would no doubt engage in other new enterprises. He was also wealthy, which meant he could sit on his haunches if that's what he desired. Now that he had reconciled with Nora, he wanted to make up for lost time—not peddle electrification.

As we talked, we divvied up tasks. I would initiate negotiations with Edison. Sharp volunteered to unload our mining interests and terminate our agreement with Big Mike. It would be my job to inform Karl Werner that his partnership with us was no longer feasible. I thought that should be done in person, but I didn't want to travel to Silverton until we had a truce with Phelps. That presented a barrier. Law was the tricky part of our plan to shed any and all encumbrances. The causes of our feud with Phelps and his gun hand were twofold. We felt confident that we could resolve our business conflicts. They were only a matter of money. But we had humiliated Law in the hotel lobby and later in the hotel dining room. I bet Law felt he had come out ahead at the Galena Queen and outside the telegraph office, but neither of those encounters were witnessed by townsfolk. Phelps would resist convincing Law to lay aside his grievances, so we had to make muzzling Law imperative for Phelps. We had to use our mining claims. Phelps wanted the Galena Queen and our other holdings, so we would make a cease-fire part of the price to buy our claims. It sounded like a sound argument, but Sharp and I had doubts that even if Phelps agreed to our conditions, he could control Law. The man was not completely sane, and both of us were sure he had designs on the Phelps empire. Instead of abiding by the wishes of his boss, he could just kill him and take over his enterprises. Then he would come after us to close the deal with lead instead of gold.

We had a problem. We couldn't communicate something this complex by telegram, and going in person without a truce set in place would be too risky. We decided we needed an intermediary to negotiate for us.

"Karl?" I asked.

"Yep," Sharp said. "Good man. Smart too."

"How much?" I asked.

"A lot," Sharp said. "It could be dangerous." He snapped the reins for something to do while he thought. "What do you think of a ten percent sales commission?"

I whistled. "That is a lot."

"Freedom has a price," Sharp answered.

Ten percent of all our mining claims would come to a hefty sum, but Sharp was right. We either risked a deadly confrontation by negotiating for ourselves or paid for the freedom to stay out of rifle range.

"We'll need to meet up with Karl outside of Silverton," I said, almost to myself.

"Is that rail line done?" Sharp asked.

"No idea. Must be close. Come to think of it, I'll bet Karl has to tidy up all the excess materials left along the path. I'll wire him to meet us along the line somewhere. We'll wait outside of town until he tells us it's safe."

Virginia asked, "What if Phelps wants to cooperate, but Law sets an ambush anyway?"

"Then we shoot the bastard an' save Mr. Phelps's highly coiffed hide." Sharp laughed but then turned serious. "It's a risk. That boy is waitin' to defy his boss."

"Why do you think Law didn't come down to fight?" Virginia asked.

A pertinent question we should have asked ourselves. Why didn't he take the bait? Had Phelps already quashed his ill temper? Was it possible he didn't care about us? Maybe he smelled a trap.

Sharp spoke up first. "He'd need lots of men, an' it's a long ride. Maybe he didn't think it was worth it. Maybe they got some other scheme goin'. Maybe he's all bluster." He snapped the reins again. "Hell, I don't know."

Sharp deftly kept the wagon moving along the ruts, but the ride remained uncomfortable. I hated buckboards. My butt already hurt, and we had traveled only about six miles. I wished I had ridden my horse. I had heard that Wyatt Earp preferred to travel by buckboard so he could bring along a more comfortable bedroll. If true, I believed he had his priorities mixed up. Travel comfort was more important than sleeping comfort. I didn't enjoy sleeping on the ground, but I hated bouncing up and down on a hard board with only my pants to cushion the shocks.

Since silence had ensued, Virginia asked, "Where do you and Nora intend to live?"

"Ya assumin' we'll live together?" Sharp asked.

"Won't you?"

"Depends." He shrugged. "But it looks that way. We ain't got all comfortable with each other yet, but it's comin' along." He rode silent a moment. "Yer askin' if we intend to settle in Durango, aren't ya?"

"She is," I answered.

Sharp's long hesitation concerned me. Finally, he said, "Nora doesn't want to live in Durango. Too close to Silverton, for one thing. She hates that town. Maybe Denver . . . but more likely New Orleans."

"How soon?" Virginia asked.

"Soon as ya marry, I suppose. Wouldn't miss the weddin'. Besides, I'm not as keen on New Orleans as she is. Denver's more to my likin'."

"You seem happy," Virginia said.

"As a clam in high water."

I had always thought of Sharp as happy-go-lucky, but I must have been mistaken, because his newfound joy was palpable since reuniting with Nora. I felt conflicted. I was pleased with Sharp's good fortune but disappointed that we'd see less of each other. Then I realized he might have felt the same way about Virginia and me. Damn. If I had to choose between him and Virginia, we both knew I'd pick Virginia. Evidently, it was time for us to move on to another part of our lives.

McAllen suddenly pulled up and raised a hand for us to stop. One of the Pinkertons was riding toward us at breakneck speed. I reached under the seat and pulled out my rifle.

The Pinkerton pulled up.

Breathless, he said, "Riders. A dozen or more."

Chapter 33

red as a cooked lobster

In a moment, we saw the second Pinkerton approach, riding hard, but not recklessly. Nine against a dozen or more. The numbers weren't too lopsided. McAllen ordered the buckboards turned sideways against the trail, and we clamored behind the wagons. I yelled for everyone to lie down and scoot under the wagons, because pine shields wouldn't stop a pistol round. After ensuring that Virginia, Maggie, and Masters were on the ground and armed properly with rifles, I walked around the wagons to stand next to Tom and Sharp. Tom held his trusty shotgun, while Sharp cradled a Winchester casually in his arms. McAllen and the two Pinkertons remained on horseback on opposite sides of the wagons so anyone approaching would ride into a deadly cross fire.

The situation felt tense, but we didn't have to wait long. In a few moments, riders approached, spewing a cloud of dust behind them. They rode in pairs until they spotted us, then fanned out wide into a single line. Most of the riders pulled rifles from sheaths and rested them across their saddle horns. I didn't see Phelps, nor did I expect to. He'd left the dirty work to Law, who rode in the center of the long line of riders. As they got closer, they slowed their horses to a walk and halted no more than twenty feet in front of us. For some reason, Ben Law appeared exceptionally pleased with himself.

Since I stood in the center position, I offered greetings. "Mr. Law, what a pleasant surprise. Is this a social visit?"

"I came to settle affairs with you . . . and your friends." He pointedly stared at Sharp and flipped McAllen an angry look. Then he swept his eyes over our obviously defensive positions. "Expecting trouble?"

"Are you trouble?" I asked.

"Like you've never seen before," Law snarled.

"Let's just kill 'em all now," Sharp said in a matter-of-fact tone.

"Hold on," Law said, irritated. "I don't fight women. Let them walk on down the road, and we men will fight this out."

"Don't fight women?" Sharp said. "Nora says ya bullied and threatened her well-bein'. Maybe ya don't want to fight these women . . . 'cuz they got rifles." Sharp smiled. "Make no mistake, they know how to use 'em. Now, make yer move or git."

"I never brandished a gun at Mrs. West. If she says so, she's lying. Quit hiding behind these women. Tell them to leave."

"I'm not going anywhere!" Maggie yelled.

From the side, McAllen said, "You're the one goin', Law. Either down that road or to hell. Make up your mind."

"I don't shoot women!" Law yelled. "This ain't fair. Damn you! Tell them to leave."

No one said a word.

Law turned red as a cooked lobster. He pressed his lips so tight, they were a straight white line running between crimson cheeks. Was he about to explode? Or have a heart attack? No such luck. He gradually controlled himself and then examined his men lined up on either side of him. I could tell he wanted to order them to kill us, but he didn't. Instead, he pointed a finger at Sharp and fixed him with an angry stare.

"You son of a bitch. You called me yella, and here you stand hiding behind your lady friends' skirts. You're the one that's yella. If you got any manliness in you, you'll meet me all by your lonesome. But you won't. You're a coward. Well, let me tell you something. If you don't ride up to Silverton to settle this once and for all, I'll show Mrs. West what a real man feels like."

I immediately used my rifle to bar Sharp from charging Law. That would start the fight in earnest. Law had basically said he was riding off, and we should let him go. Phelps might still be able to control his gunman, but if not, I'd rather fight without Maggie and Virginia in the line of fire.

223

"Law, go now," McAllen said easily. "We'll meet up with you in Silverton. If you want, your boss can buy these men's claims, and we'll leave you be. If you'd rather fight, we can do that too."

"No need for you and your Pinkertons. My gripe is only with these two. Stay with your ranch . . . and daughter. She's the one who needs your protection."

McAllen bristled. "Are you threatening my daughter?"

Law leaned forward in his saddle so he could clearly see McAllen. "Stay out of this . . . or maybe she'll learn the way of men before she means to."

McAllen snapped his reins and rode down the length of the wagons to face Law directly. Before he could speak, Maggie scooted out from under the wagon and jumped to her feet. She kept her rifle below the level of the wagon, but everyone heard her cock the hammer back.

"Mister, if you think you can rape me, you got another thing coming!"

Law ignored her and spoke directly to McAllen. "This ain't your fight."

"You just made it my fight."

Chapter 34

dying with your boots on

Law and his men rode away. A fifth confrontation had come to nothing. We had to stop these stand-offs because one was bound to get violent. As I watched them leave, I realized that odds were against our grand scheme to free ourselves from Phelps and Law. On the brighter side, they no longer threatened McAllen's ranch, so we could take the entire Pinkerton contingent to Silverton. We wouldn't need the whole team for a fair fight, but as Sharp had previously pointed out, Law always showed up with a larger force than necessary. The Pinkerton team would provide insurance against Law cheating on his promise to fight fair and square. As I thought about it, I realized that Law never actually promised to fight even up. He had just said that Sharp should meet him in Silverton all by his lonesome.

We had better be ready to barter, but prepared for war.

After a brief discussion, McAllen sent one of the Pinkertons back to round up all but two of the team. He wanted two to remain at the ranch to protect the property while we were away. The rest of us rode into Durango to drop Maggie off with her ma and Virginia at our house. Next, we bought the supplies and materials needed to continue work at the ranch. As we rode from place to place, town activity seemed normal. We saw nothing of Law or his gang. Since Tom and Masters hadn't hired on to fight, McAllen wanted them to resume building his ranch, so he instructed them to haul the materials back to his place. He told the rest of us that we would depart for Silverton in the morning.

After a couple of beers in the hotel bar, I bid good afternoon to McAllen and Sharp. Virginia hadn't invited them to dinner, so I didn't offer either. I hoped she had other activities in mind.

When I opened the front door, Virginia looked ashen as she stood perfectly still in the center of the parlor. Without a thought, my gun was in my hand. Was there danger? From where? Whipping my head around, I saw nothing untoward. Suddenly, she leaped into my arms, sobbing.

"What is it?" I asked.

When she got control, she said, "Tom and Mark are dead."

"What?" That didn't make sense. "How would you know?"

"Tom made it back to town. Barely. They shot him three times. He died just—"

"He came here?"

"The doctor did. He just left. He's known both men since they—"

"First, tell me what Tom said. What happened?"

"Ambush. Law and his men lay in wait and opened fire with no warning. Tom urged the doctor to warn you. That's why he came right over."

I ran to the front window and examined the neighborhood while standing out of sight. I couldn't spot anything abnormal.

Over my shoulder, I asked, "Anything else?"

"No. The doctor said he died quickly. His only words were to beg him to warn us. Do you see anything?"

I checked outside again. "No."

I needed to warn Sharp and McAllen. Was it safe to walk to the hotel? Why hadn't they ambushed us on our way into town? Why wait for Tom and Mark to drive the wagons back to the ranch? In fact, how could they even know Tom and Mark would return this afternoon? There could be only one answer. Someone at the mill or general store had told them. Oh hell, we split up. We had strength when we remained together, but now we were scattered all over Durango. It would have taken only a couple of men to ambush Tom and Mark. Horsemen could easily have overtaken the heavily laden wagons. If I was right, they were here, and they were also at the hotel. They had at least ten men in town to our four. Maggie? Damn. We were all in imminent danger.

I told myself to calm down. Nobody had shot

at me coming into the house, so maybe there was no one out there. Then it hit me. They didn't know where I lived. There was no reason for them to even suspect I owned a house. But they had probably followed me from the hotel. Damn it all!

I calmed myself and slowly examined the outside surroundings again. We lived on a short street that ended against a foothill covered in brush. If someone followed me, he must be on foot, because I would have noticed a rider. What would he do once I entered my house? Only one of two choices. He would either continue to the foothill to hide in the brush or cross the street to conceal himself behind my neighbor's house. Or perhaps the outhouse, which was in his side yard. Which would I do? Suddenly I knew. Both. They had a large enough gang to send two men after me, with plenty remaining for my friends at the hotel.

I watched both areas. Soon, a partial face peeked out from behind the outhouse. Concentrating on the brush, I soon discerned an inappropriate shape just at the end of our hardscrabble road. I closed my eyes for a long moment, and then opened them again to get a fresh image. I was sure. The man at the end of the street was peering through the brush, but he foolishly allowed the top of his darkish hat to jut slightly above his cover.

"Two," I said.

"Oh, dear. Now what?" Virginia said.

Without waiting for my answer, she went into the bedroom. I knew she wasn't leaving the room to hide. That wouldn't be her nature. She soon emerged, holding two rifles. I took mine and held my finger to my lips to signal silence. She nodded and stayed away from the window. Brave, but not foolish. I loved this woman.

I remained to the side of the window and slid it open in case we needed to shoot. Were there more? I doubted it. Law would want to personally confront McAllen and Sharp . . . and he would want superior force. He'd send only two of his hired guns after me and keep the rest at the hotel to back him up. My first inclination was to step onto the porch and shoot them both. The outhouse was less than thirty yards from my front porch, and the man in the brush was maybe fifty yards away. Since neither pine planks nor sagebrush stopped bullets, hitting both men would be easy. But shooting two men for no apparent reason might land me in jail. I had to draw their fire first . . . and do it in such a way that I remained safe.

Tom had used sturdy four-by-four boards to support the porch roof. Was it too risky to step out onto the porch and stand sideways against one of the columns? That idea had a big problem. A four-by-four wouldn't provide cover from shooters firing from different locations. I decided the risk would be small if the shots came from the man hiding in the brush. He likely didn't have a rifle if he had been inside the hotel before being told to follow me. Hitting a mostly concealed man standing sideways with a pistol from fifty yards would be a matter of luck or extraordinary skill. On the other hand, I would be totally exposed to the man across the street. He peered out from behind the outhouse only now and then. I thought about it. My need to warn McAllen and Sharp drove me to take a chance.

"What are you going to do?" Virginia whispered as if they could hear us inside the house.

"Kill them," I said, sitting on an ottoman to remove my boots.

When I finished, Virginia looked puzzled.

I said, "I never saw the point in dying with your boots on."

Now she looked frightened, so I quickly added, "The one across the way peeks around the side of the outhouse occasionally, but I'm sure he's listening hard. Without boots, I can get out onto the porch without him hearing me."

"You're going out there? Steve, no!"

"Don't worry, I have a plan. Stay inside, at this window. When the man behind the outhouse hears shots, he'll come around the corner and start shooting as well. Don't give him time. As soon as you hear the first shot, from me or from down the road, put every bullet in that rifle into that outhouse. Don't wait to see him, just shoot through the wood. Can you do that?"

She nodded.

"Okay, we need to do this right after he peers out the next time. We can't wait, because we need to warn Sharp and McAllen they're in danger."

She nodded again. Her lips were pursed in determination. She looked frightened, but she understood the urgency and would do her part. I knew that with certainty.

I went back to watching the outhouse.

Almost immediately, the man peeked out and quickly withdrew his head when he saw no activity in front of our house.

I carefully opened the front door and stepped onto the porch in my stocking feet, leaving the door open to avoid making noise. I held my rifle along my left side so my body shielded it. I hesitated a moment in plain sight, pretending to enjoy the view. I visualized the shooter's actions. I stepped behind the support beam . . . and nothing. I had miscalculated. Then I heard shots. Two. One right after the other. Pistol shots. One bullet hit the pillar, and another flew by my face so close, I felt a rush of hot air against my skin. I dropped to one knee and raised my rifle. The assassin stupidly stood behind the low brush, firing a pistol. He was taking his time, holding his gun with both hands and aiming with care. I put one bullet in his chest before he could fire again. Less than two seconds had passed. I swiveled around the column, resting my rifle barrel against the wood, and kept pivoting until the outhouse came into view. As I fired, I heard, or more accurately felt, shots come from behind me as well. Virginia opened fire at the same time. At least twenty bullets shredded the thin pine planks, knocking one clean away from the structure. I could see right through the outhouse, and what I saw appeared as a falling shadow. The second gunman was down.

I walked carefully across the road, watching the brush and the outhouse. The extended magazine on my Winchester '76 held fifteen cartridges, so I had a few rounds left before I would have to resort to my Colt. I needed neither my rifle nor pistol. The man behind the outhouse had at least two fatal bullet holes in him, plus a few others that would have made this a bad day. I didn't need to check the man at the end of the road. I knew exactly where my bullet had gone, and no one could survive a 45-75 cartridge to the chest.

I walked back to my house. Virginia stood on our new porch, holding her rifle across her chest. My senses were keen, and the first thing I noticed was that she looked prettier than ever. A bullet streaking alongside the face makes life more vivid and intense. I felt good . . . and then I stepped on a pebble in my stocking feet and almost stumbled as I yelped in pain.

Virginia laughed . . . and after a curse, so did I.

"We made it through another one," she said as I took her around the waist.

"We did," I said.

I nodded across the street. "But we owe our neighbors a new outhouse."

Chapter 35

not over

Since I had quartered my horse at the livery, I ran all the way to the hotel but stopped briefly outside to control my breathing. Taking a deep breath, I entered the hotel with my rifle still in hand. It wouldn't look unusual because men carried their rifles to and from their rooms all the time.

In the lobby, everything appeared normal, with people bustling here and there, showing no concern for their safety. No shots had been fired in this hotel. As of yet. I found McAllen and Sharp right where I had left them. The hotel bar was small but currently accommodated about ten customers, both men and women.

I sat next to Sharp, purposefully letting the rifle barrel thump lightly against the table edge. Since I had left without a rifle, my little drama got their attention. McAllen scanned the room, and Sharp put his hand around my rifle barrel to signal that he would use this weapon. He didn't carry a revolver, so he was generally unarmed—unless there was impending danger. His startled look told me the hot barrel had taken him by surprise.

Trying not to sound alarmed, I said quietly,

"Tom and Mark were ambushed. Both dead. I killed two assassins outside my house."

"Maggie?" McAllen asked.

"I came here direct," I answered.

A look of irritation crossed his face.

"See anythin' on the way in?" Sharp asked.

"I didn't see Law and didn't recognize any of his men. That may not mean much. At the ranch, I didn't get a good look at any of them except for those directly next to Law."

"That's one," Sharp said. His head nodded toward a man at the bar watching us through the mirror.

Sharp immediately stood and walked over to him. He carried my rifle at his left side. I had watched him practice swinging a rifle up from that position. In a blink of an eye, he could raise the rifle and press it against his shoulder, his right index finger on the trigger. His practice sessions also included bringing the rifle waist high and jamming the barrel forward at an upward angle that would catch a man just below his rib cage. I wondered which he intended for this situation.

Sharp sauntered up on the man's left side and placed a light hand on his shoulder. The friendly gesture did not calm the expression reflected in the mirror. The man was scared.

"Where're yer friends?" Sharp asked in a friendly tone.

"They returned to Silverton. I want nothing more to do with that town."

I saw him grimace as Sharp's heavy hand squeezed his shoulder at what must have been a sensitive spot. Sharp leaned over and spoke too low for me to hear, but I could tell by his lips that he had said *bullshit.*

"No. They left," he said.

But as his eyes went to the mirror, I spotted two other men in the corner who looked like they had just come off the trail. Both quizzically studied Sharp and their compatriot, obviously trying to figure out what was going on. McAllen had caught the glance in the mirror as well. He nodded, and we both stood and walked over to the corner table.

"You gentlemen seen Ben Law?" McAllen asked.

"Go to hell," one of them answered.

"Would you like to show me the way?" McAllen asked.

A staring contest ensued. Then the two men took a sip of their drinks and pretended to ignore us.

I had grown tired of these faux confrontations, so I said, "Who sent the two men after me?" When neither answered, I added, "They're both dead." Another dramatic pause. "I shot them."

Both men looked at each other with a mix of surprise and anger. As I had hoped, the men I killed were friends or possibly related.

"*You* killed them?" one said.

"I did."

Both men went for their sidearms.

McAllen and I shot twice before either man could raise his gun high enough to take aim. The noise inside the small room deafened me, and smoke burned my eyes. The half dozen people not associated with us or Law screamed or gasped but remained in their seats. Then in a sudden rush, they all shoved their way to one of the two doors. From the front of the hotel, we heard multiple shots, and a man who had run through the front door staggered back into the room and fell to the floor.

Sharp slammed the butt of my rifle into the face of the man he was covering at the bar and raced to the door. Instead of pushing through, he threw his back against the wall, quickly stuck his head out for a look, and then withdrew it. I saw no additional threat inside, so I joined him on the other side of the door frame.

"Nothin'," he said, meaning he had not spotted a target.

I grabbed a chair, flipped it over, and hanging my hat on one of the legs, dangled it so it could be partially seen from the street. I moved it in and out quickly. The second time, a barrage of bullets flew in our direction. None hit my hat. Poor, panicked shooting.

As the gunfire died away, Sharp and I took a

look. I saw smoke wafting from an alley across the street. Sharp noticed it too, and we both fired a few shots at the alley corner. We didn't expect to hit anyone but wanted to deny him time to take careful aim.

As I reloaded, I got a nasty look from Sharp. I had been so intent on warning my friends that I hadn't reloaded the rifle or gone back into the house for additional ammunition. I pointed at the unconscious man at the bar. Sharp went over to get the man's pistol, but not before giving me another exasperated look. Sharp preferred fighting with a rifle.

Luckily, the gunfight was over. The marshal and three deputies charged into the bar from the hotel lobby entrance. All three of us held up our hands, our pistols aimed at the ceiling. The marshal surveyed the carnage and barked something I had difficulty understanding because my ears were ringing. I soon realized he had ordered his deputy to disarm us. I looked at McAllen, who nodded, so I complied without resistance.

Three men were dead: the two McAllen and I had shot and the poor unfortunate soul who ran outside to be killed by Law or one of his men keeping an eye on that exit. The man Sharp had knocked unconscious hadn't stirred, but he was obviously breathing. I told the marshal we had shot at another gunman in the alley across the way. My own words sounded as if I were talking inside a train tunnel. He dispatched two of his deputies to investigate. When they hesitated, he gestured that they should go through the hotel lobby and circle around to come at the alley from behind. They left, looking relieved that they didn't need to walk through the bullet-ridden front door.

I had been in similar circumstance before and knew to keep quiet and let McAllen handle the authorities. He projected the deportment of a lawman, which generally gained him respect and credibility. After some brief introductory remarks, McAllen gently led the marshal by the elbow to a corner of the room. I had regained most of my hearing, but the ringing hadn't gone away entirely. I knew from experience that it would gradually fade. When I heard Sharp answer a question from one of the deputies, I realized that he had been speaking to me as well. I had been standing around in kind of a deaf stupor.

To let the deputy know I could answer questions, I said, "I can hear again."

He asked me what had happened. When I told him about the two dead near my house, he ran over to tell the marshal, who told him to ignore them for now. I took that to mean that he had only three deputies, and two were across the street.

Soon the two deputies returned to tell the marshal that there were no additional dead bodies lying in the alley. The marshal ordered one of his men to hurry to the parsonage to find a young girl named Maggie, to stay with her and keep her indoors. McAllen was thinking more clearly than I. I suddenly wanted to get back to Virginia.

I was about to ask permission to leave, when the other deputy said, "There may have been no dead in the alley, but someone got shot. They wrote on the wall in blood. I think it was for these men.

When he didn't offer any more, I asked, "What did it say?"

"not over."

Chapter 36

grab the girl

Because witnesses corroborated our stories, the marshal released us until an inquest. Sharp bounded upstairs to retrieve his own rifle and then handed back mine. McAllen and Sharp then rushed to the parsonage. The marshal wanted me to show him the shooting scene at my house. I took off in a hurry, not because of the marshal's request, but to check on Virginia. The marshal and a deputy huffed and puffed in a vain attempt to keep up with me.

As I opened the fence gate, I pointed out the locations of the two bodies. The deputy went to one, the marshal to the other. A relieved Virginia greeted me at the front door. After a quick hug, I nudged her into the safety of the house.

"Anything since I left?" I asked.

"No. What happened? I heard shooting."

"We got into a fight. Jeff and Joseph are unhurt. Can't say the same for a couple of others."

She gestured outside. "Trouble with the marshal?"

"I don't think so. We had witnesses at the hotel . . . and I think he accepts my story of what happened here. He'll probably want to question you." I hesitated. "We may have wounded Law. Have you seen *anyone* outside?"

241

She gave me an exasperated look. "How would Law know where we lived? Those two followed you, and I don't think they were very talkative after we shot them."

"You're right." I paced. "We killed four of his men, and the marshal has another in custody. That leaves seven or so." I quit pacing and looked directly at Virginia. "What will Law do?"

Virginia immediately said, "Maggie?"

I nodded. "Jeff and Joseph went over there." I paced some more. "Law won't just hang around. Unless he needs a doctor, he'll go to the parsonage . . . or maybe ride back to Silverton."

"Let's visit the doctors in town," she said excitedly.

I was going to argue that she should stay inside the house, but I could tell when she had made up her mind. Checking doctor's offices made sense, but not until the marshal came back from viewing the bodies to ask me questions. With that thought, I heard his knock on the door. Before inviting him into our parlor, I showed him the bullet hole in the porch column. Since both dead men had drawn guns, he accepted my actions as justified. After a few more questions, he left, leaving his deputy to keep busybodies away from the corpses until the undertaker could cart them away. I assumed that he would hurry right over after he'd handled the other dead bodies in town.

Although few buildings in town were more than

a ten-minute walk away, I wanted to use the buggy because it would somewhat conceal us, and I could move fast with a snap of the reins. I told Virginia to change into her riding dress while I retrieved her buggy horse from the livery. She knew what I meant by her riding dress. She owned one with a heavily lined concealed pocket for her small pistol.

After hitching up the horse, we were soon prancing down Main Avenue. To my knowledge, there were two doctors in Durango. I figured they could tell us if there were more. After denying that they had treated any gunshot wounds that day, both assured me that they were the only doctors in town. Disappointed that I hadn't found a gravely wounded Law, I drove the buggy over to the parsonage. Everything was quiet, at least on the outside. There was no sign of bad men, Sharp, McAllen, Maggie, or her parents. I handed the reins to Virginia and told her to ride away at the first sign of trouble. Her expression told me that my words had been a waste of breath.

Sharp answered the door, rifle in hand. He assured me that everything was safe, so I went out to the buggy and escorted Virginia into the house. The environment inside was tense. I had barely met Maggie's stepfather and didn't know him well. The timid man paced nervously and wore a worried expression. I suddenly heard shouting from the adjoining room. When I got further into the parlor, I saw the preacher's wife wagging a finger in her ex-husband's face.

"Damn you, Joe, I left you because bad elements always swarm around you. You enjoy trouble. You like to boss men around, egg ruffians into a fight. I wanted to protect our daughter from that kind of man. Now what have you done? You moved next door . . . and brought these outlaws right back into our lives. Damn you! Don't you understand that's exactly what I didn't want?"

That got her husband's attention. He chastised her from the parlor. "Dorothy, please, stop the blasphemy. It's unbecoming."

Maggie jumped out of her chair, yelling, "And stop shouting at my father! He didn't mean me harm . . . and if I'm in danger, I want *him* to protect me."

Her stepfather winced at the indirect criticism. I hadn't noticed Maggie because she had been burrowed into a corner chair, listening to her parents argue. I knew she idolized McAllen, and previously she had indicated that she had little respect for her stepfather. The implication of her last sentence was that she didn't think her stepfather could protect her. I wanted no part of this family squabble. On the other hand, a shooting war had started, and we owed this family protection from Law and his gang.

I looked at Sharp and shrugged. He hooked a finger at me, and we stepped out onto a small porch. Since I had picked up ammunition at my house, we both carried rifles. As we stepped into the yard, we carefully surveyed the surroundings. I spotted no one lurking in the area, so I pointed to a large tree in the center of the yard that provided more protection than the four-by-four holding up the roof of my porch.

"Gettin' kinda ugly in there," Sharp said, keeping an eye on the street.

"Yes, indeed. If Law doesn't know where we are, that yelling may well tip him off."

"Hell, he'd run away from that shriekin'. Figure it'd be easier to take on Joseph by his lonesome."

"No doubt." I hated to turn serious, but I had to ask. "Nora?"

"Hell, no matter how mad she got, she never screeched like that."

"That's not what I meant. Have you checked on her safety?"

Sharp smiled. "I knew that's what ya meant. She's at the hotel, in our room. The marshal has deputies in the lobby, but after the undertaker leaves with the bodies, Law or one of his men could return. Don't see why, but they could. Figure I got another half hour before I need to return."

The parsonage sat in a beautiful setting at the end of a dirt road that sloped down to the Animas River. We could hear river water splashing against the rocks and birds singing as if all were right in the world. Mature trees and the soothing sound of babbling water made the house feel peaceful, as befitted a home committed to reverence. The neighborhood was fully built out, with no empty lots. Our area, on the other hand, was sparsely built, and our road ran in the opposite direction, toward the mountains. Because the Animas River presented an effective blockade to the west, there was only one way to approach the house: straight down the rutted road that led off Main Avenue. Peaceful *and* secure. A good home for Maggie, especially in these circumstances.

Then I thought I might have seen something disturbing. Out of the corner of my eye, I thought I saw a head bob out from the corner of one of the houses up the street. I might have been mistaken, or it could have been a homeowner curious about strange, rough-looking men at the preacher's house. I turned slightly toward Sharp but kept an eye cocked in the direction of where I had seen movement.

"Did you see something move?"

"I did," Sharp answered.

"Trouble?"

"Hope not. Had enough today. Why can't that bastard just head back up the hill?"

"Maybe he did. Let's not kill some busybody."

"Yer right. Step out into the street. Let's find out if he's friend or foe."

I ignored his rib. "If it's Law or his men, how did he find Maggie's house?"

Sharp took a few moments to respond. "It's well-known that Maggie is McAllen's daughter an' that Maggie's ma is now married to the town preacher. Nobody would hesitate givin' directions to the parsonage."

I kept my eye on the house across the way. No inquisitive head appeared.

"We could split up and approach from alternate sides," I said.

Sharp didn't answer. He merely stepped out from behind our tree and headed to the right of the house. I went left. Without cover to hide behind, crossing the street presented a hazard, but I saw nothing troublesome. After reaching the other side, I ducked between the next-door houses so I could come around from behind. Sharp did the same from his side, and we met at the back of a grassy gap that ran alongside the home where we had seen movement. When we stood to either side of the pathway, Sharp signaled for us to simultaneously come around to confront our prey, if indeed there was a prey.

There was. I recognized the man as one of those riding with Law.

"Move and I'll kill ya," Sharp said, his rifle tight against his shoulder.

The man instantly put both hands as high in the air as possible. "Don't shoot."

"Who else is about?" Sharp asked.

"No one. Just me. Law told me to watch this house."

"For what purpose?" I asked.

He didn't answer, but by this time, we had walked the length of the pathway and stood in front of him. I disarmed him, remembering McAllen's admonition to check for knives and a second gun. I found a knife in his boot.

"Why did Law send ya to watch a preacher's house?" Sharp asked.

He kept his arms stretched right up to the sky and looked at us stony-faced. Sharp jammed his rifle barrel into his chest, and he bowled over, gasping in pain.

"Why?" Sharp asked again.

"To grab the girl if need be," he choked out.

"Did he tell you what might make a need?" I asked.

"If he didn't get you in town, he wanted to make you come to him."

"So he wanted McAllen's daughter as a hostage?" I asked.

"And Mrs. West."

"He put another watcher on Nora?" Sharp asked.

"Two. Didn't matter how things went, he planned on grabbing her anyway. Law hates that woman. Said he'd get even with her for her highfalutin ways."

"What highfalutin ways?" Sharp demanded.

The man looked at Sharp's rifle barrel, afraid of another jab. He finally said, "She laughed at his advances. Law wants her to watch you die . . . but only after you watch her get her comeuppance."

Chapter 37

a red bandanna

Sharp slammed his rifle butt alongside the man's head and sent him to the ground unconscious. Using a rifle as a bludgeon was becoming routine for Sharp. He ran toward the hotel with me in pursuit. I wondered if I was following to help or to keep Sharp from committing a hanging offense. When I had feared for Virginia's life, the marshal and sheriff had had difficulty keeping up with me. Now I had trouble keeping up with Sharp. I took a deep breath and ran harder, carrying my rifle in one hand and using my other to make sure my Colt remained holstered.

When we arrived at the hotel, everything looked as usual, except for the closed door to the dining room. Sharp took the stairs two at a time, with me close behind. At the first landing, he barged through a door at the head of the stairs. Sharp kept yelling for Nora, but I could see that the room was empty.

Finding no trace of her, Sharp bounded down the steps and slapped the reception counter to get the attendant's attention.

"Have ya seen Mrs. West?" he demanded.

"She left with three gentlemen ten minutes ago," he said.

"Gentlemen? Was one wounded?"

"Wounded? No. Not that I could tell."

"Did one wear a red bandanna?" I asked.

"He did. I think his name is Ben Law."

"Damn it, man, she was under duress. Couldn't ya tell?"

"I never saw her clear. One of the men walked in front of her. I recognized the dress after she passed."

"Jeff, ten minutes," I said.

"Yep." Sharp went for the door.

Outside, Sharp looked left and right, and then his face turned worried. Suddenly, I felt stupid for not using our buggy, which still sat outside the parsonage. We could have been at the livery in a few moments. As it stood, Law and his men probably had horses waiting outside the hotel, and we were a five-minute fast walk to our horses. Then we would need to saddle them. If Law had ridden off right away, he would have at least a twenty-minute head start when we rode after him.

"The train!" I exclaimed. "I heard it's running now."

Sharp ran toward the livery. "After we make certain they left town."

Good thinking. It would be a shame to race up to Silverton if Law remained in Durango.

Besides, the train was fast. So fast we would arrive in Silverton well before them, even if we couldn't leave until tomorrow. As soon as we arrived at the livery, Sharp barked orders at a boy casually shoveling hay into stalls. Soon, the boy and a stable hand helped us get mounted and on the road. Sharp rode hard for the edge of town, then got off his horse and slowly walked the trail. I remained mounted, stood in my stirrups, and craned my neck in every direction, hoping to glimpse Law and his band. Nothing. Too many trees and bends in the trail to see any distance. Having grown up in the city, I knew nothing about tracking and hadn't picked up the skill in the couple of years I had been on the frontier. Sharp, on the other hand, could track horses, men, or game. Since I had no interest, I had never asked him to teach me. I knew only enough to keep quiet until he was done.

From the ground, Sharp said, "Many riders just came through. In a hurry."

"Do you know it's them?" I asked.

"No, but it's likely." He remounted. "Let's give chase for a couple hours. If we don't catch sight of them, we'll double back an' take the evenin' train."

He didn't wait for a reply. We both rode hard for twenty minutes or so but didn't run across any riders. Sharp pulled up and dismounted again. After another examination of the churned-up trail, he indicated that we should continue chasing our phantom riders. Another hour didn't bring anyone into view. This time we both dismounted to walk the horses.

"They didn't have that big of a head start," I said.

"Unless they lollygag, it takes a long time to catch someone with a twenty-minute head start. Besides, that innkeeper may have said ten minutes because he could tell I was ready to explode." He looked down the empty trail. "Coulda been longer."

That made sense. If they had a lead of a half hour or more and rode at a steady pace, we'd be hard-pressed to catch them before dark. I looked questioningly at Sharp.

"We should go back," he said. "Buy tickets an' check the town while we wait. If we find no sign of 'em in Durango, then they're on their way to Silverton. They'll camp along the trail tonight, so we'll be waitin' for 'em when they ride in tomorrow afternoon."

I nodded.

We remounted. Instead of turning toward town, Sharp sat very still in his saddle and examined the trail ahead. His expression turned forlorn. Finally, he said, "Steve, I need a favor."

"You know I'll do it. Tell me."

"Go back an' catch that train. I'm gonna stay after 'em. If they show up before me . . . well, I probably won't be comin'."

"What's your plan?"

"Save Nora . . . kill 'em all."

I felt miserable and heartsick for Sharp's predicament. I nodded assent. Then I said, "You think they have plans for her tonight, don't you?"

"I know they do." He snapped his reins against his horse's neck. "I gotta stop 'em."

Chapter 38

this awful feud

By the time I got back to town, the remaining Pinkertons had arrived from the ranch. With their help interviewing townspeople, I soon learned that Law had been seen riding out of Durango with other riders. We even found a bystander who claimed that one of the riders had been a woman. As best as I could gather, Law appeared to have between six and eight men in his party. The lower number would present a tough challenge for one man, even from an experienced fighter like Sharp.

I had time to visit Virginia to let her know our plans. I anticipated that she would insist on going, but before she could ask, I told her I needed McAllen and the Pinkertons to even up the odds in Silverton. McAllen would never leave Durango with his daughter unprotected, so would she promise him to stay with Maggie? I explained it would make my job safer. Thankfully, she agreed.

When we returned to the parsonage, McAllen had other ideas. He took me aside and insisted that the Pinkertons remain in Durango as guards for Maggie, Virginia, his ex-wife, and her husband. Evidently, knowing an outlaw had been skulking outside their home had further unnerved his ex-wife, and she demanded that their protection be a priority. McAllen insisted that the three of us could easily handle the bunch in Silverton. I tactfully reminded him that Sharp might not make it up the hill. He harrumphed that if he didn't make it, he would have whittled down their numbers so that the two of us could handle the rest. When I told Virginia that the Pinkertons would remain behind, she said she would stay as well. She had already promised Maggie that she would remain by her side, and her mother was so distraught that Virginia thought Maggie might need emotional support. I didn't object.

It irritated me that McAllen kept making decisions about Pinkertons under my employ. I had engaged a large team to give us more guns against Law and his gang. Instead, they were stuck in Durango, protecting McAllen's daughter, her family, and Virginia. The remainder of the team was stationed out at the ranch. Oh well, McAllen was probably worth the bunch of them anyway.

McAllen and I gathered up clothes, travel gear, rifles, and ammunition, and headed for the train station. The fifty-mile ride would take three hours because of the climb and curves, still a great improvement over a two-day horse trip. The railcars were so new that the blond wood benches shone with a yellowish luster, and the drapes remained unsoiled from dirt spilling in from the windows. It was a clear, early autumn day, so we slid the windows open. I wanted to see and hear clearly. I sat with my rifle between my legs, and once we were well out of town, I kept an eye on the trail that often snaked alongside the railroad tracks. Trees regularly obstructed my view, but sooner or later the trail would come back to parallel the tracks again. Disappointingly, I never spotted Law or Sharp. Thankfully, I never heard gunshots either.

McAllen seemed indifferent to the goings-on outside the car. He told me that the engineer would never stop the train on this grade, and we couldn't jump from a moving train because an injury might preclude us from confronting Law. Also, it would be foolish to shoot through the trees from a moving train. All we would do is forewarn Law that we would be waiting for him in Silverton. He was right, but I kept my vigil anyway.

After a quiet period, McAllen said, "When we get to Silverton, we find Phelps first."

"He can't control Law," I said, not turning away from the window.

"Phelps pays more than Law's wages; he pays the wages of his men. Cut off his funds, and he's alone."

I had been leaning forward, peering out the window. I turned toward McAllen and plopped against the seatback. His comment had startled me. McAllen solved problems with guns; I was the one to try financial pressure first. I had never expected McAllen to be the one to voice a nonviolent solution to a problem with bad men. Now, he had crossed over to my bailiwick. In fact, he had often chided me for trying to buy my way out of trouble. Maybe we were both learning from each other. And his idea might work. I felt excited. Perhaps we could emerge intact from this awful feud. Of course, Law might have his own money, at least enough to deal with us. He wouldn't need much, because after he dispatched us, he could apply pressure to Phelps and take control of his empire. Still, it was worth trying.

"What's wrong?" McAllen asked.

"Nothing. I'm just surprised I didn't think of it."

"You would have before we arrived. That is, if you ever took your face away from that window."

I looked out the window again. "I'm worried about Jeff. It's him against six or more men."

"He can take care of himself."

"I'm not sure he's thinking clearly. Law intends to rape Nora on the trail. He wants to punish her for rejecting him. That's why Sharp insisted on continuing to chase him on horseback. He wants to intercept them before nightfall."

"Jeff'll be careful."

"Joseph, he's in love. Men do foolish things when they're in love . . . especially when they feel they've wronged the woman and want to make amends."

"I've noticed."

He sounded distant but said nothing further.

I knew not to pry into McAllen's personal thoughts, so I turned back to my window.

Then Joseph said something that shocked me.

"I'm in love too." He sounded resigned. "Guess it's the season."

Astonished, I asked, "What? Who? There's no one out by that damn ranch of yours."

He shrugged. "Sharon."

That stopped me for a moment. Then I recognized the name. "Your ex-wife?"

"One and the same."

"Joseph, I'm sorry."

He looked surprised at my comment. "For what?"

"I was there. I heard her yell at you."

"She was scared," he said. "Hell, she had a right to be. We get along fine when her family's not in danger."

"You get along fine?" I asked, confused. "Joseph, do you think there's a future there?"

"Of course. A platonic future, but a future nonetheless." He gave me a hard look. "Steve, we share a daughter. There's more to a relationship than sex."

"But sex does complete a relationship."

"Says the freshly in love. Hell, Steve, if we never have sex again, we'll just be like many other agin' couples. There's plenty of sex on 5th Street, but no companionship."

"Are you sure you're in love and not just lonely?"

He laughed. Rare for McAllen. "I'm lonely, sure enough, but I know I'm in love with Sharon . . . because I never fell out of love with her. She left me for stability. For safety. For attention. She may have remarried for those things, but before Maggie, she was different. Roarin' for adventure. Eager to see the world." He shook his head. "I won't pretend she still loves me, but we get along better than you suppose."

That made me wonder. Was McAllen having an affair with his ex-wife? No. I didn't believe it. Joseph said it was platonic, and he had never lied to me. Besides, his sense of honor wouldn't allow it. A problem remained, however.

"Joseph, what about Reverend Johnson? Even if your relationship's not intimate, you're going to make him wonder if you hang around his wife having private conversations."

He gave me his closed-mouth smile. "You think that preacher boy might run away?"

"No, and neither do you. But you could cause discord . . . possibly worse."

"Thought 'bout it. I joined his church, and if I restrict my time with her to church social events, it'll be fine. If not, I'll stay out on my ranch."

His expression turned resolute, and when he spoke, his voice was firm.

"Steve, I won't wreck the family of the two women I love."

Chapter 39

go to hell

Phelps was easy to find. He sat on his throne of sorts at the back of his saloon, surrounded by the same bookkeepers and guards as when I first encountered him. He was also as impeccably dressed. Unlike previously, however, no boisterous crap game was in progress, only a few quiet drinkers by the bar. Since this was McAllen's idea, I pointed out Phelps and let him take the lead.

"Mr. Phelps, I need a—"

Phelps pointed at me, "I told you to stay the hell out of my place."

"I suggest you listen to Mr. McAllen."

He examined McAllen with a slow, steady gaze. "Why should I? Who the hell are you?"

In an instant, McAllen whipped out his pistol and bashed one of the guards across his skull. He had his Smith & Wesson cocked and pointed at the second guard before the first one slid to the floor. The bookkeepers cowered against the wall. To his credit, Phelps barely flinched.

McAllen took a seat in front of Phelps, keeping his gun aimed at the second gunman. "I'm Joseph McAllen. Pleased to make your acquaintance."

"You can't do that."

"I already did."

He made a sideways flipping motion with the barrel of his gun. The guard understood and slowly pulled his pistol and let it fall to the floor. I stepped over and searched him to find a .32 pocket pistol tucked behind his back. With a wan smile, the man shrugged as if to say, can't blame me for trying. McAllen gave him a long, hard stare, then shrugged as well and waved him out of the room.

As he was about to leave, Phelps said, "If you leave, don't come back."

"I'm leavin'." He walked back, leaned into Phelps's face, and extended his hand. "But first, you owe me twenty dollars."

Phelps immediately opened a steel box on the table in front of him and flipped the man a double eagle, taking him by surprise so that he barely caught it before the coin rolled onto the floor.

"Don't just leave this saloon, leave town . . . leave the state. I'll instruct Ben to shoot your cowardly ass if he catches sight of you."

The man rubbed the gold coin between his finger and thumb, then smiled before walking out.

While I disarmed the unconscious man, McAllen said, "We're here to talk about the rest of your payroll."

"I don't discuss business affairs with strangers."

McAllen ignored his comment. "Law is on his way. When he arrives, tell him that you're firing his gang. No more money to pay them. You tell him . . . and you tell his men."

"Go to hell."

McAllen leaned forward and looked Phelps directly in the eye. "Do as I say . . . or you won't be doin' anythin' from now on."

"You threatening me?" Phelps sounded incredulous.

"Smart man. Figure out things downright quick, don't you?"

"You're the one who needs more smarts. I have more men than these. Hard men. Men who enjoy hurting showy jackasses like you. Do you even know Ben Law? Nobody challenges him and lives."

McAllen leaned back, completely relaxed. "We've met."

"I'm surprised you're still above ground."

"He ran," McAllen shrugged. "But that's beside the point. You can keep Law as an employee, but you tell his men the payroll has run dry as a bone. No more money. If they want to continue with Law out of loyalty, fine, but they'll be workin' for free. Do you understand what I'm tellin' you?"

"I understand your words, but I'm not firing my men. Besides, you need to understand I have more men than those with Law. You two are going to be kindling to the firestorm I'm going to ignite. You think you can fight off a whole army? Go to hell."

"I don't believe you," I said. "Maybe a few second-rate guards at your holdings, but no one who knows how to deal with people like us." I smiled to accentuate my irony. "Unless you're talking about that unconscious man on the floor."

"I do have more men," Phelps insisted. "Plus a dozen with Law. I suggest you get your butts out of here before he returns."

"Law has only a half dozen left," I said. "We killed four, and another two are locked up in Durango. Right now, he's scurrying back here with his tail between his legs." I struck a nonchalant pose. "I don't know how many will make it, because someone's hunting them on the trail as we speak."

"Someone? What do you mean someone? A single man?"

"He's enough," McAllen said. "He's ruthless and clever . . . and huntin' prey on a narrow trail. He'll enjoy workin' his way up to Law one man at a time."

"He'll fail," Phelps said. "I hire good men. They won't fall so easy. Besides, one man couldn't beat Law, even if he was alone. You're talking foolishness."

Phelps continued to make bellicose retorts, but his quivering voice gave him away. He was starting to doubt his convictions.

"They'll ride single file. No other way to get up that trail, especially with all that construction debris litterin' the open spaces." McAllen let that sink in before adding, "And this particular devil will take the hindmost."

For the first time, Phelps looked unnerved, so McAllen pressed the case. "Whoever makes it back, you make clear to 'em that you no longer cover their pay. That's all we're askin'. Then I'll deal with Law, one-on-one."

"And if I don't?" Now there was a clearly discernible tremor in his voice.

McAllen was done with polite negotiations.

"Law threatened my daughter." McAllen grabbed Phelps by his starched and soil-free shirtfront. He pulled him to within an inch of his nose. "What do you think?"

"Law's dangerous. You don't know what you're asking . . . or what he's capable of doing."

"Law's crazy . . . I'm the one that's dangerous," McAllen said just before he threw him back into his seat so hard that his head thumped loudly against the wall. Phelps appeared dazed. He wasn't used to people pushing him around. He was the one to push.

"What do you think firing my men will accomplish? Ben can beat any man one-on-one."

"All I want is a fair fight," McAllen said. "One-on-one."

"You'll die," Phelps said.

"Quit tellin' me how big a man he is. Are you gonna do as I say, or do I start breakin' arms and legs?"

"Go to hell."

McAllen appeared exasperated. "We've already had that conversation. Your time is up."

He reached across the table and took Phelps's wrist, bending it until he squealed in pain.

Phelps cried out, "I'll do it! I'll do it! Stop for god's sake!"

McAllen twisted one more time and let go.

Phelps looked totally beaten. He was used to being feared, not fearful. I didn't know if our ploy would work, but it certainly was worth a try.

We got up to leave.

"Law will arrive tomorrow afternoon," McAllen said. "Tell him immediately."

"I will. But his men will stand by him . . . and me." He massaged his wrist. "In case you didn't know, Law and I are related."

"We knew," I said. "If you think that will stop Law from taking your empire away from you, you're mistaken. He has his eye on a future that does not include a prissy cousin. You may not know it, but we're doing you a favor."

"Who told you we were cousins? That's daft. We're brothers . . . or half brothers, if you will. Ben would *never* hurt or steal from me. We argue, but when we do, it's a family squabble. I've pulled his butt out of trouble way too many times for him to forget he needs me. I'm the one with the smarts to keep all this running . . . and he knows it. If you're banking on turning us against each other, you'll be sorely disappointed."

"If you're banking on him winning this fight, then you're the one who'll be sorely disappointed," I said.

"Hell, Steve, let's get out of here," McAllen said. "I'm done with this blowhard."

In a move so fast I almost missed it, Phelps popped a derringer from his sleeve and fired, first at McAllen and then at me. I had seen it coming, and without a thought, fell to my left, drawing my gun with my right. When I hit the floor, I took a split second to steady my impact with the floor before firing under the table into Phelps's lap. His scream was pure agony.

I came up fast with my gun raised against Phelps. He was bowled over, howling in pain. I swung my gun barrel around and hit him in the head as hard as I could. His screeching stopped. I glanced at his guard, but he hadn't regained consciousness. I turned around to see if McAllen had been hurt.

He lay in a pool of blood on the floor. A pool that was growing bigger as I watched.

Damn it to hell.

Chapter 40

fetch a doctor

I rotated on my knees to check on McAllen. Phelps had shot him in the chest. He breathed shallowly, wincing on every intake. I yelled for someone to fetch a doctor. When nobody moved, I put a hole in Phelps's ceiling. That got the men at the bar moving. I had little experience with gunshot wounds, so I put my ear to McAllen's mouth and asked what I should do. A garbled noise came out, but I understood enough to tear open his shirt and press my hands against the wound. I pressed lightly because I didn't want to hurt him, but he gestured with his fingers for me to apply more pressure. Damn, where was that doctor?

Someone knelt beside me and handed me a towel. It was the barkeep. He told me to use the towel instead of my hands. I was grateful for any help but had a fleeting thought that he must not have liked his boss.

I glanced at the door again, worried. McAllen was shot center chest. A kill shot. I hadn't seen much of the wound, because blood kept oozing out over my hands, and now the bar towel was turning crimson. His chest was just a wet, red pool. McAllen continued to breathe, but it didn't look good. I kept thinking that, although he had faced every type of bad man in the West, he might die from an underhanded play by a lowlife who pretended to a proper upbringing. Derringers were highly lethal in close quarters. I recognized the palm pistol used by Phelps as a .41 caliber Remington. It shot a very slow but potentially lethal bullet. The short barrel made it useless at any distance, but within a few feet, the slug was just as powerful as if it had been fired from a revolver.

Finally, the doctor arrived.

Without fanfare, he shoved me aside and took over. After a moment, he turned from McAllen to examine Phelps, but I told him that Phelps was fine. I had picked up my pistol from the floor and held it in my bloody hand. The doctor glanced at it and looked at my face. I must have appeared determined, because he ignored Phelps and went back to work on McAllen.

In a moment, he yelled for help lifting him onto the table. Five men were immediately at the ready. After McAllen had been settled on the table, I noticed a huge pool of blood on the floor, more blood than could possibly have come from McAllen. I went around the table and lifted Phelps's upper body away from the table. His wound had bled profusely, his blood flowing into McAllen's to form a single pool at the front of the table. I put my ear close to his mouth and heard a sporadic gasp or two before he went silent.

The doctor came over, and I informed him that Phelps was dead. He said he'd be the judge of that, bending to examine him. When he'd finished, he looked at me and nodded. Then he did a quick assessment of the guard and pronounced him unconscious and in need of stiches, but otherwise sound.

"What about my friend?" I asked.

He waved his hand to indicate the floor. "Most of that blood came from Phelps. That bullet drained him dry." He wiped his hands on a handkerchief. "Your friend's hurt bad, but he may make it. The bullet went clean through. Depends on what it hit."

"Then you better get back to him," I said none too kindly.

"Not much I can do. That fella's holding a compress to the wound. Blood loss is severe, but not lethal. His heart is still beating, so the bullet missed it. His chest hasn't swelled, so the bullet missed the lungs."

I was confused. "Does that mean he'll be alright?"

"No, it doesn't. Lots of other things a bullet can hit. We need to watch him close . . . but, and don't get encouraged by this, when I compare the entry and exit, it appears the bullet hit him on an upward slant and may have been deflected by a rib. It came out below his shoulder blade."

"What would that mean?" I asked, still confused.

"A straight-in shot would have damaged vital organs, but a steep upward angle may have hit only muscle tissue. It still did a lot of damage, but he may not die today." He looked me in the eye. "Maybe tomorrow. Or . . . he could live and lose the use of his right arm. Any number of other bad outcomes might afflict him if he lives. I told you, don't get encouraged by what I said. It doesn't look good."

"Does a man's internal fortitude help recovery?"

"Absolutely. I've seen men die who shouldn't, and I've seen men live I was sure would die. Your friend is strongly built. Heavily muscular, in fact. The bullet missed the two most vital organs. If he's got a strong will, he might pull through."

I smiled. The doctor started to caution me again, but I waved him off.

"If will has anything to do with his survival, then Joseph will be hammering nails at his ranch before the next full moon."

Chapter 41

foolish or brave beyond reason

My first action on waking the next morning was to run over to the doctor's office. McAllen looked bad, but the doctor felt encouraged. He told me most men would have died in the night. He still wasn't out of danger, but every hour improved his chances. I asked the doctor if I could get him breakfast, and he appeared grateful.

I returned in a half hour, juggling a pail of coffee and two plates of chops and eggs. We sat across from each other in his outer office and ate like we hadn't seen a good meal in a week.

After devouring everything but the chop bone, I sat back and sipped coffee. I had eaten so fast, the coffee was still hot. When I looked up at the doctor, I realized I had finished second.

"I presume you know about Ben Law?" the doctor said.

"He'll be here sometime today. Riding in with about a half dozen men."

He shook his head. "Then my work is far from over." When I didn't respond, he added, "He's dangerous."

"Because he's not wholly sane?" I asked.

"I doctor the body, not the mind, but I'll give

271

you this: Law's unpredictable. And capable of anything. Don't underestimate him."

"You sound like you're on our side."

He shook his head vehemently. "I'm on no side." Then he added quickly, "I'm certainly not against Law." He made an anxious laugh. "He's fed me plenty of business. If he were gone, I don't know what I'd do with all my free time."

He sounded nervous. Law certainly had him frightened.

I asked, "What about Phelps? Has he shot anyone before?"

He seemed eager for the change in subject. I don't think he feared dead people.

"Not to my knowledge," he answered. "No need with Law around. Rumor has it that they were related."

"Phelps told us they were half-brothers. Odd. We thought Law wanted to take over Phelps's operations."

"I'm sure Law had thoughts along that line, but I doubt he ever would do anything. Law's not quick-witted, but he's smart enough to know he needs Phelps. Needed, I should say. You did what he probably never would have done on his own. Now, all that was Phelps's is his for the taking."

"He won't enjoy the fruits of our labors," I said.

"You plan to stop him all by yourself? You said there were half a dozen men with him." He looked toward the door to his treatment room.

"Your friend may live, but he won't help you. I admire your confidence, but you're in serious trouble. When Law finds out you killed Phelps, he'll come gunning for you." He took on a more worried expression and nodded toward his treatment room. "Your friend too . . . and he won't wait for him to heal. As soon as he dispatches you, he'll storm in here and finish Mr. McAllen." He threw out his hands, palms up. "I can't stop him."

"He'll never get this far," I said. "There's someone shadowing him right now. He'll either kill him on the trail or whittle down the numbers so I can handle Law . . . or what's left. Even if he fails, it doesn't matter. I'll still face Law."

"You're foolhardy, not brave," the doctor said. "I suspect you'll soon be the undertaker's concern."

"I'm not nearly as foolhardy as you think," I said. "Besides, what would you have me do?"

"An intelligent man would run. Run like the dickens. Facing those odds isn't a fight, it's suicide. You're smart, educated even, but you're not running." He gave me an appraising look. "So . . . you tell me, are you foolish or brave beyond reason?"

"Neither, I'm loyal. Loyal to my friends who would do the same for me. One lies near death in your treatment room, and another is chasing Law to save the woman he loves from being abused in the worst possible way." I glanced through the door at McAllen. "I don't need a bigger reason than my two friends."

"What woman? I don't believe you. Law's never harmed a woman. He's not completely sane, but he draws the line at abusing women. I know. Phelps wanted him to rough up one woman in town, a mine owner. He not only refused but said he'd kill any man who harmed her. He has his own odd code, and that code excludes harming women and children. You must be mistaken."

"You're referring to Nora West," I said.

He nodded, surprised that I knew her name.

"Law took her away from Durango by force yesterday. She's with him and what's left of his gang. Law fancies himself in love with her, but she spurned him, so he intended to rape her during the ride back here."

He appeared confused. "Nora West? Law took her from Durango?"

"Yes. That's who Jeff Sharp is trying to protect."

"Your friend loves Nora West?" It wasn't really a question. There was wonderment in his voice.

"He does," I answered simply.

He shook his head. "As do I. Three men in love with her . . . hell, maybe more for all I know."

"You love her?" I blurted.

"Is that so surprising? She's a wonderful

woman in a town full of harlots. Of course I courted her . . . after her husband died."

"What happened?"

"It ended months ago. At the time, I fooled myself into thinking she did it to protect me. Law doesn't attack women, but he truly enjoys savaging a man a woman cares about. I'm no fighter, and he would have had an easy time with me. But I was wrong." He looked sad. "She didn't do it to protect me. She put an end to our courtship because I couldn't measure up to her true love."

"How do you know this?" I asked.

"I got tipsy and went to see her one night. Said I wanted an honest answer, or I'd hound her day and night. She told me her true love was lost, but she measured every man against him. He deserted her and broke her heart. She had no idea why. Nor do I. How could any man desert her? It makes no sense."

"My friend is the one who left her. Big misunderstanding. They got together again by accident a few weeks ago and made amends."

His face knotted up in a weird expression that looked like he couldn't quite smile or allow himself to cry. He wanted to do one or the other.

Finally, he said, "Then I'm happy for Nora." But he didn't sound happy. "And your friend is trying to rescue her?"

"He is. Law grabbed her because he knew

about their reconciliation. He wanted to hurt them both."

Without enthusiasm, he said, "I wish your friend luck. And I hope they have a good life together."

I doubted that but kept my mouth shut. I finished my coffee in a gulp and stood. I had things to do before Law made his way into town. I handed the doctor a ten-dollar note and instructed him to take good care of McAllen. I had no doubt that he would, although it might be a different matter if Jeff Sharp were lying on his treatment table. McAllen still may not recover, and Sharp could easily be dead. I left the doctor's office with an uneasy feeling. The idea of losing both of my friends depressed me. On the other hand, Law might be as dead as Phelps, although it seemed doubtful. The odds were just too great.

If Sharp was dead, he had failed his true love. I thought a moment about Virginia. I knew what Sharp or McAllen would do if I died trying to save her. I could do no less.

As I marched toward the Silver Nugget, I vowed to clear my head and finish the job.

Chapter 42

nothing comes for free

About halfway to the Silver Nugget, I turned around and went back to my hotel. I didn't expect Law until early afternoon or later, but there was no reason to take chances. I wanted my rifle and a full box of rifle cartridges in my coat pocket.

With only a few minutes' delay, I walked into the saloon and asked the whereabouts of Mike Fletcher. It was still early, and I was told Big Mike was at the café around the corner, eating breakfast. I found him by himself at a back table and impolitely sat down without asking permission to join him.

"I need to talk," I said.

"Indeed you do." He wiped his mouth with a cloth napkin. "You killed George Phelps. The town smelled cleaner this morning." He made a show of sniffing the air. "But I detect a foul odor on the horizon."

"How much do you know?" I asked, a bit surprised.

"I know your friend got shot by Phelps. Hurt bad from what I hear. He shot at you too, but missed, so you hit him with a low blow. His undignified demise is the talk of the town. I'm told his saloon gals found it apropos. I also know you're carrying a rifle into an anodyne eating establishment, and Law is nowhere to be seen. That means you're expecting him . . . soon."

I nodded. "Probably early afternoon. We killed a number of his gang in Durango. He fled, and he grabbed Nora West as a hostage. He holds a grudge against her, so she won't be treated well. Jeff chased after them on horseback up the Silverton trail. He asked McAllen and me to take the train to get here ahead of them. I don't know how Sharp has fared, but the odds are heavy against him." I gave him a second to absorb what I'd said. "That means I'm probably alone. I intend to kill Law. For what he's done to me and my friends . . . and further, because he intends to kill me."

"Reason enough." Big Mike mulled over what I'd told him. "You want help. The shooting kind."

"I do."

"I do like a direct man." He chuckled. "Phelps was the big dog in this town. I survived because I didn't directly challenge him. If I had, I would have had to face Law. He's an unpleasant sort, and I value my life too much to get into a needless fight with a crazed savage." He ate another bite of his breakfast. "Now you want me to take him on for you . . . a near stranger."

"We're business partners," I offered.

"Who haven't transacted a single piece of business."

"Nor will we." He looked annoyed at my comment. He probably thought I was going to use future business opportunities as leverage to coerce him into action.

I quickly explained. "Let me lay this out for you. First, what I'm about to tell you has nothing to do with Phelps or Law. Sharp and I came to this decision prior to our present difficulties. We no longer want to electrify the West. We'll recommend to Mr. Edison that he transfer our license to you. Since you're a successful businessman and related by marriage, there's a good chance he'll be receptive to our suggestion, especially since you know Barney Ford, our only contract to date. We also no longer want to own mining interests in Silverton. We intended to sell them to Phelps if he would call off his bastard brother. Now, that's out of the picture. Instead, you may have the Galena Queen and Mr. Sharp's other recent mining acquisitions for fifty cents on the dollar. You may also acquire the Edison electrification inventory warehoused in Denver for fifty cents on the dollar. Barney's the warehouse landlord, by the way, so he can act as your agent. With a proper resolution of our current troubles with Mr. Law, the Phelps operations will be unclaimed. Mr. Phelps has already run off most of the capable men who could compete with you. If you handle these mining interests and the Edison license as well as you've run your saloon, you could be one of the wealthiest men west of the Mississippi. So . . . don't take him on for me, a near stranger . . . help me put him away because it will make you incredibly wealthy."

Big Mike finished his breakfast, fastidiously folded his napkin, and lay it across his plate. Then he waved the waitress over. After the table had been cleared and coffee refilled, he gave me a long, hard stare.

"I run a damn good saloon and a few other enterprises, but I'm not a big-time businessman. You're trying to tempt me with wealth I don't want or need. I'm happy with things the way they are. I don't need more. I have no idea how to install that equipment . . . or run a mining operation, for that matter. You're dangling a carrot I have no appetite for."

"You can hire people. In fact, we already have a deal with Karl Werner. He says you know each other."

"Karl's a good man. Knows his trade."

With the mention of Werner, Fletcher appeared intrigued, so I explained Werner's responsibilities, compensation, and ownership interest. I said that he could continue with the agreement that made Werner a junior partner, or we would take care of severing the arrangement.

"I don't understand why you want to do this." he said. "With Phelps and Law gone, you could become the kingpins. What are you and Mr. Sharp planning to do?"

"We plan on getting married. Both of us. We have plenty of money, and at least for the next few years, we intend to enjoy it with our brides."

"And what would I need to do to be the recipient of this largesse?"

"Help me put Ben Law in his grave. I need a couple of your men . . . tough ones who've been in fights before. When Law arrives, he'll have only a few men left."

"You don't know that. It's a hope, not a fact.

"I know Jeff Sharp. He'll ride into Silverton alone, or Law will stumble into town knowing he has been in a nasty fight."

Fletcher drank his coffee and appeared contemplative. I didn't interrupt his thoughts.

"I don't have a gang. Only a few men to keep Phelps at bay and take care of rowdies in the saloon. They can take care of themselves, but they're not gunmen."

"I don't want help with Law. Only the men who ride with him. I'll be in the forefront. I'll be the one to kill Law. So the question is . . . can your men handle what's left of Law's crew?"

"Possibly, especially if I join them." Those were his words, but he didn't look fully convinced. "It could get bloody."

"Nothing comes for free."

Chapter 43

damn him to hell

Our plan was not complicated. Fletcher was a simple man and wanted a simple plan. I would wait in a chair in front of Phelps's saloon because it had a clear view of the trail as it entered town. When I saw Law, I would walk into the street to challenge him. Fletcher and three other men would hide along the street or inside businesses that provided a good sightline to the trail end. They would make themselves visible after I stopped Law's progress. Fletcher and his men would carry rifles. After Law noticed that he was surrounded by armed men, I would demand a fair duel.

If I could fight one-on-one with Law and win, we surmised that his men would scatter without further argument. If I lost, Fletcher failed to confide in me what he would do, except that he promised to hide McAllen until he recovered. That was fine with me. If Law killed me, I'd rather my revenge come from McAllen anyway.

To show good faith, Fletcher had McAllen moved to his private quarters above the Silver Nugget. He was a clever—and careful—man. While we moved McAllen on a stretcher, he had one of his men play drunk and shoot up the opposite end of the street. The diversion worked, and no one paid any attention to our part of town. We placed McAllen on a cot in Fletcher's sleeping quarters and then used a screen to hide him in case anyone made it past the guard Fletcher had positioned at the bottom of the staircase.

At Fletcher's suggestion, I bribed the undertaker to say he had buried a large man who had died in the doctor's office. I insulted the doctor by offering him money to collaborate the story. In a huff, he said he had already been compensated. He further promised to look in on McAllen whenever he went over to the Silver Nugget for a beer.

McAllen appeared to be recovering. The man was tough. His breath was regular and he spoke now and then. However, the doctor had dosed him with laudanum, so he was too groggy to make sense. I watched him for about a half hour after we moved him and became convinced that he would live. The doctor had warned me that the use of his right arm remained uncertain, but I was confident that even a maimed McAllen could revenge my death in the event I lost the fight. Then I thought about Virginia. Revenge would not satisfy her. I needed to quit thinking about what would happen if I lost and concentrate on winning.

I pulled a captain's chair onto the boardwalk in front of Phelps's saloon and sat with a cup of coffee, ready for a long wait. At first, I felt uncomfortable sitting in front of Phelps's place of business, but the rowdies and ruffians that frequented his saloon only gave me odd glances as they entered or left. Perhaps they were intimidated by the rifle I held with one hand behind the lever and the other on the forend, or possibly they didn't want to confront someone ruthless enough to shoot Phelps in the groin. Besides, they knew I was waiting for Law. That was a show they didn't want to miss by foolishly dying in a gunfight.

The afternoon wore on with no sign of Law or Sharp. One of them had to emerge from the woods. I worried. It was late afternoon, and someone should have ridden into town. Then a thought struck me. No one had emerged from the trail. No one. The train route had been completed, but the trail should have remained a busy thoroughfare. People were always going between Durango and Silverton, and not all of them had the wherewithal to buy a train ticket. Something had happened to hold up traffic. Now I had a predicament. Did I stay put or ride down the trail to see what had happened? I decided to wait another hour. I couldn't wait longer than that because it would grow dark before I could get too far down the trail. Time passed.

Still nothing. Just as I was about to go see about renting a horse, Law rode out of the forest with four men. No woman. What had become of Nora West?

I rose from my chair and slowly walked to the center of the street. When I needed to be quick, I felt more confident with my Colt, so I had left my rifle lying across the arms of the chair. Besides, a rifle would be more provocative, and I didn't want to unnerve Law before I could get close enough to use a handgun. When he spotted me, he and his men pulled up. Hooking his index finger, he beckoned them to spread wide across my path.

I continued into the street until I faced Law from less than ten feet. He remained on horseback, so I looked up to meet his eyes. He displayed no wound. Then I spotted a rider at his side with a bandaged forearm. Law had used another man's blood to write us a warning message in that alley across from the Durango hotel. I guessed he wouldn't be considered a compassionate boss.

"Where is Mrs. West?" I asked.

"Gone."

"What does that mean?"

"It means she ain't here. What difference does it make to you?"

That took me aback for an instant because it was true. It made no difference. I intended to kill him in any case. Keeping that to myself, I said,

"She was with you when you left Durango. Did you kill her?"

With a smirk, he said, "If I were you, I'd be more concerned about me killing you."

Now I hooked my finger. From different directions, Fletcher and his three men came into the open, each with a rifle snugged against his shoulder. Their aim was unmistakable. Each had one of Law's men in his sights. In an instant, they could all be dead.

"Gentlemen, my argument is with Mr. Law. If you slowly ride to the livery and allow Law and me to settle our differences alone, these men will fade back to where they came from. But if you remain to back him, they will blow you out of your saddles. Your choice."

"Leave and I'll hunt you down and kill you all!" Law yelled.

"That's an empty threat," I said. "Mr. Law will no longer be among the living in a few minutes. I suggest you go now or plan on joining him at the undertakers. Make up your mind. You have only seconds."

"Don't anybody move," Law ordered.

A few horses pawed the ground, but no one broke ranks.

"By the way, where are your other men? You left Durango with at least six."

"That's my business. I have enough to take care of you . . . and your newfound friends."

"Perhaps . . . but these men look smart enough to see the situation clear. You don't pay them enough to commit suicide."

Law stopped his men with a scowl so mean that his rough face looked crazed. If he lived, none would doubt that he would hunt each and every one of them down and kill them in some horrific fashion.

Regaining eye contact with me, he stormed, "These are not fair odds!"

I smiled. "Five against five. How's that not fair?"

Law whipped his head left and right between Fletcher and his men. "Damn it, they already have a bead on my men while their guns are still holstered, their rifles in scabbards."

"It's going to stay that way," I said easily. "At the first jerk, your men go down in a hail of bullets. You alone will be spared. My orders. They're here to even out the odds, so you and I can fight it out fair and square." If possible, the scowl became more contemptuous. "Are you too weak to face me alone? Does your bravery depend on being backed by more guns than your opponents?"

"Are you calling me a coward?"

"I'm not calling you anything. I'm merely pointing out that your actions might be viewed as cowardly by the townsfolk."

"Go to hell."

"After you." Never taking my eyes off Law, I spoke to his men. "You boys don't have much time. Lead will fly any moment. If you're here, you die."

The wait seemed long, but it was probably only a few seconds before Law's men peeled off and started walking their horses in the direction of the livery. Fletcher and his men kept their rifles aimed at their backs until they were well down the street, then they faded back into their hiding positions.

Law and I were alone. The street was empty. It was starting to grow dark. It was so quiet that I could hear Law breathe. As we stared at each other, I felt as if we were the only people left in Colorado. I knew dozens of eyes were on us, but they remained hidden. Nothing moved. The only sound was a crow squawking in the distance.

Then Law frightened me. His wild look faded away, and his expression turned sanguine. I didn't like that. I preferred him mad as a hatter.

Hoping to ignite anger, I said, "Your brother's dead." I waited a couple of heartbeats and then added, "I killed him." His eyes flared. "I shot him in his privates, and he slowly bled to death." I shrugged. "He didn't die bravely."

The fury returned but abated way too fast to my liking. The man refused to be taunted into a rage. After his next words, I shivered.

"Sharp died on the trail . . . with his dead woman friend in his arms."

My face must have betrayed me, because

the smirk returned, only now it was relaxed, confident. I had tried to taunt him and failed. He'd returned the favor and succeeded. He liked the odds in his favor, so I thought depriving him of his men would rattle him. Instead, he appeared to be in complete control. I needed to do the same. I forced my mind to empty.

"That bother you, dandy? Would you like to go away and cry? I'll wait. You and I have business, and I don't want you blurry-eyed because you teared up."

He started laughing. In fact, he laughed so hard, I thought his crazy side might be getting the upper hand, but he abruptly quit and appeared supremely confident again. He tugged his reins slightly to his left, and his horse's head came around to shield his body from my view. Good tactic, but I simultaneously stepped in the opposite direction and got an even better angle on him. Law seemed displeased.

I relaxed, emptied my mind, and let my muscles loosen.

The tense moment was interrupted by a voice behind me.

"Ben, yer a liar."

I almost turned toward the voice but caught myself in time, my attention fixed on Law.

Sharp said, "I'm alive . . . and so is Mrs. West."

"How—" Law momentarily glanced at Sharp but quickly glared back at me.

Sharp laughed. "This is the 1880s, Ben. Instead of riding the trail in a pointless attempt to catch you, we raced back to Durango and took the train."

"This ain't a fair fight anymore," Law squealed. "Tell your friend to step aside."

I had no intention of saying anything. Talking required thought, and in a gunfight, it was a bad idea to think about anything other than your opponent. Law wanted me to speak so he would have a split-second advantage. As soon as I opened my mouth, he would go for his gun.

"No need," Sharp said casually. "Steve don't need any help with the likes of you."

I tried not to pay attention, but I couldn't help hearing his footfall as he moved down the boardwalk.

Now, Law and I were intent only on each other. There was nothing else in the world.

In the blink of an eye, one of us would be dead, but I never allowed that thought to enter my head. I wanted an eye-hand reflex unencumbered by extraneous thought or emotion. I waited. Law waited as well, probably hoping for a distraction. He was thinking. I could see it in his eyes. He was trying to figure out an edge.

Law suddenly jerked his horse's head up and to the right as he drew his pistol. I went in the opposite direction as I pulled my gun. I knew he intended to swing his arm and head under the horse's neck to shoot me while hanging half out of his saddle. Law leaned into the turn, keeping his body hidden behind his horse. I kept moving as fast as I could in the opposite direction. I shot him in his exposed thigh. He involuntarily jerked up in reaction to the wound. As he came up, I shot him in the chest. He immediately fell from his horse. As the horse bolted away, I put a third bullet in his head.

The echo from the gunshots receded, and the gun smoke slowly wafted away. It was so still, I could hear that crow protesting some perceived wrong. This street had witnessed many of Law's victims, and now his own mortality was seeping into the dirt. He no longer looked dangerous. He no longer looked crazed. He just looked tragic. I hated him. I didn't hate him for what he was, I hated him for what he had made me do. Damn him to hell, anyway.

Chapter 44

both dead

The silence didn't even last until I'd reloaded. People stormed out of every building, making so much noise that I couldn't tell if the crow flew away or the busybodies drowned him out. Fletcher and his men came out from behind cover as well, standing on the perimeter, seemingly uninterested in the spectacle. The townspeople gathered around the corpse, clucking like a bunch of young girls inspecting a new shipment of ribbons at the general store. I supposed the death of the meanest despot in Silverton presented cause for celebration, but the jocularity distressed me. A couple of the men walked over to slap me on the back, but most gave me a wide berth. I wasn't interested in glad-handing, so I walked away.

I never expected the sight of Jeff Sharp to lift my spirits so much. I smiled, even laughed a bit. That ornery oldster had found a way to save Nora and remain among the living. I should have known. My anger had been fueled by McAllen's getting shot and Sharp in mortal danger. We had been through so much together, it seemed unjust that they would die at the hands of some worthless little tyrants. And for what? We had already decided to forego our business interests in the San Juan Mountains. I had been infuriated by the pointlessness.

I stepped up onto the boardwalk, and to the surprise of both of us, found myself hugging Sharp.

I pulled away, a little embarrassed. "How did you save Nora?"

"I didn't," Sharp said, unabashed. "She escaped when they set camp. They didn't have her tied up 'cuz they didn't believe a woman would wander into the wilderness by herself. She ran into me workin' my way closer to their camp, so we rode double until I found a good ambush site. I knew Law an' his men would come after her, an' we couldn't outrun 'em. When they charged around a corner, I shot a couple of 'em, an' they scampered away."

He looked pleased with himself.

I said, "So you didn't save the damsel in distress. You just caught her as she made her own escape, threw a couple bullets at the villains, and left me up here on my lonesome to handle the aftermath."

I meant it as gentle ribbing, but I saw concern on Sharp's face. "Lonesome? Where's McAllen?"

Damn, he didn't know, and I had made light of the situation. In truth, I was so happy to have survived the fight and see an unharmed Sharp that I had forgotten about McAllen.

"Follow me," I said, heading toward the Silver Nugget.

As we walked, I explained. "McAllen's been shot . . . and it's serious. It looks like he'll recover, but it didn't look good for a while.

"How bad?" Sharp asked in a no-nonsense tone.

"Bad. He may not have full use of his shoulder again."

"Which shoulder?"

"Right."

"He ain't gonna like it if he can't use a gun or throw a punch."

"He's McAllen. If necessary, he'll become left-handed."

Sharp looked behind him. "That was the doctor's office. Where are we goin'?"

"Big Mike's. He's holed up in his private quarters . . . to hide him from Law . . . in case I lost that fight. Big Mike has helped a lot. He and his men took Law's men out of the fight so I had a chance, and he looked after Joseph." I looked at Sharp. "I made promises to Big Mike. He buys all of our business interests cheap."

Sharp nodded, and then seemed confused. "When did McAllen get shot?"

"Last night."

He grabbed my shoulder and turned me around. "Wait a minute. Law was on the trail. Who shot McAllen?"

"Phelps."

"What? That doesn't make sense. That dandified good-for-nothin' would never win a fight with Joseph."

"You mean a fair fight. That starchy ass was Law's half-brother and just as mean. He kept a derringer in one of those spring contraptions gamblers use. Caught us both by surprise. He shot Joseph before either of us had an inkling we were in a fight."

"Both? You were with him? Why would Phelps try such a thing?"

"He was practiced. Only two shots in that derringer, but he almost got us both. He shot Joseph first and then barely missed me as I dove under the table. I shot him in his balls, and he bled to death. Too quickly, if you ask me. The bullet hit Joseph in the chest and passed through. He was lucky it didn't hit his heart or lungs. Doc says he was saved by the upward angle. McAllen was standing and Phelps sitting, so the bullet trajected up from the entry point, hitting mainly muscle."

"You killed Phelps? They're both dead?"

"They're both dead."

Without another word, he raced toward the Silver Nugget.

Chapter 45

rue the day

When we got to the Silver Nugget, Fletcher's man wouldn't let us climb the stairs to his quarters. The sentry had never seen us before, and no matter what we said, he just kept repeating his orders: No one could enter but Big Mike. Not only did we not want to challenge a man who worked for our ally, but he looked completely capable of taking down Sharp. Luckily, the next person through the saloon door was Fletcher.

As we climbed the stairs together, he said over his shoulder, "Okay, let's see about getting your friend back to the doctor's."

McAllen did not greet us. He was asleep or in a laudanum stupor. Fletcher declared it a good time to move him. Sharp and I objected until the doctor had inspected him, so Fletcher dispatched one of his men to fetch him.

While we waited, McAllen remained unnaturally still, his chest barely rising and falling as he breathed. None of us spoke for fear of waking him, but he seemed so far under that I could have fired my pistol without disturbing him.

The doctor arrived and briefly examined McAllen, and then we retreated to the outer office.

"I don't want to tell you your business," I said, "but are you sure he's not overly drugged?"

The doctor looked at me as if I were a child. "Then don't tell me my business. I gave him enough laudanum to rest comfortably and sleep though any ruckus downstairs or in Mike's office."

"What 'bout now?" Sharp asked. "Is there still a need for him to look like a Chinaman in an opium den?"

"Not at all. In fact, I want him conscious enough to tell me how he feels."

"What about moving him back to your office?" Fletcher asked.

"Good idea. But only for a day or two. You gentlemen need to find him other quarters as soon as possible. Other patients need to use that office."

"What would've happened if Law had found Joseph here?" Sharp asked, sounding irritated.

"He didn't."

Sharp took a half step toward the doctor.

"But what if he did?" He continued to sound harsh.

"How should I know?" the doctor said. "He probably would have finished the job his brother started."

"An' then what would he have done to ya for treatin' him?" Sharp asked, sounding deeply annoyed.

"Why are you interrogating me?"

"What did ya fear he would do?" Sharp asked, standing face-to-face with the doctor.

"He wouldn't kill me, if that's what you mean. I treat his men all the time."

Sharp said nothing more but glared at the man.

"Probably beat me up and tell me to heal myself." The doctor sounded nervous but unafraid.

Sharp leaned in until he almost touched noses. "Ya gave him heavy doses of laudanum to keep him quiet to save yer own skin."

The doctor was unabashed. "It was for the good of both of us. Don't lecture me. I treated him knowing the penalty if I got caught. Many doctors would have sent him off to die. As it is, everything worked out, but it could have gone the other way."

"Ya were afraid of Law because ya never met me." The doctor flinched. "I've seen laudanum ruin men, make strong men weaker than a starvin' child. All they know is that they have a need, an' they'll do anything to fill it."

"Your friend has only been dosed for a day. He'll be fine."

"I know he will," Sharp said. "Do ya know how I know?"

"I suspect I don't want to hear."

"He's going back to your office. Ya'll cut out all laudanum. Ya'll care for him as if he were yer brother. Ya'll treat the gunshot *and* the addiction. Ya'll bring him back to full health. Do ya understand?"

"Thoroughly. And a proper resolution." Appearing unaffected, he turned to Fletcher. "Now I need a stretcher and four strong men to move him."

In a few minutes, four big men entered the room, peering right and left in a manner that said they had never been in their boss's inner sanctum. In short order, they had loaded McAllen onto the stretcher and carried him down the stairs.

As the doctor followed, we could hear him in the stairwell. "Gently, or you'll rue the day you met this man."

Chapter 46

kit an' kaboodle

"I don't think you intimidated him."

Sharp stood in the doorway, watching the doctor's backside as he descended the stairs.

"Of course I did," he said.

"You've seen how laudanum takes hold of people?" I asked.

"Yep. Sad. But the doc's right. One day shouldn't enslave McAllen."

"Then what was that all about?"

"I don't want the doc to use laudanum to quiet down Joseph when he has other patients in the office. He got the message." In turn, Sharp looked at me and then at Fletcher. "What's our agreement?"

Fletcher looked to me to answer. I hesitated a second, unsure of how Sharp would react. "I promised him the silver claims and Edison inventory for fifty cents on the dollar. If you think I gave away the store, I'll make up the difference."

Sharp smiled. "Sounds good to me, as long as he takes the whole kit an' kaboodle." He looked directly at Fletcher. "I want free of it all."

"He'll take it all," I said, "but only if Karl

comes with the package . . . and . . . Edison obviously has to agree to transfer the license. Big Mike needs Karl's construction experience."

He kept eye contact with Fletcher, who hadn't said a word. "Yer a smart man. Have ya talked to Karl? Measured his intentions?"

"No," he said. "But I sent someone to look for him."

"Could be a fly in the ointment," I offered. "He was none too friendly the last time I saw him. He thought we carried blame for that right-of-way issue."

"Well, that right-of-way's not a problem any longer," Sharp said. " 'Sides, if he's in town, he knows Law an' Phelps have left us for their eternal destination. That should make his decision easy."

We all looked at each other, and then Sharp stepped over and extended his hand to Fletcher. They shook with the full understanding that to Sharp, a handshake was more binding than a contract. Now we only needed Karl on our side, and we were free until we encumbered our lives once again.

After the ceremonial handshake, Sharp and I raced after the doctor to make sure McAllen received proper treatment. McAllen remained in a stupor, which facilitated the jostling movement of his bearers. A couple of times he tried to speak, his words gibberish. We had been correct in suspecting that the doctor had applied an overly heavy dosage of laudanum. We got him settled in a bed, and the carriers were dismissed. A screen shielded him from the rest of the office. Sharp reminded the doctor not to administer anything stronger than salicylic acid or Jameson's. Once the doctor appeared adequately cowed, we returned to Fletcher's office.

When we arrived, Fletcher dismissed several men from his office and waved us over to a comfortable sitting area furnished like a parlor. As I took a seat on one of the facing settees, I realized that this was in fact his parlor, as well as his office and his dining room. This large outer room with adjoining sleeping quarters was where he lived and worked.

Fletcher offered us cigars and whiskey. I accepted the whiskey, while Sharp gladly accepted both. My former habit of smoking a pipe had become too much of a bother on the trail, so I had given it up without much thought. I had no desire to try any other forms of tobacco.

"Heard anything about Karl?" Sharp asked, enjoying Fletcher's hospitality.

"He's out on the trail directing a work crew. They're collecting all the leftover materials to be shipped to the next construction site."

Sharp looked perplexed. "I didn't see him on the trail."

"Only a short distance out of town. Law had

to have passed him. One of my men rode out to fetch him. Shouldn't be long."

"What if he says no?" I asked.

"Why would he? He gets the same deal you offered. Let's assume the best until presented with the worst." He took a long swallow of whiskey. "One other thing. Something we haven't discussed yet."

Both of us sat more erect in our seats.

"And what would that be?" I asked.

"The formation of a stock company, and you accept my payment for your holdings in stock instead of cash."

"What the hell?" I stammered. "That's not what we discussed." I waved my hand around the room. "The Silver Nugget is the busiest saloon in Silverton. Surely you have cash to buy us out."

"I do, but I wouldn't have enough left over to buy Phelps's holdings. You said I could have it all if you succeeded in killing Law."

"But not on our nickel," I countered.

Fletcher sat back into the cushion of the settee. "Nor on mine, I'm afraid. I don't have enough of them."

We all glared at each other for a bit. I had violated good negotiating tactics by revealing how desperately we wanted to leave all this behind. Fletcher had us over a barrel, but I couldn't just give in. I wasn't built that way.

"Stock is not cash. There's additional risk. If

we consent to a stock payment, then we can no longer accept fifty cents on the dollar. We want full value."

I expected Fletcher to react angrily; instead he laughed. "Now we have established a basis for negotiation."

Sharp gave me a dirty look. "Damn it, Steve, ya conceded payment in stock instead of cash. I thought ya knew how to conduct business."

"Rusty, I guess." But I smiled in admiration of Fletcher's acumen.

Everything was settled over the next several hours. We would receive shares worth sixty-five cents on the dollar for our property transferred into a newly established company. We couldn't sell our shares for twenty-four months, but after two years, Fletcher had the right to buy them at a specified increase over the initial valuation. All assets, including the Phelps claims, would be held in the same company. As long as we remained shareholders, Fletcher could not dilute our interest. Upon transfer of our Edison license, Fletcher would pay us ten thousand dollars in cash.

Werner arrived during the process and accepted a deal equivalent to what we had offered him. He seemed a happy man, and why shouldn't he be? He had an excellent offer, and without Phelps or Law around, he could reunite with his family.

The deal made sense to everyone. We received

some cash up front and an ownership interest in a company run by experienced businessmen. If all went well over the next two years, we'd walk away with one hundred percent of the money we had put into these enterprises, and Fletcher would get all of the value above our buyout. Everyone benefited. Sharp and I would walk away free and clear of all business interests, Fletcher had a juicy opportunity to become enormously wealthy, and Werner acquired enough ownership interest to make him happy. An hour later, both sides had hired attorneys to hammer out the details.

Next, we visited the town marshal. He had been conspicuously absent during our altercation. He told us that no charges would be pressed, and we were free to leave Silverton. In fact, he encouraged us to do so. We informed him that we would leave as soon as McAllen was capable of train travel. He seemed satisfied but warned us about making any more trouble. I knew he had been on Phelps's payroll, but he surprised me when he put the arm on us to maintain his financial arrangements. We laughed at his awkward solicitation and gladly told him that we had no further business in his town. When he learned that Big Mike had bought us out, I could tell from his expression that he knew the graft had come to an end. My bet was that he would move to another town where he could continue to profit from unofficial activities.

Our work done, we rented rooms for the night and got roaring drunk watching the dancing girls at the Silver Nugget. Everybody bought us drinks, and neither Sharp nor I could bear to be rude by refusing. Even the dancing girls offered us their favors, but since we each had special women waiting in Durango, no enticement could lure us away from the free drinks.

At one point, Sharp looked at me with bleary eyes.

"See that blond over there?" he asked.

When I nodded, he said, "Her sittin' alone is proof I'm in love."

Chapter 47

ugly cuss

The following morning, I woke late. Although my pocket watch read nearly noon, I still beat Sharp down for breakfast by over an hour. Both of us kept conversation to a minimum to spare our throbbing heads the task of thinking around the pain. I chewed carefully because my teeth ached. The only thing I consumed with relish was hot coffee.

By mid-afternoon we felt better, so we went over to check on McAllen. He was awake, but still flat on his back.

As we came around the screen, he said. "Where have you boys been?"

"Ice cream parlor," Sharp quipped.

"Ice cream? For damn sake, I'm dyin' and you're gallivantin' around havin' a good time."

He tried to move to see us better but collapsed back on his pillow and groaned. "Damn that hurts." He threw Sharp a nasty glance. "Doc won't give me anything for the pain. Says you threatened to shoot him if he did. What the hell is that about? You enjoy seein' me hurtin'?"

"Not until this moment," Sharp said.

He meant the comment in jest, but his voice

sounded humorless. Sharp's alcohol-addled mind probably throbbed more than mine, so to distract everyone, I told McAllen about Law and his recent demise. The doctor had already told him, but I embellished a little, telling the story as I intended to write it up in my new novel. McAllen seemed pleased, either by my skill at storytelling or the fact that Law had taken up residence at the undertaker's shack.

He smiled wanly, then once again turned cantankerous.

"My chest hurts like hell. My pride hurts more," McAllen said. "I can't believe I let that straitlaced little twit shoot me." He tried to look up enough to see me standing at the head of his bed. "The doc tells me you shot the son of a bitch in the balls. Bled to death, he says." After I nodded, McAllen added, "Much obliged."

I realized that I had never talked with McAllen about the aftermath of the Phelps shooting. That fight seemed such a long time ago.

"I wish I could say I gave him a nasty death for you, but from the floor, I had no other target."

"Obliged just the same." He closed his eyes. "I'm gettin' old. Guess I'm not movin' that fast anymore. That bastard plugged me right in the middle, but you got out of the way."

"Shot you first, so I had time to duck." I smiled now. "I'm obliged to you for being such a son of a bitch that he wanted to put the first slug in you."

McAllen started to laugh but stifled it immediately. "Damn. Can't lift my head." He used a thumb to point beyond the curtain. "That stupid doctor nearly drowned me pourin' whiskey down my throat. Jeff, why'd you tell him not to give me laudanum?"

"Hell, for the life of me, I can't remember."

"Whiskey don't deaden the pain; it just makes me care less about it. Next time you're shot, maybe I'll just stand on the wound."

"I was mistaken. You're so ornery, you *should* be knocked out until yer ready to visit the undertaker."

"I ain't dyin'." He balled his fist and made a slight punch at the bedding. "I just feel stupid . . . and my chest hurts like the dickens." For a moment he said nothing, just breathed shallow and slow. "You were right, Jeff. I already crave the stuff, and I was only on it for a day or so. Hell, the pain serves me right for being so damn slow."

Sharp chuckled. "You know, Joseph, even in yer best days, ya were never faster than a bullet."

"Someone tried that on me once before. Grabbed his wrist and twisted it away before he could shoot me." McAllen made a slight noise that could have been a stifled laugh. "Come to think of it, he may have fired, but quick as a bunny, I twisted out of the way of that flying bullet."

309

"I stand corrected," Sharp said.

McAllen rewarded us with one of his closed-lip smiles.

Sharp picked up a whiskey bottle and held it up so McAllen could see it. When he gave an affirmative nod, we spent the next ten minutes dribbling the dark fluid into his mouth. Finally, McAllen lifted his left hand to signal he'd had enough. He seemed more content, but I wasn't sure if it was the whiskey or our patient attentiveness.

The doctor came in and listened to McAllen's chest. When he finished, he said, "You are one hell of a tough hombre. Your lungs are clear and your heart sounds fine. I know it hurts, but you'll be fine."

"Full use of his arm?" I blurted, regretting my question immediately.

"That's to be determined, but I'm optimistic. The muscle will heal. It depends on the tendons. Right now, if I were to lift his arm to test his mobility, the pain would be excruciating."

Sharp took the bait. "Hell, he's a tough hombre. Go ahead, doc."

"We'll give it a few days," the doctor answered with a chuckle.

After the doctor left, McAllen asked, "What do Maggie and her ma know?"

"Nothing. I never sent a telegram." Realizing my error, I added weakly, "Damn, I'm sorry."

McAllen again tried to lift his head. "Steve, that's stupid. There's been two gunfights up here. Someone has already wired Durango about them. Probably stories in all the newspapers. Go. Send a telegram. Tell them I'm slightly wounded, recovering fine. We'll be back in a few days." When I hesitated, he murmured, "Go," and let his head fall back against the pillow.

When I returned from sending the telegram, McAllen had fallen asleep, and the doctor shooed us out. After the previous night's revels, we didn't feel like drinking, so we took a walk to build an appetite for supper.

At the end of town, we started to turn around at the new train station. Sharp took my elbow and nodded toward the station. "Ya know, we both don't have to wait for Joseph to get well enough to travel. One of us could go down an' reassure the womenfolk."

"Getting lonely for Nora?" I asked.

"I was thinkin' ya should go. Stay overnight an' return the next day."

I thought about it. "I'll go tomorrow if Joseph looks better."

"Hell, go tonight. Tomorrow he'll still look like an ugly cuss."

Chapter 48

son of a gun

On the train to Durango, I suddenly had an urge to work on my novel. I needed to get the events of the last few days written down while they were fresh in my memory. The narrow-gauge train swayed around bend after bend, making my attempt to write fitful. I almost put my notebook away, but excitement kept me writing. My notations would need to be rewritten for clarity, but at least I got the major ideas down on paper. I didn't try to write a narrative, only notes to jog my memory later. I usually avoided writing about my escapades close to their occurrence, because I needed time to gain perspective about what had happened. I couldn't blend actual events into other aspects of the story without having the bigger picture in mind, and I didn't want choppy accounts of disjointed scenes. Once I had my notes down, I started writing about Hugo Kelly and New York City. That adventure had happened months ago, and I had already had an outline of a surrounding tale of western versus eastern ethos.

When I got to town, I rushed to the hotel, but a clerk said Nora was at my house. Oh, oh, that didn't bode well. It wasn't a good idea for the women to feed off each other's worries. Sharp had been right to send me down right away. Someone needed to reassure them in person.

When I approached my house, two Pinkertons stepped out into the street to impede my progress. They recognized me and waved me forward, and without a word, disappeared off the street. I peered through the shattered wood of the shot-up outhouse across the street and spied a third guard. After I reassured the women, I would need to find Lawson and terminate their services.

When I stepped through my front door, both women sat in the parlor with their heads bent together. Virginia leaped out of her chair and rushed over to hug and kiss me. Nora looked anxious, so I quickly assured her that Sharp was completely unharmed and cantankerous as ever. She showed immediate relief. I explained that McAllen had been shot but downplayed the severity, assuring them that he would recover.

"Where's Jeff?" Nora asked.

"Keeping an eye on Joseph. Making sure he doesn't climb onto a horse and ride to his ranch."

Nora and Virginia started discussing taking the train up to tend to him, but I said he had good care and would be taking the train down in a few days anyway. I explained that he couldn't travel immediately because the train would toss him to and fro with little warning.

"He'll be here soon enough," I said, shaking my head. "The man's stubborn as hell."

"Indeed," Nora said. "As are others in our party."

"What does that mean?" I asked.

Virginia said, "We need to see the two of you together."

Her tone brooked no argument.

"Me and Jeff? Together? For what reason?"

Virginia answered. "If you both intend to stand by your proposals, we want to set a date. Soon. A dual wedding."

"Proposals? Plural?" I looked at Nora. "Did Jeff propose?"

"On the trail . . . after he rescued me," Nora said.

"That son of a gun. He never told me." I shook my head smiling. "In that case, set the date. The sooner the better. On second thought, give Joseph two weeks or so to fully recover, but other than that, we're ready." I took Virginia's hands in mine and stepped slightly away from her so I could see her face clearly. "We sold everything to Big Mike Fletcher. Nothing has a hold on us."

Nora answered from the settee. "We can rectify that in a jiffy."

Chapter 49

simple, yet perfect

The wedding ceremony took place three weeks later alongside the creek at McAllen's ranch. The sky was clear, the temperature crisp. Winter felt close enough to touch. A nip in the air was far better than sweltering heat, especially since we men were dressed in our finest wool suits, and the women sported dresses with more complicated underthings than a Southern belle wore to a ball.

Maggie's stepfather officiated. Guests included his wife, Maggie, and McAllen. The only other person present was a photographer we hired to take pictures after the ceremony. He carried so much paraphernalia, I was surprised he could get it all to the ranch in a single buckboard. Since he was already there, McAllen wanted photographs of his house, barn, and corral. We got this out of the way before the ceremony, and McAllen fussed over the framing of the shots as if they were pictures of his children. Speaking of which, he also insisted on a portrait of Maggie looking like a pretty young woman instead of a tomboy. She eventually relented, but I suspected she would rather have been photographed with her horse.

McAllen had healed enough to do light work, and it appeared that he would soon have full use of his right arm and hand. With the loss of Tom and Mark, and with McAllen's impairment, the ranch house remained far from finished, but we had put in a few hard days' work to fill and tighten exposures to the outside. Our departure wouldn't leave McAllen out in the cold. Despite our protestations, he refused to allow us to hire someone to help him. At this point, he wanted to finish the house on his own. That didn't worry us, because no structural work remained. McAllen didn't know how to build things, but he surely was capable of a little nailing and painting.

The double wedding was simple, yet perfect. The reverend did a fine job of officiating. The burbling creek sounded far more soothing than organ music, and Sharon had planted mums and pansies around the site where the ceremony would be conducted. I had wondered about Sharon traipsing out here alone to do the planting, but her relationship with McAllen remained brittle. I presumed he had no problem resisting the temptation to make an advance.

Jeff and Nora picked New Orleans for their honeymoon, while Virginia and I were headed in the opposite direction. I wanted to fulfill a lifelong dream to visit San Diego, and Virginia couldn't have been more excited about the prospect. We would see the Pacific Ocean and one of the best natural harbors in the world. No train traveled to San Diego, so we would journey by horsepower. We had discussed horseback, buggies, and buckboards. Every option had its advantages and disadvantages. Buggies were too fragile for a long trip, buckboards uncomfortable, and we couldn't carry a comfortable bedroll on horseback. Virginia thought we had decided on a buckboard with horses tethered behind for riding alongside on occasion. She had insisted that this arrangement provided the best solution. I had a different idea.

After the ceremony, we gathered around a long table made from boards nailed to sawhorses. I had bought tablecloths, napkins, seat pillows, and vases for dried flowers, and Sharp had purchased plates and flatware. We would leave everything for McAllen as a housewarming gift. Virginia and Nora had spent days in our kitchen cooking food that could easily be prepared and served after the reverend had finished bestowing the vows.

As I ate a piece of fried chicken, I heard Nora say, "Jeff and I aren't leaving until Tuesday. Will you be around?"

Before Virginia could respond, I said, "No. We'll leave directly from here . . . in a couple of hours."

I enjoyed the startled look on Virginia's face.

"What?" Virginia exclaimed. "We didn't discuss this."

"No, we didn't. It's your wedding present."

"Our things are in town."

"Someone will deliver them in a bit," I said. "Along with our transportation."

She looked at the bleak landscape to the west. "You want us to spend our wedding night on the plains?"

"We'll be comfortable," I said cryptically.

She tilted her head and watched me wipe chicken from my mouth and chin. "You have something planned," she said.

"I do."

"You already said that. Tell me something new."

"After our meal," I said, pretending to be preoccupied with another piece of chicken.

"I'm not an expert on marriage," McAllen said, "but this surprise better be damn good. Your bride will remember it forever, either with fondness or . . . she'll tell the world how you ruined her wedding day."

McAllen's ex-wife said, "You're right, you're not an expert."

"That's not fair, Ma," Maggie said. "Pa didn't leave you."

"He didn't start the divorce, but he left me all the time," she said in a snit.

"Hold it right there," McAllen said. "No more talk like that. Today is our friends' wedding day."

"You're right," Maggie's mother said. She looked all of us in the eye. "I apologize."

Maggie got the conversation on a better note. "When can we see this surprise, Uncle Steve?"

I was a bit too pleased with myself. "Not long, but right now we have fried chicken, potato salad, applesauce, beer, pie, and who knows what else?" I raised my mug. "To both happy couples."

Everyone happily drank a beer toast, including Maggie.

Chapter 50

the handsome prince

For a party of only eight, we had become boisterous. Sharp was at his storytelling best, entertaining the table with hilarious stories, mostly about his own foibles. Despite McAllen often being the butt of jokes, he laughed along with the rest of us. I was hoping the day would never end, when the reverend called out that something was kicking up a lot of dust and moving fast in our direction. Peace takes a while to settle in, and I saw McAllen and Sharp glance around for weapons. Then I noticed them both remember that our enemies were in no condition to harm us. They simultaneously shot me a questioning look. I smiled and nodded to show they had nothing to worry about.

Everyone became quiet and watched the apparition charging toward us.

"That's a stagecoach!" Sharp exclaimed.

"You ought to know," I said. "If memory serves, you drove one in your youth . . . eons ago, I believe."

"Steve, you rented a stagecoach?" Virginia asked.

"Bought one . . . but I merely rented the teamsters who will drive it to San Diego."

"We have drivers?"

"Of course. I want to spend my time with you."

She beamed. "Well . . . I don't know what to say."

"Six horses," Sharp said. "That's a regular stage."

"Not quite," I said. "I made a few changes."

As the stage thundered toward the ranch house, I stood and signaled for the driver to slow down. We had finished eating, but food remained on the table. Besides, I didn't think the women would appreciate their wedding dresses getting dusty. The driver immediately pulled up with a great show of force and then proceeded to slowly walk the horses to the front of the house.

Everybody sprinted to the stage to look inside. I put one arm across the door to block access and used my other hand to pull Virginia forward.

"Ladies first," I said.

When she was in position, I opened the door with a flourish. Her gasp told me that I had achieved my goal.

The interior had been reupholstered in tan sailcloth, with additional cushioning on the seats. Tied-back, heavy red curtains could be dropped across the windows for privacy. The usual rear bench had extra padding, but the front bench had been replaced with two cabinets: one across the floor and another attached to the roof. I invited Virginia inside and sat beside her. I opened the upper cabinet and showed her bottles of fine wine, whiskey, and champagne. The cabinet also held bins filled with nuts, crackers, cheese, candy, and heartier fare in case we decided to eat lunch on the move. There were books, canteens of water, washcloths, and other paraphernalia one might want handy on a long trip. I told her foodstuffs and cooking utensils were stored in back and on the roof. I asked her to stand away from the rear bench and then lifted the seat to display our neatly folded clothes. Next I asked her to step out. When we both had exited the coach, I lifted the lid on the front floor cabinet, extending a folding contraption that joined with the rear bench. After I had finished arranging some cushions hidden within the cabinet, a comfortable bed extended across the entire interior.

"What do you think?" I asked.

"Wonderful. I never heard of such a thing." She kissed me. "This is better than a compartment on a train."

"Not really. I'm afraid this rocks more than a train on steady tracks, but we'll be comfortable enough."

We backed away to let the remainder of the wedding party examine the stagecoach. Appreciative whistles and exclamations made me feel good. I had actually worked on this for over a month, well before the events in Silverton. In fact, I had bought the stagecoach as soon as we'd decided on a San Diego honeymoon. As our friends inspected the coach, I introduced Virginia to our drivers. I had interviewed dozens of men before picking these two. They were capable teamsters, experienced at fixing wheels and caring for horses, and between the two of them, they could mend most things that might break in the middle of nowhere. As a test, I had them hunt game and prepare meals. Both were good cooks. As a precaution, I verified that they were forthright, honest men with good references. I didn't fear going into the wilderness with these men and my bride.

"This is a huge surprise," Virginia said.

"I have one more," I said.

"No, Steve, this is enough."

"The next surprise didn't cost me a penny." I felt myself grinning.

I waved Sharp over. "Jeff, we're going to stop in Arizona for a few days. Any guess where?"

"The Grand Canyon. Damn. Steve, if ya hadn't removed the front seat, me an' Nora would join ya."

"I've heard about the Grand Canyon," Virginia said. "It's supposed to be huge."

"Big ain't nothin'. I've seen big before," Sharp said. "It's beautiful, maybe the most beautiful spot on earth. Steve an' I were there a while back. We almost stayed forever."

"Should have," I said. "Then you wouldn't have got yourself nearly hanged."

"Hell, I knew ya'd get me off." He laughed "Never had a worry. But darlin', you're gonna love the canyon. Just don't let the snakes bite. They got some mean creatures in that territory."

I pointed at our stagecoach. "We'll stay high and safe."

"I'm jealous. Love to show the canyon to first-timers. Best place in the wilderness, but . . ." He looked at Nora. "New Orleans is still my favorite city. Best food in America, fine hotels, and plenty of danc—" Sharp shook his head. "Damn, almost said dancin' girls." He grabbed Nora and gave her a big kiss. "Got no use for 'em now."

"You better not," Nora said.

I looked up at the sky. "Virginia, it's getting late. We need to put a few hours on the road before sunset. You ready?"

"Couldn't be readier. Let's start a new adventure."

"Let's just say, start a new life. I need a break from adventures."

Everyone laughed as if I had said something amusing. We said goodbyes all around and climbed into our carriage. When I heard the snap of the whip and felt the rock of the coach as it headed into the sunset, I pulled Virginia close, and we kissed slowly and passionately, as if we had nothing but time.

Virginia said, "I feel like Cinderella."

"Then I must be the handsome prince."

Thank you for reading *Crossing the Animas*. On the next page is a complimentary short story, first published in *Wanted II: A Western Story Collection*. The story, *Relentless,* takes place along the southern California coast after Steve and Virginia move to San Diego.

Again, thanks for reading. If you enjoyed *Crossing the Animas*, please write a review, otherwise mum's the word.

To be notified when I have a new book, please join my mailing list by sending me a note at jimbest@jamesdbest.com.

You can also receive email updates from my blog at http://jamesdbest.blogspot.com by leaving your email address in the Follow by Email box. Thanks again.

The following short story first appeared in
Wanted II: A Western Story Collection

Relentless
A Steve Dancy Tale

By James D. Best

Gray sky and gray water made it difficult to discern a horizon. The windless morning raised nary a ripple on the surface of the Pacific Ocean. As I rode my horse along a small rise above a sandy beach, even the small waves seemed listless. *Pacífico* means peaceful in Spanish, and the ocean lived up to its name on this bright, clear morning.

I had risen at daybreak, and after a couple of cups of coffee, saddled my horse, Liberty, and started riding north along the trail called El Camino Real. Walking Liberty at a leisurely pace, I nibbled day-old biscuits and even older bacon. I was content.

Content, but not inattentive. This part of California was known for angry banditos who loved to rob the gringos they believed had stolen their country. I had some empathy for them. The United States had used the Mexican-American War to acquire territory, but that didn't mean I wanted to be an object of their revenge. California was safer than the rest of the frontier, but *pandillas* rustled cattle, counterfeited American currency, and robbed travelers. I enjoyed the ocean in the early morning light but kept a watchful eye on the rolling hills.

The trail was well-worn and clearly marked with stone cairns. Nightly accommodations were readily available in the settlements that had developed around Catholic missions built a day's ride apart. I had spent the night at San Luis Rey de Francía, and with my early start, had plenty of time to reach San Juan Capistrano before nightfall.

Growing up privileged in New York City, I had always wanted to explore the coast that stretched along the edge of the western frontier. I had taken my bride to San Diego for a honeymoon, and we had remained in a seaside cottage for three months. Now I wanted to buy property inside the bay formed by Point Loma. After my father had died, I had sold his gun shop and myriad other interests to invest in railroads, which had done spectacularly well. I now had the wherewithal to develop a commercial harbor that could compete with San Francisco.

California began at Point Loma. When Juan Rodríguez Cabrillo docked on the east coast of a long peninsula in 1542, he named it La Punta de la Loma de San Diego and declared the bay an exceptional port, a port I believed could supply the entire Southwest with products from around the world.

San Diego remained primitive in 1881. A permanent European settlement had been established a little over one hundred years previously, but New Town, deeper in the bay, had been around only a dozen years. New Town, and the potential for dredging the bay, opened the entire inlet to development, which made North Island, situated in the middle of the bay, an invaluable property. Transportation was my preferred investment, and a massive harbor at the southwest corner of the United States looked like a clear winner. The southern tip of the peninsula had already been set aside for the military, but private land still existed further inside the bay. I wanted to own a good piece of North Island, which was perfectly situated for docking dozens of ships.

I had corresponded with a San Francisco attorney named Archibald C. Peachy, who, together with the estate of William Henry Aspinwall, owned North Island. In the settlement of a dispute over a California land grant, Peachy had somehow wrangled ownership of Rancho San Diego for himself and Aspinwall, his New York moneyed partner. Evidently, not all California banditos used guns. Aspinwall had since died, but his interest in North Island remained within his estate. My family had done numerous business deals with the Aspinwalls, so my mother in New

York could handle the East Coast negotiations.

After forwarding letters of recommendation from New York and considerable correspondence, Peachy agreed to meet me in Los Angeles, where he had other business. I found this arrangement convenient, because railroads had not yet reached San Diego; thus, my solitary ride up the southern California coastline.

I rode easy and enjoyed the tranquil sea. I was fascinated by porpoises and whales, especially the way they leaped out of the water. I had seen whales off New England, but the slick and graceful porpoises were a new phenomenon. They swam in packs and appeared to effortlessly fly out of the water, twist, and dive back in with barely a ripple. I had no idea what they would do if they encountered a human, but there was slim chance that would happen with me, because I rarely ventured into the sea above my waist. Still, I kept my eyes open in the hopes of catching these animals' playful antics.

deep hatred

A motion behind a hillock caught my eye. After riding for several hours, I had been lollygagging without a care in the world.

Now I had a care.

I brought Liberty to a stop. I saw no more movement, but examining the landscape, I realized it was an ideal spot for an ambush. The terrain had gradually risen until a cliff sat between me and the beach below, and a berm extended out from the coastal hills, narrowing the trail to only twenty feet. Racing through the pinch point probably wouldn't work. If bandits lurked behind the berm, I would risk being driven over a steep cliff that fell to a rocky shoreline.

Maybe I was wrong. Maybe I hadn't seen anything.

I knew better. I hadn't survived on the frontier for the last three years by relying on wishful thinking. Trial by fire and good advice from friends had gotten me through some tough situations. In fact, one of the lessons I had learned was to accept a situation as it presents itself. Don't assume the intentions of bad men can be mitigated by gentleness. When threatened, expect that your assailant means you harm and react immediately.

How should I react? I could fight. I could submit. Or I could retreat. Or perhaps even find a way to go around. I inspected the terrain more carefully. The inland hills weren't impassable, but a determined pursuer could easily get in front of me and have no problem hiding in a fold of the undulating knolls. I carried money in multiple places on my person and my horse so I wouldn't look overly flush when I paid for something. Perhaps If I turned over one of my stashes, the bandits would let me ride on. Unlikely. They would probably search me and take every cent. If they took all my money, would they let me go? Doubtful. Rumors claimed that the Mexican banditos harbored deep hatred for gringos. In the middle of nowhere, their first impulse would not be mercy. A fight with an unknown force appeared foolhardy. That left one obvious choice: pull back and wait for other travelers to come along.

This was not a time for guile. They had seen me, and because of my dalliance, they knew I had seen them. I reined around and spurred Liberty to a gallop. I rode at speed for about ten minutes, but no one pursued, so I slackened the pace to a trot. After another ten minutes, I dismounted and walked my horse. Should I keep heading south until I ran into someone or wait for other parties to come upon me? A wide swale ahead made up my mind. I could set up camp in the recess, where I would be hard to spot but could see anyone who traveled along the trail. I led Liberty up the incline, pleased with my cleverness.

ven aquí

I didn't wait long. In under an hour, four riders came along. I came out from hiding and approached cautiously with a friendly wave. I didn't want to be shot for being mistaken for a desperado. They seemed unconcerned with my appearance, greeting me with hearty hellos. All four were dressed as ranch hands and rode good mounts.

When I got close enough not to shout, I said, "Hello, friends." I pointed. "I believe there may be robbers around a berm further up the trail. Almost certain I saw movement, and no one called out a greeting."

The men looked unconcerned. "I think you wrong, señor. Many of my *banda* wait around the corner, but we . . . we're here . . . right in front of you." He laughed. "This day not yours, amigo."

My first thought was that these were clever men. Besides wearing American rancher garb, they had not brought enough men to make me wary. They also appeared jocular rather than intimidating. Perhaps they would lighten my load by one of my stashes of money, and I could be on my way.

The leader walked his horse a step closer to mine. "Step off your horse and strip naked."

Or perhaps not.

I didn't move.

He yelled, "Hombres, *ven aquí!*" Then to me, "Get down. Take off your clothes, amigo. Leave your weapons. Leave your horse. Leave your boots. Walk away." He confidently rested both hands on his saddle horn. "All you have is mine. Do it now, señor, and you will not be harmed."

Six or seven more men stormed in a gallop out

from behind a hill, whooping with glee. They were also dressed as American ranchers. No sombreros, no bandoleros, no serapes. They evidently intended to add my clothing to their wardrobe. Clever disguise for Mexican highwaymen.

What I did next, I never thought about. Pure instinct. When the charging riders arrived, their horses kicked up dust as they twirled or reared up slightly. I drew my pistol and shot the talkative one in the center of his chest as I spurred my horse past the banditos, then raced away as fast as Liberty could carry me. After I cleared a knoll, I jerked my reins to take me behind a hill that would shield me from flying bullets.

I heard gunfire. Lots of it. What the hell? I moved fast. I didn't give them time to respond. I glanced back but saw no one in pursuit. They were shooting at my image that had already disappeared around a corner. Good. Let them waste ammunition. I bent low against Liberty's neck and urged him up the slight incline that would take me into the hills and to safety.

last stand?

The gunfire grew loud. Taking another peek over my shoulder, I saw that they had recovered their wits and rode after me, blasting away with six-shooters. I had about a fifty-yard head start, a challenging pistol shot when on solid ground, but foolish from a galloping horse. Shooting from horseback took practice. A good cavalryman developed a knack for aiming and shooting with the rhythm of his horse's gait, but it was generally not within a highwayman's expertise.

Something hit me in the butt. Reaching behind, I passed my hand across my rear. No blood. What was that? Reaching back again, I felt a ragged tear in my saddle cantle. I immediately spurred Liberty to greater speed. These vaqueros were either lucky or damn good at shooting from horseback. I needed to put more distance between us.

Liberty was a steadfast runner, possessing a good balance between endurance and speed. With luck, the vaqueros' mounts were lesser animals. In my experience, outlawing seldom generated enough income to buy decent horse-flesh. Except. They stole their horses, like they had tried to steal mine. Certainly, a few came from good stock. Another glance showed that we had increased our lead, but I knew we couldn't outrun them forever—not all of them. Eventually, a few would get close enough to put a bullet in more than my saddle. I examined the terrain ahead. If I could find a rock outcropping, I could unsheathe my rifle and possibly drive them away. To ward them off, I needed to make the price too high for them to continue their chase.

I saw something that would have to do. The cluster of rocks was high enough to shelter me if I lay on the ground, but not tall enough to stand or kneel behind . . . or shield Liberty. Since the outcropping was on an upslope, my legs also might be exposed. As I drew closer, I saw that the rocks were even smaller than I had thought. I spotted something better. At the crest of the hillock we were climbing, a large mound protruding against the skyline looked big enough to conceal Liberty. Would this be our last stand? I immediately regretted the thought. I had been to Little Bighorn, and the landscape looked far too similar for comfort. I desperately wanted a different outcome.

I wheeled around the knoll and flew out of the saddle, pulling out my rifle as I dismounted. I scrambled behind the mound on my elbows and knees until I could peer down at my pursuers. The bandits surprised me. Instead of riding hell-bent after me, they had pulled up just out of rifle range. These men were smart, at least in the art of running a prey to ground. I had hoped to pick off one or two so they would retreat, but they refused to accommodate me. Damn.

I noticed that I was breathing hard. I had no right to complain—Liberty had done most of the work and was breathing even harder. But I needed to get control of my breathing before shooting. The banditos stood not quite beyond range, but far enough away to make the shot difficult. I waited until I could breathe easy, then took a bead on the pack of desperadoes. Just before I could get off a shot, they started to scatter side to side. I threw one futile bullet in their direction, but none fell off his horse. A miss, but I had sent a message that I intended to fight, one that might give them pause about climbing the incline.

I held my fire and watched. What were they doing? Then I saw that they were forming a wide single line. Damn. Another smart move. If they bunched up, I could get lucky, but spreading out with six feet between them lowered my odds of taking down more than one.

Why did they think I was worth the trouble? Did my possessions warrant risking their lives? I had a fine-looking horse, worn but expensive tack, durable clothes, costly hat and boots, but an unknown amount of money or gold coin. They knew I was fast and lethal with a handgun, as evidenced by their dead compatriot. My rifle shot signaled that I would continue to fight. I shook my head. They should go away.

They didn't go away. The far extremes of the line started a slow march toward my position. The riders formed an arc, with every target approximately equal distance. I tried to figure out who the remaining leaders were, but they were all dressed alike, and no one gave obvious orders. Their formation told me that these men had military experience, or at least had served in a highly regimented band of outlaws. I was in trouble.

These were experienced robbers who knew better than to have their leaders ride in the center of the line. I looked behind me. The vaqueros were downhill, and by staying directly behind the knoll, I would be hidden from their view for a hundred feet or so. That would extend my head start. But first I had to slow them down. I picked a rider to the left of center. I rested my rifle barrel on the hilltop, aimed carefully, and squeezed. He fell. I immediately fired three more times in a broad pattern, then turned, grabbed Liberty by the reins, and pulled him after me as I walked away from my pursuers.

I walked because I would come into view sooner mounted. If I heard warlike shouts, I'd turn around and return to my knoll and fight from cover; otherwise, I'd put as much distance as I could between them and me. I heard shots and glanced back. The hill exploded with dirt and debris. The accuracy of the shots told me they had slowed or halted their march to send a volley at the knoll. How far could I travel before an over-shot put a nasty hole in my head? Due to the deteriorating arc of a bullet's flight, it would be prior to their seeing me. I told myself to hell with it and quickened my pace.

committed

A moment later, a bullet dug up dirt ahead of me. The first of the bandits had rounded the knoll. Sorry, Liberty, your rest is over. I swung into the saddle and spurred him up the hill. Without hesitation, he leaped forward. Glancing back, I saw his tail swish side to side as we raced to safety. I hoped it could brush away bullets as effectively as flies. We crested a ridgeline, and I immediately turned north in the direction of San Juan Capistrano. I estimated that the mission was a four-hour ride away . . . if I could ride as the crow flies. That would never happen. The bandits would herd me inland, away from any fellow travelers who might lend a hand.

I had never taken the time to count the band but had originally estimated a dozen or more. Now, two less rode after me. I needed to get away or whittle their numbers down further. Liberty felt strong and ran at a steady pace, with no indication of tiring. That couldn't last. Again, arithmetic said we could not outrun all of our pursuers. He would have to outlast ten or more horses, one or two of which might be his match. Since I had planned on being gone for over a week, he also carried a hefty load behind the saddle. Could I untie the saddlebags on the run? It would not only lighten Liberty's load, but several of the bandits might stop to inspect their bounty. Not here. I wanted an open space where they would see me drop the bags. They might even present a target as they dismounted to pick them up.

I spotted a flat area in front of me, with low brush and a few scrub oaks. Reaching behind my saddle, I untied the bag flaps and fumbled around until I found the boxes of ammunition I always carried. With difficulty, I shoved the outsized boxes into my overly large shirt pockets. Next, I untied the latigos that attached the bags to my saddle. With the bags riding free, I pulled the reins and jumped off before Liberty came to a complete stop. In one smooth motion, I released the saddlebag flank cinch, threw them to the ground, and jumped back into the saddle. I was at full gallop without drawing a single shot.

When I saw two of the bandits dismount to go after the bags, I pulled around a windswept oak and flew out of the saddle, rifle in hand. The remainder of the band kept after me, so I didn't have much time. I leaned against the tree trunk to steady myself and took three quick shots at the relatively stationary men on the ground. One fell, and the other grabbed his arm as he screamed obscenities. At least, I assumed they were obscenities. My rudimentary Spanish didn't include the more colorful aspects of the language. I leaped back into the saddle and spurred Liberty away from the incoming bullets sprayed around me by the men in pursuit.

The mounted bandits had gained too much ground, and I wondered if I had made a fatal mistake by stopping to throw off the saddlebags and again to shoot at the bandits picking them up.

I wasn't sure if the lightened load made a difference, but Liberty gradually pulled away from the band. I kept looking ahead for a place where I could have an advantage. My hope was a swale that narrowed enough so that they could pursue only in single file. Nothing ahead. I looked back, and although they were still chasing me, the bandits fell further behind. Or maybe *fell* was the wrong word. I suddenly felt like they were herding me. They let me get a lead because they knew what lay ahead. What kind of trouble was I riding into?

More bandits! That must be the answer. They were pushing me up this hill because compatriots waited over the crest. Perhaps their camp lay ahead. They allowed Liberty to pull away as long as I rode in the direction they wanted. I searched left and right, looking for an escape. None. I was committed to going forward.

pang of guilt

As I hit the crest, I saw what they were driving me toward. Nothing. A flat plain that extended north and south as far as the eye could see, with a steep incline to the east. The brown, dried-out grass rose only about a foot, and I couldn't see a single scrub oak. No cover. Lots of room to run, but nowhere to hide. Damn it, they had saved their horses for the real contest.

I felt doomed but turned Liberty north toward San Juan Capistrano. It made no sense to lumber up the steepening incline, so I would head in the direction of the closest mission. I looked back. The bandits had started to lash their horses with their saddle strings, yelping like hunting dogs that had finally treed a fox. Sooner or later, one or more of the bandits would run me down. I needed a gully . . . or a tree . . . or a mound. Anything to hide behind. Anything.

I spotted a dry creek bed. Not much, but it would have to do. My problem was Liberty. I could lay in the shallow gully, but it was not deep enough to provide cover for my horse. Would they shoot him? Cavalry horses were trained to lie down when a dismounted rider pulled the reins down and to the side. I had never practiced this maneuver with Liberty, but I had forced him at times to lie down. I leaped out of the saddle, throwing my rifle to the position I intended to shoot from, and tugged Liberty toward the ground. He didn't resist. I slid over to the upslope of the gully, picked up my rifle, and moved sideways so Liberty wouldn't be directly behind me. I took aim. They were coming fast and riding low, their heads shielded by their horses' necks. I had a split-second pang of guilt . . . then shot the horses.

The first horse stumbled and fell, throwing its rider over its head. Then another horse tripped on the first and went down as well. The second horse I shot caused all the other riders to whirl around and retreat. Now I took a bead on one of the tossed bandits as he moved shakily to his feet. He went down hard this time. The other two tossed riders kept their heads. They remained prone as they crawled backward, stopping on occasion to throw a few bullets in my direction. I took a single shot to hurry them along.

ambush

After what seemed like an hour, but was probably less than half that time, I wondered if I should climb back onto Liberty and ride away. The bandits had dropped below the crest of the hill they had chased me up, and I had seen no further sign of them. Had they left? I had now killed four and wounded another. That should make them reconsider. They had my saddlebags, which even empty were worth a week's wages. The clothing and books should fetch several dollars more. The bags also held five double-eagle gold coins worth one hundred dollars. They had no idea if I carried more money on my person. As far as they knew, my clothes and horse, plus maybe some pocket change, were my only remaining valuables.

Wishful thinking. Liberty, an obviously fine animal, would fetch a good price below the border. The men I had killed were probably friends or relatives. A grudge can induce men to do foolish things. Besides, these pursuers had shown no inclination to give up.

I thought. Just because they dropped below the crest several hundred yards back didn't mean they needed to return to this flat area from the same location. In fact, they wouldn't. I looked due west. I was about forty yards from the ridge. If they charged at me from that location, I could get off two or three shots before they overran this position. Or . . . they could ambush me. The gully curved enough so that I had cover from a sharpshooter lying perpendicular to me below the crest, but I doubted they could hit my head, because I was moving locations and didn't stay exposed for long periods. But I couldn't hit them either, and a couple of shooters from that location could easily pin me down while others charged me from another direction.

Damn. I had to get out of there.

I pulled Liberty to his feet, but instead of riding, I led him on foot in a northerly direction. I wouldn't mount until I saw pursuers. In the meantime, I wanted Liberty to get as much rest as possible. I heard a sharp yell in Spanish. As I suspected, they had someone keeping an eye on me. How long would it take for them to get after me? Not long. I saw the band down the plain emerge first, but two riders soon came up from almost the exact place I had guessed they would wait in ambush.

Another chase. This was getting tiresome.

Instead of mounting Liberty, I walked around behind him and used my saddle as a brace to lay my rifle against. These bandits had been savvy until now, but the two groups were separated by over a hundred yards. I couldn't resist shooting the two on ambush detail. I saw them recognize their error just as I fired. Five dead. The second rider turned back toward his compatriots and lashed his horse mercilessly. I took careful aim. Should I shoot a man in the back as he ran away? I could shoot the horse, but the animal meant me no harm. I shot the man. After all, the bandit had killing in his heart, and if I let him go now, he would return. Next time, the odds might not be in my favor. Besides, I told myself that attempting to assassinate me from behind cover didn't warrant mercy.

Six dead.

hounding my tail

I mounted Liberty and rode away at a leisurely pace. The band rode after me at a full gallop. Good. Let them fatigue their horses. I saw nothing but flatness ahead, so I drove over the edge of an embankment and headed back toward the trail running along the ocean. Perhaps this time I could get support from fellow travelers.

The band followed me back toward civilization. They came on stronger than ever, yelling what I assumed were profanities. For a moment, I wanted to dismount and fight it out. Kill every damn one of them. I hadn't asked for this. I didn't want to kill, but they insisted on hounding my tail with intent to murder me for a few hundred dollars' worth of gear and horseflesh. Damn it, anyway.

Reason prevailed. I had whittled their number down, but I still counted eight men in pursuit. Too many. I needed help . . . or a narrow path that would require them to approach in single file. I searched left and right. Then I abandoned the idea. I had a canteen of water, but my food had been in the saddlebags. If I hid in a narrow ravine, they would pin me down until hunger forced me to do something stupid. A narrow path would work only if I had an exit that wouldn't require me to pass by the bandits. That was too much to hope for. Better to concentrate on getting back to the trail and finding travelers willing to help.

I could see the ocean, but it looked to be over two miles away. Had I really come inland that far? Evidently. I looked back. The bandits were no longer gaining ground on me. Now they fell behind, not by intent, but because they had worn out their horses. I patted Liberty's neck and continued to ride at an unhurried pace. I smiled. I may not have beat them yet, but if my luck held, I would soon be rid of them.

It occurred to me that I would need to hire guards for the return trip. I wouldn't want to run into this band again without extra gun hands.

I checked behind once again. They had not closed the gap. When I faced front again, my mood instantly turned from pleased to frightened. Four riders approached, all with rifles braced against their legs, barrels pointed up. Riding abreast, these men wore Mexican garb and unpleasant smiles. If I had any further doubts, one of them waved a greeting to my pursuers. I was trapped in a pincer maneuver.

I pulled up. No obstacle prevented me from going left or right, but that would result in a simple horse race that I would eventually lose. Well, hell. I spurred Liberty, and we drove right at the four bandits directly ahead. I pulled my Colt and threw a shot low to spook the horses.

Their smirks went away as fast as my good mood had vanished. They hadn't expected a charge. Now I was close enough to aim at the men, not their hapless mounts. I waited a beat. Standing in the stirrups, leaning forward, I put a bullet in the man on the far right, then veered hard in his direction. Two of the bandits were trying to shoot their rifles one-handed. The third was shoving his rifle back in its sheath so he could use a handgun. A smarter play, so I shot him next. By then I was parallel to them, so I put my head down and urged Liberty to run for all he was worth. He was worth all my fortune. I heard shots, but none hit me or Liberty.

We had cleared their secondary force.

let them attack

The downhill slope to the sea allowed me to see all the way to shore. It looked to be over a mile, but Liberty was gliding down with ease. Damn, it felt good to be finally rid of those bastards. No more bandits ahead, and the ones behind appeared to have given up the chase. Then I got angry when I remembered they had taken my saddlebags. I had half a mind to go take them back, but that made no sense. I was free and clear and only ten minutes away from a well-traveled trail.

I slowed Liberty to a walk. He had earned a respite. Besides, I kept an eye on my rear and saw nothing of the bandits. After seven dead and one wounded, I guessed they had finally given up. Out of danger, I dreamed of revenge. I could hire a team of hard men and rid the trail of highwaymen. The thought gave me pleasure, but I knew I didn't want to get involved in a long-running feud.

I felt content until I saw something to the side that made me shiver. About a hundred yards north, riders were racing to get in front of me. I still walked Liberty, but these riders were galloping like there was no tomorrow. This was not over. Damn.

I pulled Liberty to a halt and dismounted. I stopped so I would have a steady shot at anyone riding toward me. If the bandits wanted to race up the hill in front of me, let them attack in the wide open. I'd wait right in this spot and allow Liberty to graze. I pulled my rifle from the sheath and shoved cartridges in the loading gate until it was full. I had an extended fifteen-round tube, so having enough cartridges would not be a problem. The problem would be not getting hit by one of their bullets before I killed them all. I also reloaded my pistol. If they got close enough, I could fire it quicker.

I cradled the rifle in my arms and stared down the slope at the bandits as they gathered at the bottom of the hill. There appeared to be nine. Where did the other one go? I suddenly became wary. Was this a distraction while a sharpshooter ambushed me? I discounted the possibility almost immediately. I was sure they would assume I would run, just like I had done all day. They'd not likely assume that I would stay in place and dare them to attack. At least, I hoped that was the case. A quick perusal of my surroundings showed no threats. In fact, the landscape provided no cover. More likely, the wounded man had died, stayed behind, or made his way back to camp to get help.

The bandits sat astride their horses, glaring at me, their animals pawing the ground and snorting. They wanted to come. They wanted to attack. They wanted to kill me.

Damn it, let them come.

slip right by them

They split up. Five went north, four south. They chose not to charge up an incline for a frontal attack. Instead, they intended to ambush me if I tried to return south to San Luis Rey de Francía or continue north to San Juan Capistrano. I hated to admit that this was the smart move. I was good with a rifle and could have brought down at least four before they got close enough to hit me from horseback. I only needed a little luck or a miscalculation on their part to come out on top.

Now, I was the one who had to make a smart decision. North or south? The odds dictated going south, but my meeting with Archibald Peachy lay to the north. I waited until the bandits disappeared before taking Liberty by the reins to walk north. I would continue my trip to Los Angeles. They would not get the satisfaction of driving me away from my destination.

I stayed on high ground. I had never traversed this terrain, and they probably knew it like the back of their hand. They'd guess I'd stay above the trail, so they'd probably set up their ambush in a spot above the coastal thoroughfare. Should I try again to find fellow travelers to help me? Yes. I decided to drop back down to the trail in a mile or so. With luck, they would have repositioned to intercept me inland, and I might slip right by them. In the meantime, I'd allow Liberty a good rest in case we needed to make another run for it.

incredible speed

When I returned to El Camino Real, I ran into no other travelers. People intent on completing the ride between missions would be further along in their journey. Because of my delays, it would be dusk or possibly even dark before I reached

San Juan Capistrano. I considered riding hard to catch up with travelers further down the road but wanted Liberty fresh in case of another run-in with the bandits.

The first hour was uneventful, and I started to think my luck had changed. Then I came upon a bend with trees clustered along what must have been a streambed in the wet season. If they wanted to ambush me, this spot would be perfect. The bend in the trail forced travelers to ride hundreds of feet parallel to the tree-lined shallow. I brought Liberty to a stop.

They were there. I knew it. They would never give up.

I could ride straight at them or try to bypass them on the inland side. Closer to the ocean wouldn't work, because the arroyo became wide where the winter stream plunged over the shoreline cliff. I examined the cliff. If I could find a way down, perhaps I could ride through the sand close by the water. I discarded the idea when I realized that I would present a perfect target for potshots from above. I stood in my stirrups but couldn't see anyone hiding ahead. That didn't mean they weren't there, only that I couldn't see a target.

It wasn't the rainy season. No rush of water carved the arroyo deeper. No matter where I looked, I could not see green. The grass and every shrub had been burnt brown by a relentless sun. I held a spit-moistened finger in the air. The wind blew from the ocean. I had a plan.

I dismounted and walked on Liberty's seaward side to the cliff, continuing along the ridge until I reached the arroyo. I pulled a tube of matches from my pocket and lit the dry grass. Then I backed away from the arroyo, keeping Liberty between me and the likely ambush site.

The fire grew fast, taking on a life of its own. I worried that it would consume the entire countryside. What would ever stop it? Were there homes in the way of the fire? I just wanted a small blaze to scare away the bandits, but this inferno moved with incredible speed. The intense heat surprised me. Despite being back from the fire, Liberty neighed as he struggled to get free of my grip.

Thankfully, the fire blew to the east and didn't jump the arroyo, but it did burn up the incline that led to some rolling hills in the distance. I couldn't see if the fire forced the bandits to run, because a smoke curtain made it impossible to see anything beyond the arroyo. Then I noticed something else. The fire subsided quickly after it burnt through the dry grass. In minutes, there was nothing left to burn. As the smoke blew inland, I saw riders scurrying away on the far side of the streambed.

I may have caused a bigger fire than I had intended, but I had accomplished my goal.

trapped

I waited for the sparks to wane so I could lead Liberty over to the other side. I waited too long. A shot rang out from behind. Then two. A quick glance confirmed that the brush fire had drawn the bandits who had headed south. Damn. I mounted Liberty and rode hard for a wooden bridge that crossed the arroyo. When I got to the other side, I dismounted and led Liberty down a steep slope to hide him under the bridge. Then I crawled up the embankment with my rifle. Now I was the one in the ambush position.

The bandits halted their progress to evaluate the situation. I took solace that they were not the smart ones. Otherwise, they wouldn't have thrown random shots that forewarned me. Perhaps they would come right at me. After a few minutes, I realized that they may not have been the smartest of the bandits, but they knew enough not to charge at a man shooting from cover. The thought triggered a glance behind me, but I couldn't see the rest of the band. Now the bullet made more sense. They had fired at me to signal to the rest of their band that they had returned.

I surveyed my position and decided to move to the other side of the bridge where the ravine narrowed so I could move quicker between the north and south banks of the streambed. I had no food and very little water, but plenty of ammunition. I wondered who had my saddlebags. I peeked at the band, but they remained too far away for me to see their gear clearly. Because of my fire, there were no shrubs or tall grass to obscure my head when I lifted it above the ridge. I visually examined the bridge, but it had withstood my fire and looked far too substantial to burn easily.

Suddenly, I heard something behind me. Sure enough, the other portion of the band had returned. They had me trapped.

escape plan

The two bands spread out wide, at least ten feet between each man. They approached slowly. Who leads these bandits? I spotted the man closest to the ocean yell and give hand signals. Others acknowledged his commands, confirming his leadership. My furthest shot. Why would men follow such a yellow dog?

The line from the south seemed to move faster, so I lay on that bank and took careful aim. I was just about to squeeze the trigger when they did something unexpected. They dismounted. Glancing behind, I saw that the other line must have already swung down from their horses, because they were all without riders. The fire had not burned the grass on the north side at all, and the bandits were concealed as they crawled toward me. The ones to the south were not so lucky. The scorched earth provided little cover.

If I stayed and fought, I would soon be dead. Not a desirable outcome. My only choice was to go east. If I followed the streambed west, I'd end up where the land dropped off to the ocean. No escape that way. Going uphill to the east, I would find many of the bandits bunched up below me. That escape route meant I had to leave Liberty under the bridge, because he was too tall to be hidden by the shallow depression, and my escape plan would be exposed.

I took my canteen from Liberty and hunched low to scramble up the incline, away from the coast.

kill them all

Once I had moved about a hundred yards, the streambed became too low to conceal me. I had expected this. I knew the water-eroded channel didn't provide escape, only a better fighting position.

I was now on foot, hunched down in a ditch, with relentless pursuers. I wanted to live, so I had no choice. I had to kill them all.

Tributary water flows had eroded the walls of the swale in places that might provide a position where I could hide from someone sneaking up the streambed. But for now, I wanted as smooth a surface as possible to lie against. I soon found a spot with clean slopes on either side, the walls close enough that I could swing from north to south with ease. I used a bush blackened by the fire to disguise my head peeking over the ledge. The bandits still crawled toward my old location, but now I lay nearly opposite the one furthest inland. This closest bandit thought I was still huddled far below, so he grew careless and failed to keep his head down.

With my first shot, I had the luxury of taking my time. I took aim at his head as he crawled high on his elbows. I squeezed. My bullet caused a plume of blood to spray the air. I quickly readjusted my aim, but everyone else had bent low to the ground. I flipped around to check on my assailants from the north. One idiot was running hunched over. I pulled two shots. Both struck him, but neither might have been fatal. Didn't matter. His injuries were severe enough that he no longer presented a threat. Again, the other bandits ducked so low, they had to be eating dirt for their noonday meal.

Now they realized I was far more inland than they had supposed. Those closest to the ocean on the north side stood and ran to the streambed. I snapped a shot and missed. Damn, I didn't have much time. Soon they would attack from three directions. The streambed meandered, so the bandits who scrambled into it could approach partway without being seen. They presented the greatest risk, but not at the moment. Yelling in Spanish, the leader, now safely concealed, gave orders at the top of his lungs. If I survived this attack, I would need to learn the local language. Checking the south from behind my blackened bush, I saw the remaining bandits moving away from the ocean and toward my position. This must have been what the leader had yelled out. Unfortunately for me, the bandits crawled with their heads in the dirt. I aimed at the movement anyway. Sooner or later, one of them would lift his head to make sure he was crawling in the right direction. Sooner. And uncomfortably close. I shot him before he finished raising his head. Now there were only two to the south.

I returned my attention to the north.

I finally made out one moving bandit. That meant three had made the run for the streambed. He kept low. I kept a bead on him, but he never accommodated me by lifting his head. I could wait until he got so close that hugging the ground wouldn't save him, but that would waste far too much time. Checking south, I saw that the two bandits had veered away from me. Killing two of their compatriots had made them cautious. Good.

If they kept to their current track, they would enter the streambed on the ocean side of me. That meant the attack would come from one direction . . . except for the lone bandit to the north. I needed to kill him so I could concentrate on the streambed.

I took another look. He crawled right at me . . . close enough to be on me in seconds. I swung my rifle around, hesitated an instant for the barrel to steady, and shot him in the forehead. No time to waste. I scurried up the streambed until I found a crevice deep enough to hide me. Laying my rifle aside, I checked my pistol load. Six bullets. Five killers. Hopefully, the two groups wouldn't join up and coordinate their attack.

quickness

I was a good marksman with a rifle, but quicker with a pistol. Growing up in my father's gun shop, I had practiced with pistols so much that I could fire faster than even a wary person could react. But I needed surprise, so I leaned back against the slope and used only my ears to tell me when they approached.

I didn't wait long. The men trudged heavily, so they must have assumed that I had raced further up the streambed. I wanted them right on top of me before I revealed myself. My sole strategy was quickness. I waited. I tried to breathe shallowly. I relaxed my muscles, especially in my gun hand. This was not a time to think. I needed to rely on instincts bred from hundreds of hours of target shooting.

I leaped up, keeping half my body shielded by the crevice. I fired three times. The first shot hit the lead attacker center chest, but he partially blocked the man behind. My next bullet put a hole into the second attacker's exposed leg. As he collapsed sideways, I shot my third bullet into his chest. Damn. These were the two who had been crawling toward me from the south. Where were the other three?

The leader had sent these two forward to draw fire while he held back. Coward. I hadn't wanted this fight, and killing repelled me, but this man deserved to die. Why would he lead men, men he had probably befriended, to attack me so relentlessly? I had proved capable of defending myself. He had my saddlebags and horse. How much money could he suppose I had on my person? In truth, I had a lot, but he had no way of knowing that. Unless. Unless that banker had forewarned him that I would be traveling El Camino Real with ten thousand dollars. How stupid of me. I had wanted to be ready to close a deal for North Island, but I should have made withdrawals from several banks over an extended period. Without conscious thought, I swept my hand across the thick money belt around my waist.

They weren't out for revenge, nor would they be satisfied with five twenty-dollar gold coins. They knew what I carried. And . . . they needed me dead to protect the banker's fraud. This had happened before. He probably pointed out any traveler who had made a large withdrawal.

That damn banker. He would rue the day I got out of this mess.

hard to spot

Now what? If I escaped up the streambed, I'd probably take a bullet in the back. If I stayed put, my last memory would likely be a muzzle flash. Only one thing to do. I crawled out of the streambed to the north side, where long grass still waved in the breeze. Cradling my rifle in front of me, I scrambled directly north as fast as I could. After a few minutes, I squirmed around and faced the streambed. I stopped moving. After reloading my pistol and rifle, I lay as still as possible. While in the ditch, I had spotted the bandits crawling toward me. If I didn't move, I would be hard to spot.

I had a decent line of sight through the grass but saw nothing. Then a head popped up and down. They didn't know where I had gone. Good. They would eventually need to come out of that swale. I could be patient. Then I thought about what I would do in their situation. I would move to the other side of the bridge. Far to the other side. As far away as possible from a potential assassin lurking in the grass. I had vowed not to move, but was that the wrong strategy? The bandits were smart. They would move away from the threat, return to their horses, and hunt from horseback, with the advantage of speed and elevation.

I had to move toward the coast. I started crawling but kept my eye on the streambed. Whenever I saw a head pop up, I stopped moving. The head never changed location. He was a decoy. He was supposed to distract me while the other two bandits made their way to the far side of the bridge. The bandit did not perform his job well. Fearing a bullet in the forehead, he popped up and down so fast, he never got a good perspective on what was in front of him. Emboldened, I crawled faster.

surrender

I saw the bridge. If I could get in a few more yards, I would be in a perfect position to shoot the robbers as they came out of the streambed. Before I could move an additional foot, one of the bandits jumped up and ran for all he was worth. I almost shot him but wondered why he bounced out of the swale all by himself.

I soon had my answer. The presumed leader

came charging out on the back of Liberty. The poor sod on foot was yet another decoy. Instead of shooting, I yelled "Hey, horse!" which was the way I greeted Liberty.

Liberty stopped and threw down his neck, and his rider tumbled to the ground. He was obscured by grass, so I swung around and shot the running man, who collapsed like a scarecrow thrown to the ground by a wicked wind. Only two of the band remained.

I scrunched over and kept a bead on where the bandit had been thrown. Liberty felt content to locate me and then graze while I killed the man who had tried to steal him. It occurred to me that the bandit might shoot Liberty for spite.

I yelled, "Do you want to live?"

"Hombre, you couldn't kill me on your best day."

"You're out of luck. This is my best day. Ask your amigos."

"*Antiguo soldados* I picked up in del pueblo. Nobodies. I'm a different breed. An officer. Now stand up with your hands raised, and I won't kill you."

"How about we stand up together with our hands in the air?"

"No, gringo. No fair fight. I kill you my way unless you surrender."

I worried about the bandit behind me in the streambed, but I saw no movement from that direction. I returned my attention to the front. We each knew only the general position of the other. Yelling would alert him to my exact whereabouts, so I kept quiet.

"You like your horse, hombre? Stand with hands in air, and I won't shoot it."

I rolled to the left. I knew his head would be down when he yelled. I waited.

"Hey, hombre, give me your dinero . . . and you can go."

I rolled left twice.

A shot rang out. Liberty raised his head but returned to grazing.

"Next bullet goes into your *caballo*. Last chance."

Two more rolls, and I cascaded into the streambed. Immediately, I checked for the other bandit. With no one in sight, I scrambled forward until I was sure I was behind the leader. I rose and spotted him not ten feet away, aiming at Liberty.

He never got off the shot.

si, señor

Now I shouted at the last bandit.

"Give up! I won't harm you!"

"Why would I trust you?"

The response came from the last of the band, still somewhere in the streambed.

I yelled again. "Do you know the banker?"

A long pause.

"I know him."

"I want him more than you. Tell the marshal . . . and you go free."

Another long pause.

"If no?"

"Then you are of no use to me. You will join your amigos."

"Then I say, si, señor."

two weeks later

I stepped into the San Diego bank two weeks later. I hadn't closed a deal on North Island, but negotiations remained open. I had made Miguel, the surviving bandit, bury the dead, collect the horses and guns, and return my saddlebags. He not only accompanied me on my travels, but we had become friends of sorts. His disreputable nature persisted, but he was a gregarious rogue who remained loyal to whoever paid him. I paid him well.

With the U.S. marshal at my side, I asked to speak to the bank president. Unlike Miguel, Mr. Blankenship was not gregarious, and he was disloyal to boot.

He sauntered over, hand extended, "Mr. Dancy, a pleasure to see you again. I hope your business up north went to your liking."

"Not yet, but hopefully soon. I'm pleased with the progress." I detected no surprise at my return, but he probably knew the robbery had not gone well. "However, I did encounter a mishap on the way to Los Angeles."

He looked me up and down. "A shame, but you look well. I hope it was a minor mishap."

"Not really. I killed many men to protect my purse. Men who tried to rob me . . . at your bidding."

He looked aghast. "Never! I don't associate with riffraff. You're mistaken."

"Am I? Perhaps you wish to tell Miguel Lopez that he's riffraff."

Miguel came forward, wearing a friendly smile. "Señor Blankenship, I have bad news. We failed in our last robbery." He bowed. "*Lo siento*, this Mr. Dancy is *un duro* hombre."

Now Blankenship looked surprised. He said, "I never saw this man before."

The marshal spoke for the first time. "Perhaps you remember Mrs. Harding. Her husband withdrew a large sum to buy horse stock. He never returned from his buying trip." He stepped forward. "Señor Lopez returned a saddle engraved with her husband's name." The marshal pulled his pistol. "There are six men besides Mr. Lopez who say you tipped them about lone riders with large amounts of money. They've all agreed to testify."

Blankenship looked furtively around for an escape path.

"Run," I said. "Please."

"Listen, I may have had too much to drink one evening and blabbed about Mr. Dancy's withdrawal. I meant no harm."

I held out a satchel. "Your money. It's counterfeit. You had me ambushed to hide that you were behind the rash of counterfeit money in San Diego."

"What? No!"

"We have additional witnesses," the marshal said as he handed Blankenship a piece of paper. "This is a warrant to examine your vault."

Blankenship started to wail. "I can give you names, men below the border who print this money. But only if we make a deal."

"Do you admit you had me robbed?" I asked.

Blankenship spoke only to the marshal. "I admit it, but I'm not the only one who passes bad bills. I can provide names. Here, in San Diego, and in Mexico. Can we deal?"

"Mr. Blankenship, you're under arrest."

| Books are produced in the United States using U.S.-based materials | Books are printed using a revolutionary new process called THINKtech™ that lowers energy usage by 70% and increases overall quality | Books are durable and flexible because of smythe-sewing | Paper is sourced using environmentally responsible foresting methods and the paper is acid-free |

Center Point Large Print
600 Brooks Road / PO Box 1
Thorndike, ME 04986-0001 USA

(207) 568-3717

US & Canada:
1 800 929-9108
www.centerpointlargeprint.com